James Stark

Dr. Kidd of Aberdeen

A Picture of Religious Life in By-Gone Days. Third Edition

James Stark

Dr. Kidd of Aberdeen
A Picture of Religious Life in By-Gone Days. Third Edition

ISBN/EAN: 9783337060893

Printed in Europe, USA, Canada, Australia, Japan

Cover: Foto ©Raphael Reischuk / pixelio.de

More available books at **www.hansebooks.com**

Dr. Kidd of Aberdeen:

A PICTURE OF RELIGIOUS LIFE

IN

BY-GONE DAYS.

BY

JAMES STARK, D.D.,

AUTHOR OF "JOHN MURKER," "LIGHTS OF THE NORTH,"
ETC.

Third Edition.

ABERDEEN: D. WYLLIE & SON.

MDCCCXCVIII.

PRINTED AT THE ROSEMOUNT PRESS,
ABERDEEN.

Dedicated

WITH FEELINGS OF SINCERE RESPECT

TO

Sir WILLIAM HENDERSON

OF DEVANHA HOUSE.

PREFACE TO THIRD EDITION.

IT is generally admitted, by those most competent to give a judgment, that Dr. Kidd was one of the very greatest religious forces with which this part of the country was ever favoured, and it is with the view of bringing the stimulating witness of his career into still wider circulation that this third and cheap edition of the biography has been issued. We are desirous that this book should have unhampered access to the homes of the people, and win a standard place in our Sabbath School and other popular libraries, particularly in the North of Scotland, and it is now given at a price which places it within the reach of all.

It is a cheap but not an abridged edition. All the printed matter that was in previous editions is here, with some additions, such as are found in pages 145, 253, 279.

Perhaps it may not be unfitting to state, and it will be interesting specially to readers in the northern parts of our land to learn, that since this book was written abundant evidence has been forthcoming of the widespread as well as abiding impression produced by Dr. Kidd's striking personality. Never much out of Aberdeen after he entered it, his fame during his lifetime was almost confined to the country on this side of the Tay, but the persons who were influenced by his robust Evangelical testimony, and their descendants, went further afield, and communications from various parts of our colonies—particularly from Canada—make us aware of the fact that the memory of the Gilcomston pastor is still fragrant to many.

J. S.

November, 1898.

PREFACE TO SECOND EDITION.

THE First Edition of this book, with the exception of a few copies on superior paper, was exhausted in less than a month after it was published. Such a graceful compliment from the public deserved the acknowledgment of a Second Edition at an earlier date; but the author, in the middle of the winter, was engrossed with other duties, and could not afford the needed time to put into shape the material which even then had come to hand. During the intervening months many memories have been awakened, without any pinching, and important documents have come to light, which being placed at our service, we have been able to add about forty pages to the book as it was in the First Edition.

Slight changes have been made, and a few additions introduced in some parts, notably a letter from Dr. Beattie, the author of the "Minstrel," in Chapter V., and three entirely new chapters are given:—"The Anti-Patronage

Battle," "The Gilcomston Pastor from Home," and "More Kiddiana."

Warm thanks are due to numerous friends who were moved to render service in our effort to make this book a fitting memorial of Dr. Kidd, and to some extent a mirror of the religious life of our city as it was three or four generations ago.

J. S.

November, 1893.

PREFACE TO FIRST EDITION.

It is no easy task to write the life of a man who passed from this world fifty-eight years ago; yet there were many who thought it ought to be written. It was scarcely possible that a unique and striking personality like that of Dr. Kidd could fail to leave an impression, which found its way more or less into print; but, owing to various circumstances, a detailed biography, founded upon documents in the custody of relatives, has not till now appeared.

An account of his early life was inserted in the "Imperial Magazine" in 1826; a brilliant monograph from the pen of Professor Masson appeared in "Macmillan's Magazine" in 1863; the late Dr. Candlish, in introducing a second edition of Dr. Kidd's work on the "Sonship" in 1872, published with it a summary of the principal facts in the career of this remarkable man; in 1888, Mr. J. Martin, in his "Eminent Divines in Aberdeen and the North," gave a brief, but faithful narrative of the experiences and labours of Dr. Kidd; and, besides the above mentioned, numerous sketches have appeared since his death, more or less fragmentary and fugitive: but such a Memoir as is possible only when the author has access to the inner life of the deceased, as it comes out in diaries, letters, and other private memoranda, has not been put into the possession of the public.

It is a memorial of that kind—a tribute of respect which has often been less tardily paid to men of far less consequence—that it is the design of this book to supply. It must be owned, however, that the writer had a desire, with the materials freely placed at his disposal, not only to delineate the life of a man who, by his breezy and forceful manner, had become an interesting local figure in the gallery of the past; but also to depict the religious aspects of the times in which he lived, while he was a dweller in this northern region. What lies before the reader is intended to be a contribution to the illustration of that transition period in our national history at the beginning of the present century, when Evangelical life and doctrine came once more to the forefront.

Some of the matter in these pages appeared

a few months ago in the columns of local newspapers; but it has all been recast, and ten
entirely new chapters have been added.

Assistance in gathering and sifting material
has been cheerfully rendered by friends in Aberdeen, and some now residing elsewhere, who,
from their special knowledge, are entitled to
speak with authority. Advantage has been
taken of the memories of surviving members of
Dr. Kidd's congregation—and there is a considerable number of them still to the fore—to
verify what, by lapse of time, is rapidly becoming a tradition. Different versions of the same
thing have occasionally come from persons whose
word was of equal weight, and in such circumstances we have tried to give effect to what is
probable and congruous. We have done our best
to make this book an authentic and reliable
record of that part of the past with which it
deals; though it is to be expected that all impressions should not agree regarding things so
remote, many of which are now being put upon
paper for the first time.

We thank all friends most sincerely for their
courteous attention and valuable aid, and only
regret that to give the list of names of those

who have favoured us with oral or written communications would be too serious an encroach-
ment upon our space.   Special mention, however, must be made of Mrs. H. Oswald, without
whose unwearied and enthusiastic co-operation
the work could not have been done.

J. S.

ABERDEEN, *22nd October,* 1892.

CONTENTS.

DR. KIDD OF ABERDEEN.

CHAPTER I.

INTRODUCTORY.

ONE of the first duties which a self-respecting community owes to itself is to keep in vivid remembrance the men belonging to it who, by their character and work, have shed lustre upon its annals, and bring healthful moral stimulus to its succeeding generations. What an advantageous natural situation and sustained enterprise in improvements and extensions are to the material side of a town's prosperity, an enthusiasm for righteousness, made conspicuous in the lives of some of its most notable citizens, is to the inner core of its well-being. We cannot be too advanced in the introduction of well-considered sanitary appliances; but neither can we have too much of the wholesome influence of noble example in life, more especially when it is

B

illumined and enforced by extraordinary talent and natural genius.

One of the wisest men of Ancient Rome said: —" You will do the greatest service to the State if you shall raise, not the roofs of the houses, but the souls of the citizens; for it is better that great souls should dwell in small houses rather than mean souls to burrow in great palaces." But there is no reason why material and moral progress should not keep pace. They do go together when tasteful monuments—real things of beauty, that are a joy to look at—are erected to the memory of persons who have won distinction. In the absence of stone or bronze statue, which tells its tale and points its moral, a plain, unvarnished narrative of the career of one of our local heroes may be of use.

We propose to do that service for Dr. Kidd. We shall do our best to tell the story to the present generation so as to make that man, if possible, one of the moral forces of the time in which we live. Ours is the humble task of imitating "Old Mortality," who went about the country retouching the lettering upon the tombstones of the Covenanters, that the inscriptions might have more legibility.

It is said there was a dearth of "saints" in this part of the country in mediæval times, but if canonisation had been carried over from the Roman to the Protestant Church there is little doubt that there would have been at least one "saint" made in Aberdeen within the last fifty years, and that is Dr. Kidd. "Saint James" might have led to confusion with scriptural personages, and to have taken the surname Kidd, besides being unusual, would not have been euphonious, but the prefix has often been added to names far less worthy of it.

Of all the men associated with this region during at least a hundred years noted for sterling moral worth and power for good over the people, made all the more striking by a strong dash of eccentricity, Dr. Kidd, it will be generally admitted, stands without a peer. He made a mark in this city which more than half a century has not effaced. Several generations have passed away since his head was put under the sod, and yet amongst native Aberdonians his name is as much a household word as ever. In the houses of not a few you still see the print of his portly Johnsonian figure reverently framed, and also his remarkable "Farewell," which was found after his death amongst his papers.

It will be our endeavour to unfold the causes of such widespread and unexampled popularity, which is becoming a tradition, but one that should not be allowed to die. The delineation of the character and the recital of the life and work of this remarkable man may disclose the secret of his power, so as to afford needed direction and stimulus for the duties and opportunities of the present time. Success of the kind that Dr. Kidd achieved is not the accident or the perquisite of any particular age. Geologists are now telling us that most of the great changes which have taken place upon the surface of the earth are due to causes still in existence, and more or less in operation. Certainly, true human greatness has its roots in what belongs to man as he always has been and ever will be. The great man gives one of the proofs of his greatness in bringing himself into close alliance and sympathy with the requirements of the period to which he belongs; but that in him which constrained him so to do would, speaking generally, have made him the man of whatever hour the hand of the clock of time pointed to; and, therefore, in perusing the story of Dr. Kidd's life, we may expect to glean some hints which, if well used, will contribute to make our lives of more consequence to ourselves and to others.

It will throw helpful, and occasionally much-needed, light upon what is to follow if we remember at the outset that the subject of our sketch came from the north of Ireland, and, being a typical and eminently favourable specimen of the race bred in that part of the world, he had in him, as we shall see, a combination of the fiery impetuosity of the Celt and the invincible pertinacity of the Scot.

CHAPTER II.

EARLY DAYS IN IRELAND.

*J*AMES KIDD was born near Loughbrickland, in the county of Down, on 6th November, 1761. He had, like many in that part of Ireland, the inestimable privilege of a godly though poor parentage. He was bereft of his father when he was a few months old, and, along with the three sons, of whom he was the youngest, his mother removed to her native place, Broughshane, in the county of Antrim.

The story of his early education reads like a charming bit of romance, and forcibly reminds us that the child is indeed father of the man. The first leaf of the Shorter Catechism was the mental pabulum with which his infant life was nourished. No wonder that he became a mighty man when at that early age he could take such strong food! From the first leaf of that compendium of theology he learned his alphabet, and after spelling and reading each question in rotation he committed the whole to memory.

It has been remarked by those who have had wide opportunities for observation that memory is a most important part of the basis of intellectual pre-eminence. The information we can

gather regarding the early training of James
Kidd bears out this high estimate that is taken
of the function of memory in mental and moral
development. When he was a mere child he not
only read, but was able to repeat without book,
the greater part of the Gospel of John. Every
day his mother gave him his portion, causing
him to commit to memory the passage that was
read, and putting questions to him to induce him
to ponder and digest what he had acquired, so
that the truth entered into his growing intelligence, and was not a mere mechanical appro-
priation. When he was an old man, Dr. Kidd
often spoke with grateful emotion of the gracious
wisdom of his mother in being at such pains so
to present Jesus Christ to his mind as to beget
in him reverence and love that hallowed the
springs of his life.

That this quick-witted and faithful mother
knew her business as an instructor of her fatherless children is amply proved by the fact that her
youngest son fell in love with the New Testament, and read it with the absorbed and glowing
interest which that most precious of all story
books can arouse when intelligence, heart, and
imagination are enlisted in the reading. The
miracles and parables recorded in the New Testament stirred the fancy and feeling of the child as
much as could the story of the Arabian Nights
or other nursery tales, and left a rich deposit of

knowledge of more use for the future. Instead of the Bible being associated in his mind with weary task-work it became the companion of his brightest hours; it was put under his pillow at night, and was read with avidity when he awoke in the morning. With such pure and elevating influences shed upon a naturally ardent and aspiring spirit, and such tastes wrought into the texture of character and habit, into what fair form might we not expect this young life to blossom?

When about eight years of age, he went with his mother to the church in Broughshane on a communion Sabbath. He was placed in a pew in full view of the officiating minister, who, according to what is said to have been the ancient usage of the Scottish Kirk, was clothed in blue. The appearance of the venerable man of God in this uncommon dress, the white covering of the sacramental table, the bread and wine spread upon it, the peculiar solemnity of the discourse, and the rapt, subdued demeanour of the assembled people struck the susceptible nature of this child; he was in an ecstasy, and before leaving the place he made a vow that he should endeavour to acquire needful qualification for the sacred office of the ministry, which his kindled imagination regarded as nothing short of an angelic, if not indeed a divine, function.

Consecrated in heart, in vague and childish

fashion, at this early age, he yet found it difficult
to pay his vows.   The widowed mother was not
in circumstances to give her youngest son the
education he coveted as a means to a great end.
But the young Irishman, fired with a noble ambition, was not of the sort to be easily daunted.
He borrowed some school books, and, literally
committing them to memory, needed little more
assistance than that a competent person should
hear him repeat his lessons.   The ingenuous
youth was so terribly in earnest that he awakened
a sympathetic interest in some teachers in the
district, who gave him gratuitous assistance.   No
one with a spark of generous manhood in him
could fail to offer help to one who by his own
exertions proved himself to be so worthy of it.

Goethe says that all things come into the service and use of the man of culture.   Is it not so,
also, with the person earnestly in pursuit of
culture ?   James Kidd found, when inspired with
the love of learning, and the desire to count for
something among the better forces of the world,
that, while there were formidable difficulties
arrayed against him, there were still more powerful ministries at hand to further his interests and
carry him on to the object he was pursuing.
People delight in snubbing the *uppish* youth, but
they cannot help giving a word of good cheer and
a helping hand to one who is truly aspiring.
What is best in us goes out in admiration for

pluck in the undaunted uphill search for the finer things of life.

So, we are told, a youth, belonging to the neighbourhood, of good social position and splendid parts, named James Ritchie, hearing of the struggles of the young scholar, offered to help him in his spare hours. James Kidd, not able to pay the fee for attendance at a Latin class in the adjoining Academy, borrowed a grammar, committed it bit by bit to memory, and repeated it as he learned it to his honorary tutor, who gave the fatherless boy the benefit of his superior classical outfit. This friend in need was several years older than James Kidd, yet a David and Jonathan like friendship sprung up between them, which lasted till the premature death of Ritchie divided them. As long as he lived, this generous youth was James Kidd's good angel, and the companionship not only softened the rigour of a hard lot, but rendered the youth who had to endure it the inestimable service of so presenting human nature that it could be trusted and loved.

When one friend passed away another stepped in. A farmer in the district undertook to place him for six months at the Academy which his deceased friend had attended. He made rapid progress during that time, and soon was alongside those who had for years enjoyed the advantages which he possessed for such a limited period. In an irregular and scrambling fashion he managed to pick up the elements of a fairly good education for his years. His case was, indeed, an illustration of the truth that God helps those who help themselves, that "self-help" brings help from all sorts of quarters. The youth who had a thirst for knowledge so intense that he would frequently rise during the night, and, lighting what is called in the country a *split*, that he might look at a passage in one of the classics which he had not succeeded in mastering on the previous day, and who began the practice, before he had reached his *teens*, of parting company with his bed at the first glimpse of dawn, was not likely to go without his reward.

He had an irrepressible impulse and determination to make his personality of some account. He must have an outlet and channel for his superabundant energy. What is in him cannot remain as idle ore. Life must yield its richest possibilities. His course through life is not to be a saunter, but a race, and he will so run as to get the prize.

It was noticed by those who watched his career in those early days that he could not bear to be at the bottom of his class. His ambitious spirit was wounded if classmates outstripped him. But it was spirited emulation, not mean envy that moved him. If others shot ahead of him he was spurred to do better. There was mettle in him that could not brook the pace of a laggard. That other boys should be better clothed and housed than he was never cost him a pang; but that they should excel him in repeating the prescribed lessons was more than his spirit could endure. Ah! that son of the widow was indeed the father of the man that was to be. Mind, and not circumstance, was, in his eyes, the measure of the man; and he had a passion for personal excellency.

Acting in the spirit of the military canon of the first Napoleon—that the invaded country should afford needful supplies to the invader, he resolved to make his living by teaching those branches of learning in which he was determined to attain the utmost proficiency. His thoroughness and enthusiasm drew many pupils around him. It is said that most speakers learn their art at the expense of their audiences, but James Kidd was able to do others, as well as himself, much good in his school. The boy-teacher grew in experience and fitness for his vocation, passing from smaller to larger schools, till he was called by the educational guardians of the place to a school that was erected for him in Kildownie, about twenty miles from Belfast. There he laboured for a number of years, and established his reputation as a man whose pupils bore the mark of being handled by a master in his craft.

Still no opening occurred for the higher

education needed for the ministry, which was the
goal of his desire and endeavour. While yet a
young man, he did what to many of his friends
seemed to be fatal to his prospects of success as
an aspirant to the pulpit: he married the
daughter of a respectable farmer in the district
—Mr. Robert Boyd, of Carnlea, near Ballymena.
It almost looked as if he were shut up now to
the career of a pedagogue. What with the responsibilities of married life, and his inability to
procure either time or money to attend a University, most men would have felt that constraining circumstances had released them from
obedience to their "vision."

It was not so with our young hero. The
possibilities of life were not exhausted. There
was a new world on the other side of the Atlantic
where many of his fellow-countrymen had been
able to do what baffled them in the old country.
The hard knot might be untied under the more
favourable conditions which he expected to find
in a country that, like himself, was shaping its
future. He resolved to emigrate to America.

CHAPTER III.

FROM IRELAND TO AMERICA.

WITHOUT a single letter of introduction, or any friend to bid him welcome after his weary passage of nine weeks, James Kidd, with his family, landed on the shores of what was to him the land of promise in 1784. When they disembarked at Philadelphia he was directed by the captain of the ship they had sailed in to apply to a fellow-countryman in that city, a schoolmaster of the name of James Little, who was of great service in opening up his future.

The manner in which Mr. Kidd began his career in America was truly characteristic, and had in it a prophetic significance. All through life he owed more to inherent worth than to propitious circumstance. Native force of character was left to do for him what the favours of smiling fortune do for many. He carried no letters of introduction to the new world; but he took with him what was more advantageous— an ardent and loyal nature that was generally consistent with itself, and which won the confidence and fastened itself to the affections of those who made his acquaintance. He had, under a guiding God, to make his own way, and he could make it, as there was stamina in his personality that never failed to give a good account of itself, at least in the eyes of those whose appreciation was of any consequence. It was one of his most admirable personal traits that the best men whom he happened to meet, if they came up to him with openness and discernment of mind, could not help making him their friend.

Through the recommendation of Mr. Little, Mr. Kidd, soon after his arrival, was installed as tutor in a family in New Jersey. From that he passed to a better situation in the family of Nathaniel Ewing, brother of the then provost of the College of Pennsylvania. By and bye Mr. Little, who was advanced in life, induced him to settle in Philadelphia, and become a sharer with him in the work and emoluments of his school. Discovering, however, on closer acquaintance, that Mr. Kidd, from his abilities and acquirements was capable of higher work than what was required in a common school, Mr. Little magnanimously advised him to open a classical academy of his own. This Mr. Kidd did, and carried it on with very marked success for years. Several of his pupils were men who took an active and honourable part in the public affairs of their country, amongst them being Commodore Decatur, who was well known in America at the beginning of this century.

In recalling the adventures of his life in America at that period, there was one narrow escape he described which left an impression upon him that was never effaced. When travelling through a comparatively uninhabited part of the country, his adventurous spirit led him alone into one of those trackless forests, of which America had many then, and, unable to find a way out, he was kept wandering amidst its solitude and darkness for days. At last he was found crawling on hands and feet, exhausted with hunger and fatigue. One advantage, he sometimes said, derived from the trying experience was that he "never afterwards esteemed any of God's bounties, however plain, as not good enough for him, but partook with thankfulness of whatever was set before him."

After some lapse of time, a vacancy for an usher having occurred in the College of Pennsylvania, Mr. Kidd offered himself as a candidate, and was elected to the situation. Having continued to act in that capacity for some time, he was enrolled as a student* and went through the

* Certificate received by Mr. Kidd from the University in Philadelphia :—

"PHILADELPHIA, 12th September, 1795.

"This is to certify that Mr. James Kidd, formerly of Philadelphia, in America, and now of Aberdeen, in Scotland, was a student of the University of Pennsylvania, in Philadelphia, and attended the lectures of the several professors

entire course of classics, philosophy, and all the
other parts of a collegiate training, bringing in
money at the same time for the support of himself and his family as a corrector to the press.

One day in the course of his reading he
lighted upon a book that contained the Hebrew
alphabet, and this circumstance gave an impulse
and direction to his whole future life. In a very
short time he mastered the letters and vowel-
points, and, with the tuition of a Portuguese Jew,

in Natural Philosophy, Moral Philosophy, Mathematics, and
Humanity, in the winter seasons of 1787 and 1789:—that
by the advantage of a good natural genius and diligent
application to his studies, he acquired such a laudable
acquaintance with the different branches of Science, to
which he attended, as met with the unanimous approbation
of his professors:—and that his moral and religious conduct,
during his stay with us in America, was unexceptionable
and exemplary; so that he may be admitted into any
religious society to which he may choose to attach himself.
It is with pleasure that the Provost, Vice-Provost, and the
other professors of the University of Pennsylvania, in Philadelphia, subscribe this unanimous attestation in favour of
the moral conduct and literary accomplishments of one of
their former pupils, and the Provost begs leave to add that,
from his particular knowledge of Mr. Kidd's acquaintance
with the Oriental languages, he had recommended him to
the notice of the late *Professor Robertson*, of Edinburgh, and
is glad to find that he is now employed at Aberdeen in that
important line of instruction.

> "John Ewing, Provost, and Prof. of Nat. Ph.
> "Sam Mayor, V.-Prov., and Pr. of Moral Philos.
> "Jas. Davidson, Prof. of Humanity.
> "Rt. Paterson, Prof. of Mathematics."

he was able to read the book of Genesis in the
course of a few months. He was smitten with a
passion for Oriental languages. He attended a
Jewish synagogue every Friday evening, where
he learned to read Hebrew fluently, and at the
same time acquired an insight into the modes of
Jewish thought and worship.

The exorbitant charges of his Jewish teacher,
and the expenses consequent upon a rising family,
reduced Mr. Kidd's finances to a very low ebb.
He was greatly in need of one thing, and he as
ardently longed for another, and he had not the
money with which to purchase both. What he
needed was a suit of clothes; what he lusted
after was a Hebrew Bible that he had cast his
eyes upon in the window of a Dutch bookseller.
In obedience, doubtless, to the behest of his
better-half, yielding at last to her repeated remonstrances, he went away with money he had
saved to clothe the outer man. But while going
to the clothier's he had to pass the bookseller's,
and found, alas! as many have done before,
though usually in connection with other things
than sacred literature, that he was on temptation's path. As he passed, he could not help
looking at the coveted book; he stepped in to
have a closer inspection: the Dutchman was loud
in his praises of the edition and type; the
impulse, as he felt the money in his pocket,
was too strong to be resisted. He flung the price

C

down on the counter, carried off his prize, and the enthusiastic Hebraist had to begin again, by extra toil and economy, gradually to accumulate as much as would enable him to replace his threadbare garments.

For some time he had Oriental languages on the brain, and he set his face immediately in the direction of anything that was likely to perfect him in the knowledge of that branch of study. The ardent and simple-hearted youth conceived the idea at that time that a visit to the Holy Land, which had been the scene of heaven's revelations and solemn transactions, and where Hebrew had been spoken as a living language, would render him signal service in his studies. Happily he had amongst his intimate friends Dr. Benjamin Rush, the well-known American physician and politician, who succeeded in exploding that juvenile notion. "I think," he said, "I see you coming back from Palestine and lecturing to empty benches: study men and things."

But he clung tenaciously to the splendid and beloved ideal of his childhood. He was not to be diverted from the great aim of his life, which was to acquire needful equipment for the pulpit, though he was quite willing to listen to the counsel of experience as to the best method to be pursued. That nothing might be left undone which was within the compass of his inventive genius and indomitable will to make him "a workman that needeth not to be ashamed," he resolved to sit at the feet of John Brown of Haddington, and study in the University of Edinburgh, the rising fame of which was attracting students from all parts of the world. His friends in America did all they could to dissuade him from this course, but his resolution was not to be shaken.

He left America; but he took with him what gave form and colour to his whole future life. There can be no doubt that America, which had just achieved her Independence, and was rejoicing in the exercise of her dearly-won liberties, was one of the most helpful of Mr. Kidd's "Schools and Schoolmasters." The very air which the society of that young and vigorous commonwealth breathed; the noble character and pure patriotism of most of her leading citizens of that generation; the honourable place given to those principles of right for which they had shed their blood on the battlefield; the newly-awakened powers and the consciousness of grand possibilities which were entering into the life of the nation that had just been born; the ardour, the energy, and aspiration of that race which had Washington at its head—must have told with marked effect in the formation of the character of this young, impressible Irishman.

What a rare opportunity a people have when

they, in the providence of God, are free to begin
at the beginning, having no other basis of operations for statesmanship than the principles of
justice and the eternal laws of God. The
Americans of that day were not angels, but many
of the men who took part in framing the constitution of the newly-born nation were loyal to
the holy truths, and respected, with a chivalrous
devotion, the higher sentiments which are the
inheritance of those who have received a Puritan
training. Brushing aside effete tradition and
tyrannous custom as a burden that man and not
God had laid upon them, they contributed a page
to the history of mankind that is of unique
interest, as it is the record of an experiment, the
very making of which brings us a little nearer
the realisation of that high national ideal, which,
like an orb of heaven, is very beautiful to
behold, but, as some faint-hearted ones think, is
quite as difficult to reach.

James Kidd, who arrived upon the shores of
America two or three years after its Independence had been acknowledged, was just the man
upon whom the spirit breathed around him could
not but act like a contagion. His constitutional
tendencies must have made the society congenial
to him, and they seemed also to mark him out as
a person who was destined to be one of its life-
long and leading citizens, and where unquestion-
ably his pecuniary circumstances and personal

comfort would have been what they never were in Aberdeen. The most unaccountable part of his whole career is his removal from America to Aberdeen. Truly he was led by a way that he knew not, not to the sphere that suited him best, but to the one that needed him most.

CHAPTER IV.

FROM AMERICA TO ABERDEEN.

WHAT induced Mr. Kidd to re-cross the Atlantic
and come back to the "old country" was the
desire to study under the famous John Brown of
Haddington, who was then Professor of Divinity
under the Associate Synod.   It may seem strange
to us of the present day that this ambitious
divinity student should have turned his back
upon the Theological Colleges and tutors of the
United States of excellent standing, and should
have had such a strong preference for the
Scottish Dissenter's prelections as to leave the
land where he had now good connections and
many friends who were at a loss to account for
the step he was taking.   But one of his "Irish
fits," as he himself afterwards called them, was
upon him, and he would go.

Probably he was dazzled with the romantic
story of the herculean toils in the pursuit of
learning of John Brown, who, like himself, was
a self-made man, having been once a "herd
laddie."   But, doubtless, doctrinal and spiritual
sympathy was at the bottom of this attachment.
We must not forget that, while Brown's writings
may not be part of the "master light" of the

present age, yet in popular estimation he was one of the very greatest Scotchmen of that time. His self-interpreting Bible, which was highly commended even by church dignitaries in England, and his other productions, had made him widely known and revered wherever Presbyterian Calvinism or genuine piety had a footing. He was indeed a typical Scot of the first rank in moral qualities, of whom we have reason to be proud. Even David Hume could not restrain his praise. On hearing him preach, he remarked "that old man preaches as if Christ were at his elbow."

But while man proposes, God disposes; by the time that Mr. Kidd reached the shores of Scotland the distinguished professor was in his grave. It being the personal pre-eminence and not the denominational connection of Mr. Brown that drew him to Scotland, he was free to cast about for any part of the Presbyterian fold that was most congenial and would be most helpful. Having, by his residence in Ireland and America, been all his life outside the domestic controversies and local divisions of ecclesiastical Scotland, and never having been at any time a strong denominational man, though a staunch Presbyterian, he could choose that connection which was likely to render him most service in view of his life work. He decided to cast in his lot with the Established Church of Scotland.

A letter from a fellow-student, who, like himself, had come from America to study in Scotland, and who had afterwards returned to his own
country, sheds some light upon the James Kidd
of that period :—

"NEW YORK, 2nd November, 1792.

" MY DEAR FRIEND,—You will perhaps think that
I have forgotten you because I did not write to you
before. I often remember you, and remember you
with affection, the friendship you showed me while I
was in Edinburgh I would be ungrateful to forget,
and that same friendship will prompt you, I doubt
not, to enquire how I am situated. In few words,
much better and more comfortably than I deserve.
I bless God that he has counted me faithful, putting
me in the ministry. I was licensed on the 18th ult.,
and am supplying the vacancy at New York, where I
expect soon to be settled.

" Shortly after my arrival I visited Philadelphia.
I called upon your wife and found all well. She was
extremely happy in hearing from you, and it seemed
to give her peculiar satisfaction to see a person with
whom you were acquainted. In the spring, I suppose,
you will prosecute the plan you mentioned when I left
you. Do not kill yourself with excessive study. We
are made of soul and body, and must take care of
both; intemperate application may break the flow of
your natural spirits, and then you will be able to do
very little at anything. The God of all grace bless
you. Whilst we are in a world of toil and sin, let us
give daily employment to our Great High Priest, and

our souls will prosper, and when you pray for yourself forget not your friend,

"JAS. M. MASON."

Another letter, from his eminent and valued friend, Dr. Rush, shows that, up to 1795, Mr. Kidd still had the intention of returning to America:—

"PHILADELPHIA, 19th July, 1795.

"MY DEAR FRIEND,—I rejoice to hear of your intention to return to America in the character of a minister of the Gospel. The harvest is indeed great, but wise, faithful, and zealous labourers are very few in every part of the United States—

'When He comes, shall He find faith on the earth?'

I hope you will add to your public labours in the ministry the establishment of a school for teaching the Hebrew language. I wait with impatience to see your translation of the Book of Genesis. I expect to be instructed and benefited by it, for I am engaged in preparing a work for the press to be entitled, 'An Attempt to Explain Sundry Passages in the Old and New Testaments, by the Principles of Medicine and the Laws of the Animal Economy.' I am likewise engaged in preparing a second volume for the press upon the 'Yellow Fever,' to which will be added, 'An Inquiry into the Proximate Cause of Fever, and a Defence of Blood-Letting as a Remedy in certain Diseases.'

"I deplore with you the continued effusion of human blood in Europe. How much should it lead us to appreciate the Gospel of Jesus Christ when we reflect that it contains in it a remedy for all the public as well as private calamities of mankind. The United States continue to flourish in their agriculture, manufactures, and commerce. The treaty with Great Britain, though adopted by our Senate, is disapproved of by 19 out of 20 of our citizens; I cannot detail the objections to it, not having read it.—I am, my dear sir, ever yours sincerely,

"Benjamin Rush."

Mr. Kidd carried with him letters of introduction to some of the leading University men in Edinburgh from Dr. Benjamin Rush, who had been one of its distinguished students, and other tried friends in America. A few of those men of weight and influence in Edinburgh continued for years to take a lively interest in this American Irishman, and did all they could to further his interests, and no one more so than Dr. John Hill, Professor of Humanity, some of whose letters are to appear in these pages. By their advice he began anew his academical course at Edinburgh, not content with what he had received in the College of Philadelphia. Here is a married man, with a family, nearly thirty years of age, taking his place in the class-room with the Scottish youths of that generation! Verily such pertinacity deserves its reward.

He attended Latin and Greek classes under Hill and Dalziel, also Chemistry under Black, and Anatomy with Munro; and was a student under the renowned Dugald Stewart. He enrolled himself soon after as a student of Divinity* in the Established Church. Probably no one of all his tutors influenced him so much as Dugald Stewart, who, by his attractive style more than his original or profound explorations in the field of mental and moral science, was, along with a few other brilliant men, gradually winning for the University of which they were such ornaments a European reputation. He who could present subjects usually considered dry and "crabbed," so that, as Sir Walter Scott testifies, "his striking and impressive eloquence rivetted the attention of the most volatile student," must have had a fascination for Mr. Kidd.

* From one of the Edinburgh Professors of Divinity to Mr. Kidd:—

"EDINBURGH, 29th June, 1795.

"DEAR SIR,—I was favoured with your letter of the 27th curt., and have, agreeably to your desire, written (on the other leaf) a certificate of your attendance on this Hall. I do not see from my books that you have delivered any discourses before me. I feel a reluctance to give particular advices to one of your standing, though you modestly request it. I need hardly remind you that much diligence in the study of the Scriptures, and attention to personal religion, are of the highest importance.

"With sincere wishes for your success in the important plan of life you have in view.—I am, dear sir, yours sincerely,

"A. HUNTER."

Having to find maintenance for himself and family while carrying on his studies in Edinburgh, Mr. Kidd opened classes, under the immediate patronage of the celebrated Hebraist, Robertson, as a teacher of Oriental Literature. Thus he was thrown into the current of the best thought and life of Edinburgh at that most interesting period of its history, when, by the extraordinary outburst of genius and intellectual energy, of which it was the scene, it was entitled to regard itself as more than a national capital— as a distinctive seat of letters and criticism— "Modern Athens."

His success as a teacher of Hebrew was so conspicuous that, when the Professorship of Oriental Languages in Marischal College, Aberdeen, became vacant by the death of Dr. Donaldson, he was urged by influential friends to lodge an application. His testimonials from experts were so satisfactory that the patron, Sir Alexander Ramsay of Balmain, ventured to present this stranger and Irishman to the office, which at the time was more marked for its dignity than its emoluments.

When he accepted the professorship, and it appeared to be the will of Providence that he should settle in Aberdeen, he sent for Mrs. Kidd. He was so situated that he could not return for her, and she had to cross the Atlantic alone, not knowing anything of the place for which she was bound, except that her husband was there, and not dreaming that it was destined to be her home till death came to remove her.

When coming over in one of the sailing vessels of the period, a tragedy occurred which threw the rest of her life to some extent into shadow. A great storm arose, and being frightened as the vessel was reeling under the assaults of the terrific seas, she rushed up on deck with her youngest child in her arms, when a huge wave leapt on board, knocked her down, and swept the little one from her sight. As may well be supposed, she was never quite the same person after that shock.

At last their wanderings are over. After much exploration and vicissitude Mr. Kidd finds a home. It almost looked as if he were to be as restless as the "Wandering Jew," whose language had such an attraction for him, as he found it so difficult to tie himself down anywhere in Ireland or America. What those countries could not do Aberdeen did; once his foot was planted in that city he never saw his way out of it again. What kind of place was it which held him so fast?

Aberdeen in the early days of Mr. Kidd's residence was a very different place from the large and beautiful city which now bears its name. It was then an ancient and historic town, with a romantic situation, as it stood between its two

rivers, the Dee and the Don, and fronted the vast
expanse of ocean, with no shore beyond nearer
than Norway; but it had not much more than a
fifth of its present population, and did not cover
a tenth of the space now within its boundaries.
Like most old Scottish towns, it was what
Jerusalem is said to have been, "a city that is
compact together." You could have gone from
end to end of it before breakfast and not have
suffered any inconvenience, unless from the
odours, which at certain parts were more ob-
trusive than fragrant.

Indeed, Aberdeen as it now presents itself to
the eye could scarcely be said to have existed
then; for Union Street a hundred years ago was
no more than a dream, if it was even that, and
modern Aberdonians cannot be blamed for thinking that the city, before that magnificent
thoroughfare was constructed, must have been
like a bridge when nothing else has been erected
but a pier on one side, or a palace with no
entrance hall or reception room. Union Street
is Aberdeen brought to a focus, and enthusiastic
citizens of Bon-Accord, daring, in the exuberance
of their loyalty, to link things local with the
most illustrious associations, have gone so far as
to say—What would Athens have been without
its Acropolis, or Ancient Rome if its Capitol had
only been a phantom of the brain; and what
would Aberdeen be if its stateliest and most distinctive feature were not?

The chief streets in those far-away days were Castle Street, Broad Street, Gallowgate, Guestrow, Shiprow, Netherkirkgate, Upperkirkgate, and the Green. In most parts beyond, where there are now handsome streets and terraces, there were cornfields and vegetable gardens.

The only stage coach which brought the city into connection with the rest of the world, went to Edinburgh, leaving every Monday morning at 4 o'clock, and arriving at its destination in time for dinner next day, a seat in it costing two guineas. A letter posted for London at the beginning of the week arrived at the end of it, the postage for a single sheet being not less than 1s. 3½d.

We have now between seventy and a hundred ministers of religion*: then there were only

---

* The ministers of Aberdeen in the year of Mr. Kidd's arrival, as given in "The Aberdeen Almanac for the year 1793":—

"George Campbell, James Shireffs, Duncan Shaw, Hugh Hay; College Church, James Shand; Footdee, John Thomson; Chapel of Ease, Belmont Street, John Bryce; Chapel of Ease, Gilcomston, James Gregory.

Associate Congregation, Alexander Dick.

Associate Congregation (Antiburghers), William M'Call.

St. Paul's Chapel, Mr. Deans (one vacant).

Trinity Church, William Blake.

Scots Episcopal Church, Bishop J. Skinner, Roger Aiken.

Church of Relief, Shiprow, John Brodie.

Congregational Church (Bereans), Shiprow, W. Robertson.

fifteen; and of schoolmasters, including those
for dancing and fencing, there were not more
than twenty when Dr. Kidd came. There was
one newspaper published once a week, the
Aberdeen Journal, which cost 7½d. There were
no police, no cabmen, for many years after that
date, only two letter carriers, and it is doubtful
if there was a single four-wheeled private
carriage within the precincts of the "braif
toon."

Burns, the poet, visited Aberdeen a few years
before the advent of Dr. Kidd, and summed up
his impressions of it by a brief entry in his
journal, "a lazy town." But while there was not
in those days, any more than there is now, much
noisy demonstration of activity to strike the
casual visitor, there must have been a great deal
of quiet industry; for a professor of King's
College told Dr. Johnson, when he was in the
town fourteen years before the date of Burns's
visit, that the value of the stockings alone which
were exported was never less than a hundred
thousand pounds annually. Hose at that time
was the staple product of the place, and as much
of it, along with other exports, such as raw hides,
was sent to the Low Countries, the Continent of
Europe was really in some respects in closer communication and in better commercial relations
with this northern city than was the southern
end of the island of which it formed a part. It

was then, indeed, to the rest of our country " Aberdeen Awa'."

And yet at that distant date Aberdeen had all the constituent elements out of which the present noble city has grown. It had the soil, stubborn, yet repaying labour; the invigorating air which comes from the Grampian solitudes and the unpolluted breath of the North Sea; the two Universities, the gates and bursaries of which were open to the humblest in the land; above all, it had the sturdy character of its sons that is often compared to the native granite, but which is totally unlike it in this respect, that, while accessible to formative influences which respect its individuality, it can never be hammered into shape, nor be made to yield much to the sheer force of the most persistent pounding. It can be won, however, as the sequel of this story will show, by a straightforward and heart-charged appeal, in the name of Christ, to that innate sense of righteousness and of God, which is the birthright and the crowning dignity of every human being, in whatever part of the surface of the earth his local habitation may be situated.

D

CHAPTER V.

THE PROFESSORSHIP IN MARISCHAL COLLEGE.

SIR WALTER SCOTT, in his "Legend of Montrose," makes Dugald Dalgetty say:—"By St. Andrew, here's a common fellow, a stipendiary, with four pounds a year and a livery cloak, thinks himself too good to serve Ritt Master Dugald Dalgetty of Drumthwacket, who has studied humanity at the Marischal College of Aberdeen, and served half the princes of Europe." If to have "studied humanity at Marischal College" was such an accession of dignity, what must it have been to be a professor there, before Marischal, so far as the "Arts" were concerned, was merged in King's. It was once the facetious boast of Aberdeen that, like England, which had its Cambridge and Oxford, it had also two Universities—Marischal and King's. It was really so up to 1860, when the Union took place. If shorn of some of its glory, Marischal is more imposing now in another respect. The present palatial building displaced the humbler* structure which was the Marischal College of Professor Kidd's days.

* Donald Sage thus describes old Marischal College as it was in the time of the professorship of Mr. Kidd:—

James Kidd was now a teacher in this venerable and historic school of learning, and was entitled to put the letters LL.OO.P. after his name, which, according to the device of signifying a plural by the re-duplication of a letter, stood for *Linguarum Orientalium Professor*, or Professor of Oriental Languages. But high as this position was, he had not yet reached the summit of his ambition. He took the professor's chair by the way, but the pulpit was his goal.

The professorship in Marischal College was no inconsiderable advantage to the man who was

"I remember my first session at Marischal College more distinctly than the succeeding ones. The College buildings which then existed were in a state of rapid decay. They had been erected by George, fifth Earl Marischal, in 1593; and the lapse of two centuries had reduced them to what was little better than a habitable ruin. The fabric consisted of a long, lofty, central building of four storeys, with a wing of the same height at one end, and a huge, clumsy tower, intended for an observatory, at the other. In the front of the central building, at the spring of the roof, was a clock; the windows were small, and the mason work was of the coarsest kind. On the wing were two inscriptions, the one in Greek, ... the other in broad Scotch : 'Thay haif said—quhat say thay—lat yame say.' I am told that the latter inscription had a pointed allusion to the plainness of the structure, and to the religion of its founder.

" . . . The internal accommodation consisted of a large hall on the ground floor of the central building, called 'the public school,' where all the students, at 8 a.m., met for prayer. Nothing could be more mean or wretched than this hall. It was a long, wide place,

destined to be for so many years minister of Gilcomston. It did not add much to the scanty
emoluments of his position; but in a town like
Aberdeen, which was to a great extent overshadowed by the University, it yielded a certain
measure of social distinction, and doubtless added
to the weight of his public utterances. To be
the authorised teacher of Oriental languages in
the northern seat of learning was a guarantee for
a respectable amount of scholarship, and of a
kind that was of special use to him as an ex-

perhaps 100 feet by 20; the windows, which were three
in number, were short and narrow, and were fitted with
glass in the upper sash, and boards in the lower. The
floor was paved with stone, and along the walls ran a
wooden bench on which the students sat while the roll
was called, and during prayers. There were two raised
desks in the centre of the hall, the one for the Principal
and professors on Fridays, the other, right opposite, for
any student who had a Latin oration to deliver. In
short, the whole gave one an idea of a hastily-built
granary. Above the public school was the college hall;
it was handsome, and worthy of a literary institution.
"The walls were hung with fine old prints, as well as
full-length and three-quarter-length portraits of eminent
men, more particularly of benefactors to the College.
Among others was that of Field-Marshal Keith. In this
hall the students met for the annual public examination.
Above the hall, and in the upper flat were the library,
containing a very mediocre collection of books, and the
museum, not remarkable either. The north wing, consti-
tuting the observatory tower, contained, on the ground
floor, the Greek class room, and above it was the divinity
hall."—"Memorabilia Domestica," p. 189.

pounder of Scripture. The mouths of scornful gainsayers were by anticipation closed when the eye fell upon those letters he was entitled to put after his name, and however ready some of his virulent enemies might be to stigmatise him as a mere ignorant babbler, a shallow and heated "high-flyer," yet that chair in the University took off the edge from their gibes and taunts.

In another, and perhaps still more important, respect Mr. Kidd was a distinct gainer by this long-sustained connection with the select academic circle of the town. Marischal College had doubtless an improving effect upon his general manner and bearing, and acted to some extent as a wholesome check and counterpoise in the development that would have been effected if Trinity and Gilcomston Churches with their environment had been the only potent factors. Mr. Kidd had it in him to be a demagogue if all the surrounding influences had been favourable. His irrepressible sympathy and impetuous temper might have driven him too far in the direction of overbearing popular gusts. It has been observed that the man of genius who captures for himself a place in the hearts of the people differs from them mainly in having a great deal more of that which they themselves have. But, at the same time, if he is to render the most needed help, it is well that he should have hold of much which the people themselves

may not in the same measure possess, to give
steadiness and enlightenment to his action as a
leader.

Few men can afford, any more than trees, to
hang as they grow. It is better they should be
under the eye and correction of associates competent to judge when they have diverged from
the canons of taste and propriety. Gilcomston
put no great restraint upon Mr. Kidd's natural
waywardness and occasional recklessness. He
had some of the "defects of his qualities" as a
self-made man. Naturally independent and fearless, it might have been an advantage if he could
have been daily under the influence of gentle-
born and mild-mannered Christians whom he
respected. But the elegance, the chastened style,
the cultured taste of that day were to a great
extent on the side of the Moderates, and he was
an Evangelical of the Evangelicals. It so happened, therefore, that his intimate and official
connection with the University was the principal
opportunity afforded him of mingling with men
whose presence and influence, it may be in-
sensibly felt, would tend to make the diamond a
little less rough, though none the less precious
than it would otherwise have been.

Tested by the much higher standards of the
present day, Mr. Kidd, according to testimony
handed down, could not be called a profound or
notably accurate Hebraist. Even though his

early advantages had been greater, he had not
the temperament out of which the exact scholar
is usually made. His rushing, discursive mind
was more at home in dealing with general affairs
and principles than in handling niceties of
grammar and cultivating elegancies of style.
But in the land of the blind a one-eyed man is a
prodigy; and in those days when Hebrew was
kept in the shady background, even by widely-
cultured men, he soon won a reputation for himself.

There were many things that flourished more
in Scotland than Hebrew scholarship a hundred
years ago when Mr. Kidd entered upon his professorial work. There was a strange indifference
to this study, even on the part of men whose
sacred profession should have made them alive
to its importance. That comes out in biographies
of the period, and crops up in incidental fashion
in the following letters written to Mr. Kidd by
one who bears a name that is historic in the
academic annals of St. Andrews. These letters
throw a little light upon the times, and upon Mr.
Kidd's position as professor : —

" EDINBURGH, 15th March, 1794.

" MY DEAR SIR,—I should have acknowledged the
receipt of your obliging letter sooner, but have of late
been more than ordinarily engaged. It gives me no
small pleasure to find that your new situation gives

you so much satisfaction.   The laudable ardour with
which you pursued the study of Oriental languages
does, in my opinion, give you the fullest right to every
encouragement in the line.

"My recommendation, founded on your general
attention to learning (as I am no judge of your forte),
was addressed to a patron of the strictest honour,
who was regulated by the true maxim of 'Detur
digniori.' If he is satisfied with his choice; if the
publick see and applaud the purity of his intentions;
and if you are happy in filling your chair, my reward
is complete.   My claim indeed is small, as I attempted
no more than doing you justice.

"I waited on Sir Alexander as you desired, who
was very happy to hear the contents of your letter.
He seemed to understand perfectly the circumstance
to which you refer, and thinks that without arrogat-
ing much to yourself by word or deed you will soon
claim regard in your line.   Honour is well compared
to a rainbow.   It flies the pursuer and pursues the
flier.   General civility to your colleagues is without
doubt your line of conduct, and the world judges of a
professor's merit, not by the piques of party, but by
his professional success.   I wish you heard of your
wife and family, and had them in this country.   They
are entitled to any advantage to be procured in your
literary career, which has been singular, and will, I
hope, improve.   Sir Alexander thinks a single guinea
too small a fee for you.   It may be prudent, however,
to show the world that you deserve encouragement
before you require it.

"Mrs. Hill, Norman, and my family join me in

kind compliments and best wishes to you, and I ever am, my dear sir, your most faithful, humble servant,

" Jo. HILL."

(From the Same.)

" ST. ANDREWS, 6th August, 1795.

" DEAR SIR,—I take the opportunity of writing you by my friend, Dr. Brown, who will soon be admitted your Principal. You will find him a man in every way worthy of the character he has long sustained and of the place he is about to accept. I mentioned you to him as a friend in whose happiness and success I am much interested, and was glad to find that from what he knew of your character he was before disposed to do you every service in his power. The doctor is a very learned man, and as a Latin scholar has, in my opinion, very few rivals. It will give me great satisfaction to find that your zeal and ability in your profession is duly rewarded by an increase of your class. Much is expected from your skill in Oriental literature, and I am not afraid that the general expectation will be disappointed. I saw Sir Alexander Ramsay in Edinburgh a month ago, who mentioned his intention of allocating a bursary of £25 to your salary, at least for some time. To this I gave my encouragement, and hope it may occur to the old knight that a permanent addition out of his own funds would do credit to his character now and his memory afterwards.

" Mrs. Hill joins me in kind compliments to you.

Norman, who is now as tall as myself, feels himself much obliged to you for your civility and attention at Aberdeen—which from my friend, Dr. Brown, going there I have an additional motive to visit.—I always am, dear sir, your most faithful and obedient servant,

"Jo. HILL."

The following extracts, obtained through the kindness of P. J. Anderson, Esq., from Marischal College records, bearing upon the foundation of the Hebrew chair, cannot fail to be of local interest : —

"Foundation Charter of Mar. Coll., 1593, Fasti Acad. Mar., I., 43. ' De officio Gymnasiarchae Linguarum etiam gnarus et peritus esto, imprimis vero Hebraicae et Syriacae quam propagari cupimus.'

"23rd November, 1642.

" ' The same day the Provost, Baillies, and Counsell thinks it meit and expedient that ane Ebro lesson be teachit weiklie in the colledge of this burgh till Lambmes next and ordaines Patrik Leslie provost and Doctor Patrik Dune principall of the said college to deal with Mr. John Row, ane of the tounes ministers for that effect.' (Town Council minute. Fasti, p. 264).

"1727.

"Rev. Gilbert Ramsay, Barbadoes, bequeaths £1,000 to found a chair of Oriental Languages in Mar. Coll.—Sir Alex. Ramsay of Balmain, patron. (Will in Fasti, p. 412.)"

The following statement, made by Professor Kidd before a Royal Commission of Visitation in 1827, gives the reader a very vivid idea of the conditions of his work, of which in his evidence he is taking a survey :—

" To the Very Honourable and Very Reverend the Royal Commissioners appointed by His Majesty to Visit the Colleges and Universities of Scotland,

" The Memorial of the Undersigned

" Most humbly sheweth,—That your memorialist has taught for 34 sessions; that the want of a power to enforce attendance has all along been a subject of deep regret; that few attend the class for Oriental Languages, and these few attend only as they please— one day, perhaps, in a week, and that for a short part of the session; that this prevents progress, and is a great annoyance; that it is not possible to make a Hebrew scholar in one session, so short as three months; that the mode of examination by the Presbytery greatly retards a knowledge of the Hebrew Scriptures; that at present the Presbytery of Aberdeen examine only on the first 12 chapters of the book of Genesis, and perhaps on nine or ten Psalms; and when the students can with difficulty go so far, they stop, and will not read farther; that this can never make a scholar in the Hebrew Scriptures; that two years at least would be necessary to understand the poetic and prophetic Hebrew Scriptures with tolerable accuracy.

" That the salary annexed to the class for Oriental
Languages in Marischal College is never above £80
per annum, and during the income tax was only £75;
that for the three years last past it has been little
above £70, on account of the low interest of money;
and last year it was not £67, as the returns to the
very honourable Commissioners will show; that the
smallness of the salary for the Professorship of Oriental
Languages compelled your memorialist to seek a living
in the church—a circumstance loudly reprobated by a
party in the church; that if your memorialist had a
living by his class, he would give up that he holds in
the church cheerfully; that, in general, the resources
of the students who attend the Hebrew class are so
limited that they are unable to pay a fee, and in consequence of this for many years back, your memorialist has discovered the very great difficulty which many
of them laboured under to pay a guinea; that, therefore, in order not to hurt the feelings of the poorer
lads, your memorialist made the fee of the class
optional—a few shillings, four or five, as the class
agreed; and he yearly put the proceeds into the hands
of one of the magistrates of Aberdeen, that at some
future time they might be the foundation of a fund
for building a Female Orphan Hospital in this city,
of which there is the very greatest necessity. With
most profound respect, from your memorialist,

" JAMES KIDD, LL.OO.P."

In the foregoing statement he expresses his
willingness to give up the work of the pulpit for

the sake of the professorship, but it has to be borne in mind that he was nearly seventy years of age when he said that. In giving further evidence before that same Commission of the way in which he carried on his work for so many years, some suggestive remarks are dropped:—

"What grammar do you use?"—"I, in general, lay down upon a board everything that I call a rule. You can bring any grammar, I say, that you please in this class; and many times they have taken away grammars from my class, just from those specimens. It is the same thing to me, in general, what grammar they bring."

"Do you discipline your students much in the knowledge of the verbs, and declining the different forms of Hebrew verbs?"—"I do every day most particularly and regularly through the whole class."

"Do you find those that continue to the end of the course able to consult lexicons for themselves with facility?"—"They might, perhaps, be able to do it for a little while after they leave the College, while it is fresh in their memory; but if you let them remain for a year and then try them, they could not do it."

"Do you mean to say that Hebrew is very much neglected?"—"I think it is very much neglected. I think it is a pity; probably I am partial to it as a pursuit I have followed so long."

" Do you think that the disposition for receiving instruction in Hebrew is rather increasing? "—" I rather think so, because when I came here there was scarcely any such thing taught in the north."

" Do you think that attendance upon your class should be made imperative by the Church? "—" I think so, because we cannot get them to attend."*

Professor Kidd and his students, as may be readily supposed, often relieved the dry studies and technical talk of the class-room with sallies that had more of human interest in them than the average youth finds in Hebrew roots. The rafters of the old chamber occasionally rang with peals of laughter which must have been provoked by something else than Oriental languages. Mr. Kidd was always present in the professor, and while he believed in hard work for himself and all under his charge, yet he could not prevent a witticism from crossing his brain and leaping to his tongue now and again.

* This is how the Rev. John Milne, of Perth, one of his students, wrote of the Professor in a letter to a brother minister:—" I shall begin Deuteronomy on Monday, five verses, and read critically. It is a pity you have not the points, but it is more a matter of sound than of sense, and you cannot now help it. . . . . . To teach Hebrew in a way that made our knowledge of it of no use if we wished to hold intercourse with living Jews! Luckily my teacher, Dr. Kidd, got his knowledge of it from a Rabbi."

The students, like the children of Aberdeen, revered him, and yet came close to him. He often had them in his home and at his table. It is remembered that when he and they were at dinner one day under his roof the young fellows took advantage of the favourable opportunity for having all sorts of subjects discussed. So one after another peppered him with questions, which did not evoke a single answer. Silence was maintained, and their friend went on with his dinner like a man who had a piece of business on hand. At last, when dinner was finished, pushing aside his plate, the Professor said— " Now, young gentlemen, I am ready to answer all your questions; but I make a rule to do one thing at a time ; so I don't talk much while I am eating." They did have a delightful and profitable evening.

A story of Mr. Kidd in relation to his fellow-professors has been widely circulated, and is generally believed, though there may be some doubt as to the actual amount of the sum subscribed. The professors of the day were expected to head the list in a subscription for some work to be done in connection with the University buildings. Some of the leading and richer members of the Senatus, zealous for the prosperity of the institution of which they were guardians, with a zeal that was tempered with a prudent regard for their own purses, proposed

that Kidd as their senior member should be the
first to put down his name. They knew he was
a poor man, and they thought that by paying
this honour to him they would at the same time
get off easily, as it would not do to put the good
man to shame by exceeding the figure he wrote
upon the paper. The Hebrew Professor, who
was not blind, saw their little dodge, and with
the gleeful feeling of one who was constraining
others to be virtuous against their will, he put
opposite his name, "My Year's Salary—£50."

In closing what we have now to say of Dr.
Kidd's professorship, the annexed letter, valuable as being from the pen of Dr. Beattie, the
author of "The Minstrel," will fittingly come
in :—

"ABERDEEN, 24th May, 1798.

"DEAR SIR,—I thank you for your very kind and
learned letter, and as soon as my health will permit,
which is not the case at present, I shall be very
anxious to attend to what you say of Daniel's prophecy, which I consider as a matter of very great importance. At present I attempt nothing further than
to answer the last part of your letter. Though I am
not personally much acquainted with Mr. Gavin
Mitchell, I am no stranger to his merit as a scholar
and a clergyman, and will most heartily co-operate
with you in procuring for him a Doctor's Degree in
Divinity, which I think he very well deserves. The
College is, I think, obliged to you for suggesting what

I should have been happy to propose, if the thing had occurred to me. You will please to mention it to the Principal and the other professors, who, I flatter myself, will make no objection.—I am, with much regard and esteem, dear sir, your most affectionate, humble servant,

"J. BEATTIE.

"To the Reverend Mr. Professor Kidd,
Marischal College, Aberdeen."

Through the kindness of the librarian of Marischal College, we have had access to an old volume which contains a record of the books taken out by the professors from 1752 to 1832. The books that stand most frequently against Professor Kidd's name, besides those required for ordinary class work, are the Tragedies of Euripides in the original, and works on prophecy—a characteristic and significant choice.

CHAPTER VI.

LECTURESHIP IN TRINITY CHAPEL.

In addition to the two sessions Mr. Kidd had spent in Edinburgh in the study of Divinity, he attended two courses of lectures in the Theological Halls of King's and Marischal Colleges. While a student in the latter he had to deliver a trial discourse before Dr. George Campbell, who was Professor of Divinity as well as Principal of the College. Being a busy man, and not very particular at any time about form and appearance, Mr. Kidd had not been at pains to elaborate his sermon upon sheets of paper in the ordinary way, but brought a sheaf of loose MSS. with him to the desk, the outcome of which, as might be expected, was rather disjointed and crude. At least it was so in the eyes of Dr. Campbell, who had a classic finish and neatness in all he said and did. "Now, Mr. Kidd," said the Doctor, "it would ill become me to criticise severely the production of a gentleman holding the position of a colleague; I would just advise you, when you next come up with a discourse, to have it arranged a little more methodically."

In due course Mr. Kidd presented himself

before the Presbytery of Aberdeen,* and was
licensed as a preacher of the Gospel. His first
sermon was preached in the Church of Kinellar,
where, it appears, the Presbytery of that day
often sent licentiates to preach their maiden discourses, his text being—Isaiah xlv., 22, "Look
unto Me and be ye saved all the ends of the
earth; for I am God and there is none else."

* Extracts from Minutes of Aberdeen Presbytery
relative to the examination and licensing of Mr. Kidd:—

"11th June, 1795.—Mr. James Kidd, student of
divinity, and professor of Oriental Languages in
Marischal College, called to this meeting, and the Presbytery, having seen some of his certificates, and having
reason to believe that he is entitled to be entered on
trials, and he having undergone questionary trials with
approbation, the Presbytery agree to recommend him to
the Synod, provided he produce at next meeting the
additional certificates required of him this day, and the
Presbytery appoint the Moderator to write circular
letters to the different Presbyteries of the Synod recommending him to probationary trials."

"29th July, 1795.—Moderator reported to the Presbytery that he had written the circular letters to the
different Presbyteries of the Synod recommending Mr.
James Kidd to be taken upon probationary trials; and
Mr. Kidd, being present, gave in the certificates required
at the former meeting, with which the Presbytery were
satisfied. The Presbytery prescribed to Mr. Kidd the
following subjects:—A Homily on Luke xvii., 32, and a
Lecture on Psalm xxxvi., which they appoint him to
deliver as soon as convenient."

"12th August, 1795.—The Presbytery appoint Mr. Kidd
to prepare an Exercise and Additions on Heb. i. and vii."

In a journal containing rough jottings, which he kept during the earlier years of his ministry, he says, regarding this sermon :—" The first text on which I have composed anything for public instruction is Isaiah xlv., 22. I delivered the sermon on the foregoing text on Sabbath, 28th February, 1796, in the Parish Church of Kinellar.

"13th October, 1795.—It is found that Synod have allowed Messrs. Smith and Kidd to be taken on trials, whereupon the Presbytery sustain the specimens already delivered as a part of trials. Mr. Kidd delivered his lecture on Psalm xxxvi., which was approved, and appoint him for his Exercise and Additions, first three verses of Psalm cxx., and to prepare an exegesis on the necessity of Divine Revelation."

"3rd February, 1796.—Mr. Kidd delivered his exegesis and his popular sermon, and general questions on the chronology of the eighth century, read Psalm lxx., in Hebrew, and explained, and the Greek Testament, *ad aperturam libri,* and underwent all his trials, and was approved. The Presbytery, having considered all his trials *in cumulo,* judge him to be fit to be licensed ; and he having answered in a satisfactory manner all questions appointed by active Assembly to be put to such as are to be licensed, and having promised to subscribe the Confession of Faith and Formula, and being qualified in terms of law to His Majesty, and the Acts of Assembly against Simoniacal practices being recommended to him, the Presbytery did, and hereby do, in the name of the Lord Jesus Christ, and by his authority, license Mr. James Kidd to preach the Gospel of Jesus Christ, under their inspection, and appoint him to preach at Kinellar, Newhills, and Belhelvie between this time and the meeting of Presbytery in May next, and the ministers to report."

The congregation was larger than usual, owing to the want of sermon in some of the neighbouring parish churches. Although I had not such a frame of mind as I could have wished all the morning, yet, when I began to preach, I found myself much revived by the attention of the audience, but whether their attention was due to the novelty of the preacher, or was the effect of the sermon, I cannot say. But I felt myself to be more impressive towards the close of the discourse, when I began to commend Christ."

About this time he obtained the evening lectureship in Trinity Chapel, which he held for five years. His first appearance as a preacher in Trinity Chapel was not at all auspicious, according to his own account. This is how he writes of it:—"On Sabbath, 6th March, I delivered a lecture on Isaiah xxxv., in Trinity Chapel, Aberdeen. But, ah! what a want of utterance. Never did I see how little man could do in explaining Scripture as I did this day! I felt the most exquisite distress, and was several times ready to stop. I was so much awed by the audience that I could not look up the whole time of the service. I was so much overcome that I grew quite sick, and had nearly fainted. Never shall I forget the distress of mind I laboured under." He adds:—"I preached on the afternoon of the same day on Isaiah xlv., 22, the same sermon I had delivered at Kinellar.

The Lord was gracious in giving me more
assistance than I experienced before noon."

He goes on in his journal to explain the
causes of the want of self-possession when
preaching his first sermon in Trinity Chapel:—
" I am inclined to think the grief of mind which
I laboured under for weeks before was one remote
cause of my distress. The idea of never seeing
America again, but still more the thought of
never again seeing the only man that ever I
could sincerely call a friend, had, the two preceding weeks, several times thrown me into tears.
Another remote cause was the want of time for
preparation. The Thursday morning before I
had to preach, I had not a word of my lecture
put upon paper. I had written no prayer, nor
prepared anything. I may also add that my
professorial avocations were so embarrassing all
the former part of the winter that I had scarcely
time to think of the ministry. I have always
thought, and always said, that I never could
follow my profession and the ministry with equal
success. And I apprehend it will be found true
that Oriental languages are as remote from the
immediate object of preaching as the study of
astronomy is from that of navigation, or the
actual conducting a ship to her intended port.
The study of Oriental literature is as remote
from actual preaching as anatomy is to the
manual operations of surgery."

But confidence grew with practice. On Sabbath, 20th March, 1796, he was in Greenock assisting at the communion in the Gaelic Chapel. Of this occasion he writes :—" I consider this the greatest honour ever I have received, to be permitted to close the Sacramental week. When I entered the pulpit I remembered that at the time I was a boy, about eight or ten years of age, I got leave from my mother to go to the Presbyterian meeting house in Broughshane, in the north of Ireland, on a communion Sabbath. I was then dressed in a white drugget coat. I thought I would be happy were I permitted to see such a sight every Sabbath. I often wished sincerely I had been the minister. I thought him the happiest man in the world. The remembrance of all this came to my mind most sensibly as soon as I ascended the pulpit on this occasion, and when I considered how nearly my early wishes were now completed, I was filled with joy and gratitude."

The journal contains many severe self-reproaches, much lamentation over his personal shortcomings, and bitter regrets that the sermons he had preached were so devoid of unction and power. It is interesting to think that while this self-depreciation was the burden of the record of work done in Trinity Chapel and other places, the great majority of the people of Aberdeen were receiving a very different impression. What

he was so often ashamed of, gave them satisfaction and profit, such as they had seldom experienced before. A poet has said that the reason
why one of his poems was read with so much
ease and pleasure was because it had cost him so
much in the composition. So doubtless the toils
and pangs Mr. Kidd had endured in the preparation and delivery of his discourses had something
to do with their efficiency and power as they were
heard by the congregation; and, probably, if he
had been better pleased with himself, they would
not have profited so much. By his incessant
labour and indomitable perseverance in the dis-
charge of his duty as evening lecturer in Trinity
Chapel, he laid the foundations of his future
eminence as a preacher.

It is evident that during those early years of
his ministry he was under heavy pressure, and
not a little of his frequent complaint about "a
cold and dead heart" was, perhaps, due to an
overstrained nervous system. He certainly did
not eat the bread of idleness, nor did he bring
to the pulpit what cost him nothing. A very
common phrase in the journal is—"Was employed all the week in preparing a lecture," &c.
In his entry for Sabbath, 8th October, 1796, he
says:—"I have been employed all this week in
preparing a lecture on the 89th Psalm, 9-15, and
a sermon on John vi., 10. I have met with
several interruptions which have interfered re-

markably with my studies. I have great reason
to fear I am very ill prepared. I have had only
since this (Saturday) morning at 10 o'clock for
the composition of my sermon, of which I have
only got a skeleton made out. This is the first
sermon I ever delivered with so little preparation."

He had his favourite sermons, and in circumstances of stress and difficulty he preached them
over again when he went from home. He says,
after resorting to this practice when in Edinburgh, " I am not fond of a servile repetition of
the same lecture or sermon, but time and circumstances do not permit me to study as I could wish
at present, therefore I am constrained to act
against my own inclinations in a certain degree."
But as if offering a salve to his conscience, he
adds, " I have made several additions and, I
hope, useful improvements to the lecture."

He very often preached in the Gaelic Chapel,
Aberdeen, and he seems to have had a " good
time" generally in that place; for, in his references to it, there are fewer complaints of
" desertion," " want of assistance," " deadness
and inability." Here is a specimen entry when
he went from home:—" Leith, Sabbath, 9th
April, 1796.—I preached in the tent in the yard
adjoining Mr. Colquhon's chapel. I thought I
had many valuable additions to the sermon—an
old one—but, alas! I left out as many in the de-

livery which were equally as valuable. My delivery was strained and broken. I laboured under great want of spiritual assistance. Alas! alas! such a poor, sinful, pithless preacher as I am! I much fear many of the poor hearers were very little benefited."

There are many references to his memory in those entries:—

"I committed the introduction of another discourse to memory before going to bed:" "Here I was most at a loss, I forgot some of my favourite expressions, which mortified me much:" "After the lecture, upon recollection, I found I had omitted several things I intended to mention:" "I was enabled to proceed with considerable freedom, but my sermon was not exactly uniform to the subject; in the last part I struck out into a path rather foreign to my line of thought:" "I found considerable freedom in the delivery of the first part of my discourse, but when I entered on the second head I had very nearly stopped altogether; I immediately considered this as the reward of my lazy preparation."

It is interesting to notice that, occasionally, while his work of preparation for the pulpit has been done with some degree of success and satisfaction, yet the record of the actual delivery of the discourse is one of failure. That is an experience not unknown to preachers. Here is an example:—

"Aberdeen, Saturday, 7th January, 1796.—I have been busy preparing a lecture on the 91st Psalm this week, and I have great reason to be thankful I have had considerable impression of mind, notwithstanding the subject is difficult; indeed, I have had great labour to collect the literal meaning of the passage; but still have great reason to be thankful. My mind has been serious, and I trust in God I find the power of sin is dying in my nature."

Then follows, as usual, an account of the delivery of what he had prepared:—

"Aberdeen, Sabbath, 8th January, 1796.—I delivered my lecture on the 91st Psalm in the Trinity Chapel in the evening, and, alas! I found great uneasiness, great desertion, and inability, O, my God, when shall I be enabled to serve Thee aright! My mind was away from the subject, and though I was talking of principles of the most engaging and necessary kind, yet I did not feel their power."

The next entry is one that will come home to the hearts of young preachers:—

"Sabbath, 10th April, 1796.—I failed in this service most in my prayers, which smote me to the heart. It is a bad symptom of a preacher who cannot address the Lord with fervent and suitable prayer." It was noticed by all intelligent worshippers that Mr. Kidd had singular power in prayer. The secret of this power was

that he was a praying man, and ever was at pains
to collect his thoughts, and arrange his topics
beforehand. Very often at the end of the account
of the Sabbath services there is a reference to
the particular subject for prayer—" petition,"
"adoration," "thanksgiving," and sometimes
particulars are given.

Progress is being made:—

" Aberdeen, 16th July, 1796, Saturday Evening.—I have been employed since Tuesday preparing two discourses, a sermon and a lecture.
I begin to see religious things in a very different
light from what I ever did before. I see plainly
that the Holy Ghost is the only teacher of
Divinity that can profit a preacher of the Gospel.
I feel great wants, but am willing to wait with
patience till I be further enlightened. May God
grant this very soon, for Christ's sake."

One signal advantage Trinity Chapel had for
him in those early days was that he was engaged
there only in the evening. He had thus many
opportunities of preaching in other places. He
was serving his apprenticeship for a higher
sphere. The wages, too, were those of an
apprentice. Under "Aberdeen, Saturday, 5th
April, 1797," there is the following item:—
"This day received the last payment of forty
pounds sterling for one year's salary as evening
lecturer in the Trinity Chapel."

CHAPTER VII.

SIDE LIGHTS FROM THE DIARY, 1796-97.

THERE is evidence, as has been already shown, that at the very beginning, as well as towards the close of his career, Mr. Kidd kept a kind of diary, which was about as free from careful elaboration as anything of the kind could be. In it there are no sentimental musings, no philosophical reflections, scarcely any of the results of his keen observation of men and things. It is intensely practical and spiritual, and in it he appears as a man who is keeping a vigilant eye and a firm hand upon himself, with the view of obtaining the best possible results out of life. He tells us, too, what he thought of himself, and how he felt about his work from Sabbath to Sabbath. In that diary, written during the first two years of his ministerial career, the young preacher comes before us as one who is actually agonising to attain perfection as an expounder of Scripture and a herald of the cross.

But, while there was only one idea which possessed him when jotting down these notes, and it is obvious nothing was farther from his mind than to take himself, or anyone who chanced to read them, away into fields that are

interesting to the antiquarian or historian, yet,
as a matter of fact, he does incidentally drop
remarks which shed side lights upon the period,
as well as upon the man we have to do with in
this book. Just as when you enter an express
train, your contract is not that you shall be
shown so much of the picturesque, but that you
shall be taken from one point to another; yet,
as you are hurried along, vistas are opened up,
and glances are afforded of surrounding scenery,
and you get more than the terms of the engage-
ment promised; so, in following the record of
the breathings and wrestlings of this young
minister, we need not expect to feel much more
than the throbbing of the master passion of a
consecrated heart as it struggles onwards and
upwards to the high shining ideal that is in the
distance; yet, as if by accident, allusions are
made to current events and things which give us
interesting glimpses of the fashions and manners
of byegone days. Let us, with that view, give a
few of the entries:—

"Pencaitland, Sabbath, 1st May, 1796.—I
preached in this parish church for the Rev. Mr.
Pyper. *I continued an hour in explication
and nearly three quarters in the application of
the passage,* and only intermitted a few minutes
by singing and prayer. I have great reason to
bless God I was considerably helped and found
much freedom in applying the subject. What

account shall I render at the last day for this day's labours? Merciful God, give me more of the spirit and temper of Jesus Christ my Lord, and let Thy glory be my chief aim, for His sake, Amen."

"Aberdeen, Saturday, 11th June, 1796.—I prepared a lecture on the 19th Psalm, from the 7th verse to the end. This was the first passage of scripture I ever cast my eyes on with a view to explanation. It was prescribed to me by Dr. Hunter, Professor of Divinity, in the session 1792-3. I then looked at it, but found no manner of capacity whatever for explanation. I did not read it since with any intention to preach or lecture on it until the week preceding the 28th of May last, when I studied it very attentively, and preached on it in the church of Nigg on the following Sabbath."

"Aberdeen, Sabbath, 12th June, 1796, Evening.—I delivered a lecture on the 19th Psalm. I do not remember ever to have had more freedom of utterance. The Holy Spirit graciously assisted me before I went to the church. Just whilst kneeling down to pray for direction, a thought struck me all at once to turn all the views of my explanation towards Christ, which I did, and oh! how sweetly I was enabled to show the sufficiency of revelation, in all its parts. Oh, to lead men to the blessed Jesus."

"Aberdeen, Sabbath, 24th July, 1796.—I

delivered my lecture on Job iv., 12, in the West Church for the Rev. Dr. Brown. I found considerable freedom in delivery, but not such warmth of the divine assistance as I could have wished. I felt somewhat awed by the assembly, and was conscious of restraint and timidity. I slept too long this morning, which marred my spiritual exercises. I have much to lament the desire for the praise of men which I found accompanying my thoughts this forenoon. After divine service I forgot to make my obeisance to the corps of officers after I had bowed to the magistrates, and this neglect, which happened purely by timidity and embarrassment, gave me more uneasiness than the thought of any omission or defect in my lecture had done. Ah! what hypocrisy."

"Glen Muick, Sabbath, 21st August, 1796.— I went up Deeside on a jaunt for pleasure, and came to Glen Muick meeting house on a Sabbath to hear sermon; and just as I entered the minister's house, his father-in-law, the Rev. Dr. Brown, was going out to preach, and upon seeing me he held up his hands, and declared he would preach none, seeing that I was come. So I entered the pulpit in about five minutes' warning and lectured on the parable of the barren fig tree. I did not get my mind so impressed as I could have wished, neither am I much inclined to think that I was very useful to the people, my lecture, as was to be expected, was ill digested, and could not be delivered with energy.

The interruption to his studies by this little interval of pleasure was, it would appear, felt on the following Sabbath : —

"Aberdeen, Sabbath, 28th August, 1796.— Alas! this has been a lonely Sabbath; I have had little communication with my God. I blame my jaunt to the country last week for unhinging my mind and deranging my studies, so that I could not command my thoughts."

"Aberdeen, Sabbath, 4th September, 1796. —I preached in the West Church for Dr. Shirreffs in the afternoon. I found great desertion in the first prayer, but, blessed be God! I had considerable assistance in the delivery of my sermon and my last prayer. I delivered also my lecture on the first nine verses of the 88th Psalm. And just in my outset I missed, or rather forgot, a quotation out of II. Chronicles xxv., 5, 6, 7, which deranged and distressed me in a remarkable degree. I had placed great dependence upon the verses, and, therefore, I was much confused."

"Aberdeen, Saturday, 17th September, 1796. —Yesterday and to-day I have been employed in preparing two lectures on the 55th of Isaiah, from the 6th to the end; the other, on the 88th Psalm, from the 10th verse to the end. Alas! this week has been remarkably ill spent. I

F

think the practice of feasting after the Sacrament, so common in this country, is very injurious to spiritual exercises. All this week I have been visiting and dining out; and, oh! what deadness do I feel after a communion Sabbath. Oh! how ill I am prepared to preach to-morrow."

Sometimes he had a happy experience in the pulpit when he went to it with great trepidation:—

"Aberdeen, Sabbath, 25th September, 1796. —I delivered my lecture on the first four verses of the 89th Psalm in the Trinity Chapel in the evening. And blessed be the God and Father of the Lord Jesus Christ for the assistance I received. I had laboured all the week, and yet could not get my mind in that composure for study which I wished. I went with great fears to the pulpit, and thought I could say nothing, yet, to my thankful surprise, I was mercifully helped."

"Aberdeen, Saturday, 12th November, 1796. —I have been employed all this week in preparing a lecture on the 89th Psalm, 30-37. Several avocations have distracted my studies. I find it no easy matter to attend to the affairs of this world as far as is necessary, and to attend to the great matters of eternal life as much as we ought. I attended Mr. Copeland's lectures on Natural Philosophy for three evenings, and this

led me to see directly the difference between
Philosophy and Christianity. They appear to
depend entirely on different principles of the
human mind. Philosophy depends on analogy,
Christianity or real religion depends on testimony. The first affects our reason, the second
our faith. And yet all the power of the mind
may be employed in both. Now, if we believe
the witness of man, the witness of God is
greater."

"Aberdeen, Saturday, 26th November, 1796.
—Yesterday and to-day I have been employed
in preparing a lecture on the 5th Matthew, 1-6.
I prepared the heads of a lecture on the same
passage some time ago, and delivered it in the
West Church. I think my present views are
more enlarged and much superior to the former.
But I have been disturbed by an invitation to
dinner to-day, and do not feel so much master of
my subject as I would wish."

"Aberdeen, Sabbath, 18th December, 1796.
—Oh! if the Lord will bless what I have said,
how happy should I be. I know and believe He
can work by any means and instrument; but,
oh! if I do not share in the salvation which I
preach. Oh! if I do not know that Saviour
whom I recommend, what shall I do? My God,
I desire to give myself to Thy service in the
Church. Accept of me, a poor, unworthy, and
guilty sinner, and apply the blood of Jesus to

my conscience. Grant me Thy blessing, and bless the labours of this evening to my soul, and to all who heard the Word, for the Lord Jesus Christ's sake. Amen, Amen."

"My first prayer began with adoration; it touched upon the greatness of God in creation, and the greatness of Jesus in His Godhead in this respect."

"Aberdeen, Saturday, 24th December, 1796. —All this week I have been employed in preparing an introductory lecture for my class (at College), and a lecture on the 76th Psalm, 7-12. The two last days of the week have been so intensely cold, and my place of study so very open, I have not been able to work; adding to all these the power of in-dwelling sin has been so prevalent, that if the Lord do not help me I am undone. Oh, Lord, help me for Christ's sake."

"Aberdeen, Saturday, 21st January, 1797.— I have great reason to bless the Lord for such serenity of mind as I have enjoyed this week, and I have also particular reason to bless the Lord for one sweet glimpse of the Lord Jesus my Saviour. This mercy was granted to me last Thursday evening betwixt four and five o'clock, and what an overpowering sensation it was. What a soul-comforting glance of redeeming love. Oh! for another return to my poor soul. Grant me this, blessed Lord, for the Lord Jesus Christ's sake."

"Aberdeen, Saturday, 6th May, 1797.—I went to a ball with great reluctance; indeed, God knows, it was not with my desire, but my little daughter, being a scholar of the man who had it, and she having nobody to go with her to take care of her, I went; if I have done wrong, may God forgive me, for Christ's sake."

"Aberdeen, Sabbath, 28th May, 1797.—All this day I have had sweet impressions of the sufficiency of Christ—His fulness, His power, His mercy, and His love seem so delightful and comforting, that I think I could, and do give myself wholly to Him in this transporting transaction. I view my weakness, my ignorance, my sinfulness, and my unworthiness in everything; yet, as He invites me to come to Him, and He promises me rest, I most heartily come to Him to be made all things to me—to Thee I come for Thy blessed rest, blessed Jesus, be it so. Amen."

"Aberdeen, Sabbath, 25th June, 1797.—I delivered my lecture on the ciii. Psalm, 6-10, in the Gaelic Chapel, before noon, for the Rev. Mr. MacKenzie. The reason why I lectured in the Gaelic Chapel is as follows:—There is a regiment of Highlanders, mostly from Argyleshire, lying in camp a little way out of town; they have no chaplain, and there are many of them well-disposed sober men; their officers, much to their honour, have desired to have a man to preach to them, and could get none, for they want one who can preach in the Gaelic language. I heard of this affair, and lamented much that I could not supply them; therefore, I offered to preach once a day for Mr. MacKenzie, if he would go and preach in the Gaelic in the camp: he consented."

"Aberdeen, 30th July, 1797.—In the evening I delivered a sermon in the Gaelic Chapel on Hebrews xiii., 20-21. I had but a few minutes to prepare, but I availed myself of sermon skeletons, and, for ever blest be the God of Mercy, I was graciously assisted, and I hope I was useful. My first prayer was mostly confession. I took occasion to address them on their situation as Christians likely to lose their present pastor."

"Aberdeen, Tuesday, 7th December, 1797.— Yesterday and to-day I have been employed in preparing a sermon on Ephesians i., 3. The occasion was a general thanksgiving appointed by Government for the interposition of Providence since the commencement of the war, and in particular for Admiral Duncan's victory over the Dutch fleet on the 11th October last."

The last extract we make from the venerable document before us, the writing of which is fading with the hundred years that are upon it, contains the first allusion to Gilcomston Chapel, with which his name was to be linked for the rest of his life:—" Aberdeen, Sabbath, 2nd July, 1797.—I delivered my lecture on the ciii. Psalm, 11-16, in the forenoon, in the chapel of Belmont Street, for the Rev. Mr. Bryce. I have much reason to be very thankful; I was mercifully assisted, and in some measure useful to the audience. In the interval between sermon, I went to the Chapel of Ease at Gilcomston, and there met Mrs. Kidd by appointment. It being the communion in that place, we both went to the Lord's Table."

CHAPTER VIII.

CALL TO GILCOMSTON CHAPEL.*

THE light which shone with such brilliancy for
five years in Trinity Chapel was deemed worthy
of a more commanding sphere, and when, by the
decease of the previous pastor, a vacancy occurred
in Gilcomston Chapel of Ease, Mr. Kidd was
called by a large majority, "the patronage
having been vested in those who had subscribed
one guinea to the funds of the chapel." This
place, which still stands, renovated, and a fully-
equipped church of the Establishment, was
erected in 1770, to accommodate dwellers in the
southern part of the large parish of Old Machar,

---

*Copy of the Call from Gilcomston Church to Mr.
Kidd, as the original document now stands:—

"We, a majority of the legal electors of a minister to
the Chapel of Ease, on the south side of the parish of
Old Machar, being destitute of a pastor; also, having
good information, and our own experience of the ministerial abilities, wisdom, and prudence; also, of the suit-
ableness to our capacities of the gifts of you, Mr. James
Kidd, Preacher of the Gospel, have agreed, with the
advice and consent of the parishioners subscribing, and
concurrence of the Reverend the Presbytery of Aberdeen,
to invite, call, and intreat: Like as We, by these
presents, do heartily invite, call, and intreat you to
undertake the office of a pastor

and in what was then a suburb of the city of Aberdeen. It was built on rising ground, as is patent to every observer yet, notwithstanding the changes that have taken place in the surroundings; and for many years it was a solitary and conspicuous object, the ground stretching westwards, where Skene Street and Carden Place now stand, being then under the plough or spade.

Down in the Denburn district, close by, there was a considerable population, mostly weavers and shoemakers, who had their homes and plied their occupations there, because rents were lower and taxation less than in the city. Beyond the lands of Gilcomston, in Jack's Brae, Leadside, Loanhead, also in Hardgate and Rubislaw, there were little communities of working people, who had come in from rural parts, and had much of the robustness and simplicity of the country in their character.

charge of our souls. And, further, upon your accepting of this our Call, we promise you all dutiful respect, encouragement, and obedience in the Lord. In we have subscribed this Call, written by Andrew Spalding, Clerk to Alexander Shirrefs, Esquire, Advocate in Aberdeen, on paper legally stamped, within the said Chapel, the eighteenth day of May, one thousand eight hundred and one years, before these Witnesses.

" Mr. William Middleton, Schoolmaster at said Chapel of Ease; and James Birnie, Gardener at Rottenholls.

" Witnesses—

" WILLIAM MIDDLETON, Witness.
" JAMES BIRNIE, Witness."

Gilcomston Chapel was intended to meet the spiritual wants of those outlying districts; but, in course of years, after Mr. Kidd's acceptance of the pastorate, it would have been as difficult to define the local habitation of the members of his congregation, and confine them within the bounds of a territorial connection, as it was to keep the minister himself under the restraint of ecclesiastical precedent and conventional rule. In this place he ministered to one of the largest congregations in Scotland till death came, and he received a higher call.

So at last, after much tossing and thwarting, enough to daunt the spirit of one less resolute than James Kidd, the golden dream of childhood becomes a fact in manhood's prime: he is now a fully-accredited and empowered minister of Christ. The course of preparation had been long and trying, but what ample return for it all was to be found in his subsequent career. The experience he gained in wrestling with difficulty, and the sympathy he was able to show to those whom he met, who were, as he himself once was, "sair hauden doon," was an invaluable part of the capital he had at his command as a "succourer of many."

The evening lectureship in connection with Trinity Church afforded him an opportunity of "trying his wings" as a preacher before he was weighted with the full responsibility of the

pastorate. Gilcomston came to him when he was
in the full vigour of manhood, and the fame he
had won as a preacher to the people in Trinity
gave him at once a position of commanding influence; and though he did not get his degree
till 1819, we shall now, for the sake of convenience, call him Dr. Kidd.

That Dr. Kidd, a stranger and an Irishman,
and in a city where learned and able men
abounded, should at once have leapt into a position of almost unexampled popularity and influence as a preacher, is a fact that needs to be
explained. It will be generally admitted that,
with the exception, perhaps, of Andrew Cant,
who had been in his grave for more than a
hundred years before Dr. Kidd appeared upon
the scene, no occupant of the Aberdeen pulpit
took such a hold of the people, and left such a
vivid and lasting impression behind him, as the
one whose career we are now following. Various
considerations, arising from the time, the place,
and the man, can be adduced, which throw
light upon the grounds of the extraordinary
favour with which he and his utterances were
received.

Dr. Kidd began his public work at the dawn
of a period of revived interest in religion. It
was his distinction and privilege to be one of the
heralds of better times for the church and the
world. He began to speak when the ears and

hearts of the people were opened after prolonged apathy. The eighteenth century was certainly not a period of high ideals and noble enthusiasms. Mediocre, artificial, shallow, wedded to traditional routine, substituting conventional respectability for aspiring heroism, in literature, politics, and religion, it was, up to the second last decade, a background sufficiently dark for the splendid era that was about to emerge.

A variety of causes contributed to the general awakening and stir which, about a century ago, were so general all over Europe, the most potent and striking of which was the French Revolution. In its effect it was like the shock which sometimes brings back healthy tone and action to the debilitated system. The civilised world was shaken out of its lethargy. Emancipated from the spell of the goddess of dulness, men began to think, to put questions, to see visions, and dream dreams. Rising out of the rut of custom and formalism, first principles began to be of consequence to them, the deeper wants and problems of life came to the front; and, with the energy of those who had awakened from a long sleep, men wrestled with the foes of their freedom and happiness. A spirit of enquiry was abroad, the horizon of thought was widened, men's interests were multiplied, existing institutions were brought to the bar of judgment, hope was on the wing, and the past and the present were no longer regarded as the world's goal and consummation.

There were also local reasons for the very cordial welcome which was given to Dr. Kidd and his teaching. The evangelical message, delivered with the human interest and the impassioned earnestness of a man who had both genius and heart, was, at the time, if not a new, certainly a rare thing. Nearly fifty years before Dr. Kidd became a power for good, John Bisset, and others less known, were noble witnesses for the truth, forerunners of the great Evangelical Revival; but they were solitary lights, and no general movement sprang from their labours.

It is very remarkable that Aberdeen, which has been so pronounced in its Evangelicalism for nearly a hundred years, should, before that, have been so much under the sway of " Moderatism." How can it be accounted for that a people so clear-headed, and with such activity, as well as vigour of intellect, should have been so slow to take in the thought and leaven which came with the Reformation and Covenanting periods? No town in all Scotland of its importance and intelligence offered such stout resistance to the entrance of the better religious ideas which had become the common property of most of Scotland. So much was this the case, that the ecclesiastical opponents of the Covenant considered it a safe thing to send such a fiery spirit as Samuel Rutherford to exile in Aberdeen. They hoped, perhaps, that his environment would cool his ardour, just as a sea laden with icebergs lowers the temperature of the encompassing atmosphere. Writing of Aberdeen as it was at the time he was in his "prison," Rutherford said:—"The people showed me, at the best, a dry kindness." He adds, in his own quaint style:—"There are some blossomings of Christ's Kingdom in this town, and the smoke is rising, and the ministers are raging; *but I like a rumbling and roaring devil best."*

The remoteness of Aberdeen in those days of slow travel and infrequent communication with the national centres, where stirring deeds were being done; the immense influence of such a territorial magnate as the Marquis of Huntly, and almost all the Gordons, always thrown into the scale against the cause of progress; and last, but not least, the inveterate hostility of the Aberdeen clergy and professors, with a few noble exceptions, to those views of doctrine which eventually gained the ascendancy—all the above causes contributed to put Aberdeen on a lower level than most other towns in Scotland in point of Gospel privileges. Men like Dr. Kidd were like angelic visitants, who came at rare intervals, and the common people heard them gladly.

In accounting for the success of this ministry, it should be mentioned there was something in

Dr. Kidd's own striking personality, his raciness of manner and originality, not to say eccentricity of character, that drew attention to him. It is said that Aberdeen shares with Fife the distinction of being typically Scottish—having all the characteristics of the nation intensified; and to an audience of that description, composed of persons who were habitually cautious and self-restrained, there must have been a piquancy in the preaching of a man who was effervescing with the fervid enthusiasm of the sister isle.

The people saw at once that he was a genuine bit of humanity, with many of its limitations, and some of its infirmities, but, on the whole, consecrated with a consuming zeal to high and holy ends. Had he been a mere vulgar adventurer, playing for popularity, and working for his own hand, he would soon, notwithstanding his great abilities, have passed away from public notice as a pulpit bubble that had burst. "People are soon tired of fireworks, but never of the stars." The conviction was deeply wrought in the hearts of those about him that he was a man whose soul was on fire, whose conscience was burdened with a message from heaven, whose heart went out to his fellow-men with a true, Christ-like compassion, and his odd ways and forms of speech were looked upon as the accidents, the natural excrescences of a man who was determined to be himself and nobody else in the pulpit and elsewhere.

It has to be remembered that, in those days when places and their inhabitants were shut up so much within themselves, local custom and manner, the idiosyncrasies of a community, were more pronounced, and constituted a greater barrier to a stranger, more especially if he was a public speaker, than they do now. Distance, in space, though not very great, meant some degree of aloofness. The people at the other end of a country were really foreigners in many respects.

Railways, telegraphs, and a cosmopolitan press are rapidly effacing local individuality, and reducing all to a uniform pattern, so far as differences in blood and climate will allow. But, before those adjuncts of civilisation rushed in upon us, there was much more that a man from another part of the world had to "get over" before he could be in touch with those whom he addressed. But what a breaker up of walls of separation, and, at the same time, what a bond of union is that Gospel which seeks what is central and common in world-wide humanity. Circumstances of nationality, locality, social position, and educational advantage, are lost to view when the Son of Man, through faithful preaching, appears upon the scene.

It has been said that the strong secular understanding of the northern Scot, which is so apt to absorb all available energy, puts him in great danger of becoming sceptical or formal in religion, unless its truths not only touch, but inflame his heart; and it is, in part, the secret of Dr. Kidd's extraordinary power that he was not content with enlightenment, but strove to bring kindling power to bear upon the feelings of his congregation.

He was a man of large, heroic mould, his big, burly frame being the fitting sheath to his broad, massive manhood. He kept himself to the end of his life in close alliance with heaven, and in partnership with God, subordinating all interests and aims to the one dominating desire to do good. No wonder that woman—a member of his congregation—said what she did when she heard that the Premier of the day (Mr. Perceval) had been assassinated. She was told that the *Prime Minister* had been shot. "What!" said she, "oor Dr. Kidd?"

G

CHAPTER IX.

THE PEOPLE'S PREACHER.

DR. KIDD was a man of versatile genius: in view
of the numerous channels in which his exuberant
energy flowed, and the varied resources and apti-
tudes which his public life subsequently de-
veloped, he almost appeared to be several men
rolled into one.   But preaching was the supreme
function of his life.   "Did you ever hear me
preach?" said Coleridge one day to Charles
Lamb.   "I never heard you do anything else,"
was the facetious reply.   In like manner it could
be said that whatever else overlaid, nothing ever
did conceal the preacher in Dr. Kidd.

Dr. Kidd was a born preacher.   He was a
teacher, but he was more than that: he was
emphatically a preacher.   The teacher deals with
truth; the preacher with truth and men.   Con-
sequently, the true preacher has not only logic,
and the power of lucid statement, but he has
also that persuasiveness which is the offspring of
warm and lively sympathy.   With all the ardour
of his Irish nature, which faith in Christ Jesus
had intensified as well as purified, he threw himself upon his audience as one who was under the

imperial constraint of conviction and heaven-inspired enthusiasm.

His preaching was decidedly evangelical. There is no ministry that so stirs the human heart as that which gives a large and honoured place to the Gospel. That is easily accounted for by a reference to some of the deepest and noblest feelings of our nature. The Gospel, intelligently received, at once inspires confidence and implants aspiration—two things which have more to do with human happiness and progress than any other two that could be mentioned. The minister who can tell people that God is willing to take them as they are, and make them better than they are, has a message which covers the whole breadth of human need. He addresses an appeal to the heart and conscience as well as to the intellect, and opens up springs which can never run dry. An evangelical ministry, when it is truly vital, and not aridly dogmatic, succeeds in awakening in men's minds a new and well-established interest in life, which can draw supplies for itself from the righteousness as well as from the love of God.

There was, moreover, in Dr. Kidd a singular combination of powers, which accounted for his rapid and long-sustained popularity as a preacher. In the first place, he was a man of sterling moral worth and profound spiritual feeling. His heart, everyone saw at once, was in the right place. His religious life was unmistakably real and spontaneous, the man himself coming forth in the name of the Lord on Sabbath, as to his native sphere and congenial employment. Dr. Kidd the man, and Dr. Kidd the preacher, were ever one person, identical in aim and spirit. There was nothing, professional or otherwise, "put on," except the gown. There was power in the man's character; for, according to the old proverb, his word thunders whose life lightens.

Then it has to be remembered that his intellectual ability was far above the average. His personal goodness had a strong understanding as a fitting instrument. As faith without works is dead, being alone, so goodness is, for the purposes of leadership and public usefulness, inoperative, if it be not accompanied by vigour of mind. A man may be well qualified to adorn a private station with nothing but sound principles and upright aims, but, in public life, he needs the commanding abilities of a leader, else the position is more than he can rise to. In addition to having something to say that was worth listening to, he had also a powerful voice and an imposing appearance to make him effective in delivery. His light was well seen, as it was placed upon a suitable candlestick.

Furthermore, to enhance and widen his popularity, especially amongst those who could not be attracted by his more solid and spiritual qualities, he had a strong and picturesque individuality. He did not cultivate eccentricity. He was no mere vendor of oddities. His singularity was the irrepressible outcome of the man's idiosyncrasy, as much as the gushing torrent that comes brawling from the mountain side is a bit of Highland scenery. The people, with a wondrous and almost unerring instinct, can quickly distinguish between the self-conscious Merry-Andrew in the pulpit, and the true man of God, who, being endowed with a fresh and racy nature, allows it to have free play, untrammelled by mere conventional rules and usages. A Christian brother, objecting to the flashes of wit with which a friend was brightening an argument, received the answer—"Would you not use wit too, my friend, if you had it?" So might Dr. Kidd have replied to many of his sober and eminently prosaic critics.

There was not the same staid reserve in the pulpit then that there is now. A freedom and familiarity were allowed that would be considered irreverent and vulgar in the present day. But Dr. Kidd, even in those days, was deemed to be out of the common. As Dr. Kidd he had a chartered independence. It was nothing extraordinary for him, when making an appeal for Sunday School teachers and visitors, to say—"I see William —— sitting in the front gallery;

you might come and help." A little confidential
talk might occasionally take place also between
the minister and the precentor or beadle, as, for
example, the Doctor said to the latter one
Sabbath evening, when the light was passing
away—"Bring the candles, Saunders, and not
keep me up here in the dark like a crow in the
mist."

He had much of that dramatic instinct which
carries a man into the situation of others, and
so identifies him with their circumstances and
experiences that he almost for the time being
loses his personality in theirs. An honoured
father in Israel still alive tells of a sermon he
heard Dr. Kidd delivering on Belshazzar's feast,
which had in it many dramatic touches. When
in his discourse he came to the writing which
appeared upon the wall, the Doctor, representing
the King, cowered in the pulpit till he was
almost out of sight, and his astonished and
terror-stricken face made every one in the building realise the scene that was being depicted. His
vivid imagination and intense feeling put him
for the moment into whatever situation he
described, and those who were brought under the
contagious influence of his fervid oratory could
not throw off the spell without an effort. He
often preached the annual sermon for the Shipwrecked Mariners' Society, and his discourse on
such occasions was like a strong whiff of the salt

sea. He was a sailor for the time being, and
nautical terms, such as "starboard" and "lar-
board," came as naturally to his lips as if he had
been an ancient mariner. He has been heard to
describe a shipwreck so graphically as to draw
tears from most of his audience—they, with the
help of his vivid discourse, feeling as if a dread
catastrophe were happening before their eyes.

A gentleman who had come to Aberdeen to
introduce chain cables for ships, was sitting in
the minister's seat on one of those occasions. The
Doctor was describing the storm which Paul, as
a prisoner, encountered, a wonderfully graphic
account of which we have in the 27th chapter of
the Acts of the Apostles. Rising to a grand
climax in his oratory, and putting the wild and
tragic scene in the strongest possible light, he
turned round to the pew where the English
stranger was seated, and, addressing him, he said
—"Where would even your chain cables have
been then?"

A very common theme of discourse with him
was the deceitfulness and treachery of the human
heart. His illustrations of that subject were
wonderfully diversified, and, as might be expected, homely and forcible. Explaining the
scriptural words where the god of this world is
represented as blinding the eyes of men, he took
two half-crown pieces out of his pocket, and,
suiting the action to the word, placed one over

cach of his eyes, which was an impressive, if somewhat odd, illustration of the text, not likely to be soon forgotten.

On another occasion, referring to the depravity and falseness of the heart of man, he, in an impulsive outburst, the recollection of which probably scourged no one more than himself, said—"You are all rotten at the heart like J—— C——'s potatoes," naming, as the owner of the said useful vegetable, one of his own congregation, who was doubtless more surprised than pleased at the public attention that was drawn to the quality of the article which he had reared. Not long before his death, Dr. Kidd happened, in the course of his sermon, to quote from Scripture the verse, "The heart is deceitful above all things, and desperately wicked; who can know it?" a portion of his commentary on which was—"Ye know no more of your own hearts than a grocer does of a sugar loaf before he breaks it up."

Professor Masson, in his admirable sketch of Dr. Kidd, which appeared in "Macmillan's Magazine" many years ago, gives the opening passage of a sermon delivered on April 3, 1797, the text being Eccles. v., 5—"Better is it that thou shouldest not vow than that thou shouldest vow and not pay." It may be taken as a specimen of his style when, like the apostle, being crafty, he was catching men with guile:—"My brethren,—It never was, nor is it, my desire to make the pulpit a scorner's chair, or to gratify private resentment by taking an unmanly advantage of the place where I stand; and yet I suspect there is an individual here this evening against whom, I promptly declare, I have composed the discourse which I am now about to deliver. Now, that it may not be said that I have deviated from candour, honesty, and fidelity, or that I have brought ' a railing accusation ' against anyone, I call upon you, aged fathers! and upon you, discerning men and brethren! and upon you, ye female part of my audience—whom I should have named first—and ponder well what I shall say—to weigh with Christian impartiality the force of my arguments, and to declare the truth when ye leave this house. 'Ye are witnesses of these things.' I cast myself upon the whole of this assembly, and for once request attention, without the disturbance of coughing or throat-clearing, which so frequently obstructs both speaking and hearing. As in the Divine Presence, then, we shall proceed."

Nothing could be more beside the mark than to suppose that those toothsome morsels give any idea of the general character of Dr. Kidd's preaching. Some of them are no more to it than the " flies " were to the apothecary's ointment. In every sermon that came from the

Gilcomston pulpit there was a solid body of scriptural instruction. Dr. Kidd was strong in exposition, the books of Daniel and Revelation and the Epistle to the Romans being specially remembered as the subject of many lectures. He was often highly doctrinal, and sometimes metaphysical, but he could never be dry. The printed discourse may show a little ability in that way, but not as it was spoken by the living man. Yet, let it not be imagined for a moment that because he was popular he was superficial and frothy.

Preaching three times every Sabbath to the same congregation for more than a third of a century, and that, too, with unabated interest and undiminished popularity to the very end, was ample proof not only of exceptional natural ability, but also of sustained application. He was at pains to secure variety and freshness in his preaching. He not only kept up his habits as a student and a reader, rising every morning at three o'clock, but he was always looking out for helpful illustrations and pregnant hints. No artist could have been more eager to put upon canvas some vision of beauty, or striking aspect of nature that caught his eye, than was Dr. Kidd to enrich and give point to his preaching, by what came under his notice, in the course of his perambulations.

It was not his practice, except in the early

days of his ministry, to write out his sermons
fully, but to satisfy himself with a solid, well-
compacted "skeleton," trusting to his ability in
extemporaneous address to find the necessary
clothing of flesh in the pulpit. It would have
been impossible for him, with such a daily
burden of duty upon him as professor, pastor,
and general helper, to find time to put his
thought into finished literary form. Besides, it
was quite unnecessary, and would have been, in
his case, a waste of time. He had such a command of vigorous and appropriate diction, that
all he needed was a well-conceived plan to prevent repetition. It was evident from these
"skeletons," that he did not bring to the pulpit
what cost him nothing. His mind was active,
open, and was ever being replenished with reading. He was the theologian as well as the pastor
in the pulpit, and did not scruple sometimes to
introduce subjects which must have taxed his
hearers' powers of understanding. That Church
of Gilcomston was a place where the people had
their intellects whetted, as well as their souls fed.
His main endeavour was to instruct the conscience and influence the life; but he honoured
his audience by assuming that they had intelligence as the basis of their religion; and, while
theirs was occasionally toiling and panting to
keep up with his, yet the exercise, upon the
whole, did them good.

In the note books that he left behind him,
there are jottings of scenes of distress he witnessed, intended for use in the pulpit. In some
of the outlines of sermons which were published
after his death, there are numerous allusions to
passing events, and to historical facts. Everything of human interest that came within the
scope of his knowledge was made to pay tribute
to him as a preacher. As might be supposed,
he was not always happy in his allusions.
Occasionally the incongruity was ludicrous, and
defeated the end he had in view. The following
entry in his journal is suggestive:—"I have
dabbled too much in politics. I must have done
with them. I must wait to see what God is about
to do." But Jupiter is Jupiter, though he sometimes nods. The people readily distinguished
between the man and his occasional breaches of
good taste in extemporaneous speech. An exhortation such as the following, which often came
from his lips, soon undid the effect of any "slip
of the tongue":—"Oh! my people, try to feel
and to know these doctrines. Do not go from
this house thinking that you have got good, if
you have only learned that these things are true."

One noticeable circumstance in connection
with his preaching was the intense dissatisfac-
tion he often felt with regard to his own part in
it. To be in the pulpit was to be where he was
most conscious of power, and the exquisite joy

which comes from its exercise; but, judging
from entries in his journal, he had frequent
occasion to reproach himself for some defect in
himself or his preparation, which hindered him
from attaining to the highest degree of power
of which he, as the instrument of God, was
capable:—"Aberdeen, Sabbath, 11th December,
1796.—I delivered my lecture in the Trinity
Chapel in the evening, but, ah! how dead and
listless did I feel. I have reason to bless the
living God I was not confounded altogether.
May the Lord pity and pardon me. Oh, when
shall I be enabled to serve him aright; when
shall I love my Saviour and my God; God forgive my iniquities, and grant me His acceptance,
for the sake of Jesus Christ, my Lord!"

He was at pains to realise his ideal; but had
often cause to lament that he had not come up
to it. Preaching was not to him a "performance," "doing duty," a piece of routine work.
It was the most vitally important business that
could be transacted upon the earth. Preaching,
to some who engage in it, is like a military
review which ends in smoke. To Dr. Kidd it
was "action," a real, stern battle, that was expected to do something. But sometimes he
missed the mark, or made a rash and clumsy
stroke, and he was angry with himself for it.
The natural ardour which made him cry when
a child, if he was not able to repeat his lessons,

became, in manhood, a consecrated thing, which often caused him to be impatient with himself. It was part of the secret of his power. He was never found in tears like the artist who wept because he had reached his goal. Dr. Kidd's ideal was ever ahead of his achievement.

This is how his example told according to the testimony of Professor Masson :—

" Ere long the taste for this style of preaching spread beyond his own congregation, till the whole city became in the main Evangelical in its notions of doctrine, and the other pulpits in it were filled with men supplying similar doctrine, after their various native fashions, and only in the country round did Moderatism still prevail, though even there largely modified. All this was not owing to Kidd, for the *Zeit geist* was at work ; but much of it *was* owing to him. He was a flame at which many lit their candles."

The doctrine delivered at Gilcomston, like all things real and vital to their generation, had the hue of the times. No man preaches effectively who does not breathe an atmosphere which is more or less charged with the thought and sentiment of his own day. Were anyone, from a misguided reverence for Dr. Kidd, to attempt to reproduce the exact shade of his doctrine, and slavishly repeat his phrases, he would show himself to be worse than obsolete.

Life claims freedom ; true freedom is life true

to itself and its source. Every generation of men, like every year in nature, has its own independent characteristics. Every generation likes to hear its own accent; to hold up its own "earthen vessel" for the blessing which comes from above; to see the truth with its own eyes, and tell the vision in its own way.

But the great facts contained in the message, and in those who receive it, are identical from year to year—human sin that has to be repented of, and divine grace that is to be thankfully taken. There is nothing creative in the varying dialectics of the generations. It is faith that, in its essence, cannot alter which brings the power from God. Reason merely sifts and sorts: it has no originality, no creative power. What served Dr. Kidd's generation must serve ours. Nature is permanent in its principles and forces, though its aspects vary: so is Grace.

For a generation to be so self-conscious, and so wrapt in admiration for its own theories, as to put the stress of its thought upon the fact that doctrine has been sifted and methods improved, and not upon the practical use that is to be made of them, is to be as far from sanity as the soldier would be who was so much occupied in comparing his weapons of precision with the clumsy fire-arms of former days, that he overlooked the obvious duty of turning them against the enemy that was before him.

CHAPTER X.

A SABBATH IN GILCOMSTON CHAPEL.

GILCOMSTON CHAPEL was a large, square-built, plain building, with galleries on both sides, the pulpit at one end, and a gallery at the other, with a "cock loft" above it to accommodate the increasing congregation attracted by Dr. Kidd's powerful preaching. The exterior was more than severely simple; it was bald and barn-like. The interior made no pretension to elegance of any kind; the only thing visible which hard, matter-of-fact utility did not demand, was the model of a ship (the "Agnes Oswald") hung in front of the end gallery, a symbol of the consequence of the seafaring calling to the population of that period, which was to be seen also in some of the other places of worship in the city. The only recommendation the edifice had, was that it provided shelter and sitting accommodation—not on too liberal a scale for the sitter, for the seats were narrow beyond all modern endurance—for a large multitude of people who wanted to worship, and, above all, to hear. In those days of Spartan hardiness, there was no appliance for generating warmth in winter, other than the lungs of those who were present; and in summer there was no ventilation, except by opening a door or a window, and that only when things were becoming desperate. A minister belonging to the North, with some originality and wit, once said, that if he were to preach in a bottle, the beadle would be sure to put in the cork; in like manner Dr. Kidd often suffered from an insufficiency of God's air, *i.e.*, pure air, when preaching. Try to imagine the state of the atmosphere, after a two hours' service, in which nearly two thousand people had taken part. Is it matter for surprise that sleeping in church was a practice which the pew, with the aid of the pulpit, had to fight against? So bad was the air, occasionally, in those days of defective, or rather neglected ventilation, that, it is said, the candles, in some places of worship, have been actually seen to go out from sheer exhaustion of the needful oxygen.

On going to Gilcomston Chapel, people seldom asked if it was to be " himsel' the day." It generally was " himsel' "; occasionally he went to communion services in Dundee and elsewhere, but his absence from his own pulpit was phenomenal. He once went, by earnest request, to London, for a month, to aid in recruiting what was afterwards the Rev. John Macdonald's congregation : but he never forgot his own people in his public prayers when in the far-distant metropolis.

H

There being no vestry attached to the chapel, the Doctor, as was his wont, made a virtue of a necessity, and walking from his house attired for his ministerial duty half an hour or so before worship began, made the pulpit his waiting place. There he sat primed and ready like a man who was longing for the opportunity in which he gloried as a preacher of Christ's everlasting gospel. He had been engaged in work already in the early part of the Sabbath, which only whetted his appetite for more. Besides meditating and praying from an early hour in his study, he had opened a class and addressed one or two of his Sabbath schools, and so it had been proved beyond doubt that the pump was not *off the fang.*

As the Doctor sat there on his lofty pedestal surveying the assembling multitude, he, with his observant eye and wonderful faculty of recognising individuals, was able to keep up acquaintance with his members and their families. The faces of most of those before him indicated the grave purpose and alertness of persons who had come to do business and to get something. They had not the dull, sleepy air, not unknown in parish churches of the time, of churchgoers who were merely conforming to decent custom, and meritoriously assisting at a formal celebration. No doubt they were a mixed multitude, with not a few black sheep amongst them; but, take them.

as a whole, they were a *douce*, earnest-minded hard-headed people, the progenitors of a great deal of the robust Evangelicalism of the town.

On his yearly communion Sabbath in July the immense congregation must have presented an imposing spectacle. People came then from other congregations in town and country in large numbers, and the place was packed with human beings, many of whose faces revealed that their spirits were touched with the exaltation and solemnity of the occasion. No wonder the Doctor, when standing up in the pulpit to begin the service, and looking out upon this vast sea of faces, should have been constrained to remark, as he once did, " This is a day for a death-bed ! "

The scene was not without its touches of picturesqueness and human interest, even to the ordinary observer who laid no claim to intense spiritual sympathy. The communion Sabbath was the great day of the year for putting on one's finest and newest clothes. It is a true instinct which prompts one to put on " his best " when appearing before God in His public sanctuary. So on that day the young women had on light dresses, and the men drill trousers. With a profusion of white "mutches" and a sprinkling of red-coloured cloaks among the elderly dames, there must have been something to please the eye even of those who were not " on the mount," and saw nothing that lay beyond the outward and earthly aspect of the scene.

As the people were taking their places in the pews under the Doctor's eye, occasionally little incidents occurred which told their own tale of human vanity and selfishness, and revealed the fact that Gilcomston Chapel had not yet fulfilled its task in seeking to bring Aberdeen men and women to perfection. One day he spied a young fellow in the "cock loft" who was doing his best to display a pair of white trousers. The restless movements of this youth were a disturbance, and the minister at last, rising up, sarcastically observed, "You may sit down now; surely by this time the ladies must have seen your small clothes sufficiently!" On another day, as will happen sometimes even yet in the house of God, strangers who wanted to go into a certain pew where there was abundance of room met with a passive resistance on the part of those sitting at the end of it, and as passing people in the narrow space between seat and bookboard was next to impossible, they could only stand and look and wonder at the inhospitality of professed worshippers of God. Roused to anger by this incivility shown to visitors, the Doctor, who took in the whole situation at a glance, thundered out, "Sit up, proud flesh, and let the people have a seat as long as there is one to give them." So great was the demand for sittings that there were folding seats in the passages, which were usually filled. Old men and women might be seen sitting on the pulpit stairs, and on stools on any empty space not too far from the minister.

Having a keen appreciation of the value of time, punctuality was a virtue which Dr. Kidd practised with conspicuous constancy. But his was an Irish kind of punctuality, for, as Dr. Bain tells, he regularly rose to begin the service five minutes before the hour. The first exercise was a brief exposition of the psalm that was to be sung. In that way he helped the people to give reality and significance to the praise, and when the time came for it, they were better able to sing "with the understanding." An old woman of those days, but belonging to another parish, once said, " I thocht the psalms were jist to gie the minister a breath." They knew better than that in Gilcomston. He took up the psalms in consecutive order, giving so many stanzas each Sabbath. So much was that generation impressed with the importance of this exercise that, after Dr. Kidd's death, when candidates to fill his place were being heard, it is said that explaining the psalm turned the scale in favour of Mr. Bryce, who became the minister. It was remarked in his hearing that none of the other aspirants for the place had explained the psalm. He took the hint, and got the charge.

In like manner, when he announced the passage of Scripture to be read, the Doctor proceeded to give a brief analysis of its contents,

and a summary of the lessons taught. His great
aim was to make every part of the service real
and vital to all who were before him. He was at
pains to enlist their intelligence and sympathy,
and to shut dull apathy and dreary formalism
outside the gates of Gilcomston. Having stated
the general scope of the chapter, he proceeded
to read it with that true and powerful elocution
which does not draw attention to itself, but to
the matter in hand. His sonorous voice was well
modulated, and the rich Irish accent, instead of
detracting from the effect, must, to Aberdeen
ears, have lent the charm of piquancy to his
delivery. Professor Masson says:—"His slow
and impressive reading of the psalms was, I remember, a never-failing source of admiration
and delight to the Aberdonians. He was a real
Chrysostom."

Then came the prayer, in which the man, in
the depth and tenderness of his nature, stood
revealed. Prayer was to him the very soul and
breath of religion. He knew the value of it for
himself, and he pressed its importance upon his
people, sometimes in the pulpit taking up a prose
psalm, and, there and then, like a father dealing
with his children, showing them by actual experiment how it could be turned into prayer.
Dr. Bain and others, who attended Gilcomston
in their youth, testify to the unique power, the
freshness and seraphic fervour of the man in

prayer. Dr. Bain says:—"The first occasion when I resumed attending the church, I was taken all of a heap with listening to his first prayer; the easy flow of language, the choiceness of his topics, and the brevity of the whole, came upon me like a new revelation." Dr. Bain also tells us that it was a common habit with the Doctor, in his prayer, to "address the three persons in the Godhead in consecutive order, adapting the petitions to the specific personality of each," and, he adds, "I never heard this done by any other preacher." One secret of Dr. Kidd's extraordinary power in prayer, was that he did not trust entirely to the mood of the moment for the subject matter of his petitions. Besides constantly breathing the atmosphere of prayer, he secured coherency, freshness, and variety in those all-important exercises of the church, by prolonged premeditation and careful selection of topics.

The sermon was also the outcome of well-digested knowledge and intense thought, though delivered extemporaneously. His method was exposition, having from beginning to end a practical edge. "He was mighty in the Scriptures." Generally, though not invariably, he took for exposition the historical books of the Old Testament in the forenoon, the Gospels in the afternoon, and the Epistles in the evening. In the course of his Gilcomston pastorate he, in

his expository discourses, went over the whole
Bible twice, and had begun the third series when
he died.   An old man, whose character in youth
was formed under the preaching of Dr. Kidd, in
recounting the scenes of Gilcomston, used to
wind up his remarks by saying—alluding to the
fervour of the ministrations, as well as to the
crowded congregations—"Eh, sir, it was a het
hoose."

The Sabbath spent in Gilcomston was an
educational as well as religious force to the great
body of the people of that generation in Aberdeen.   Many young men, some of whom have
won   distinction   in   their   chosen   spheres   of
activity, had their mental powers awakened by
grappling with the doctrine of the Gilcomston
pulpit, and reproducing for the benefit of others
the arguments and illustrations with which it
was supported.   For the Doctor, though he was
ever impelled by a consuming spiritual earnestness, allowed himself considerable latitude in the
topics he chose, and the manner in which he
treated them.   The millennium, the evils of
Popery, and the glories of prophecy might be
sprung upon his people at any time.   Things
civil, political, and local, the resources of literature and the examples of history, as well as the
general information which could be gathered
from all parts of the world, were woven into the
texture of his Sabbath discourses.   It would be

a stretch of fancy for even the most enthusiastic
Kiddite to lay it all to the credit of the Gilcomston pastor, but it is certainly, to say the least of
it, a most remarkable coincidence that so many
youths belonging to the district, and who were
brought more or less under the influence of its
chief luminary, should have risen to place and
fame.   Phillip, the painter; Dr. Bain, the
logician and metaphysician; Hill Burton, the
historian; Dr. Duncan, the Hebrew scholar and
theologian; Dr. Masson, professor of English
literature; and Dr. Walter Smith, the minister-
poet, occur among many names that might be
mentioned in this connection.

Many others, too, whose distinction is known
only to the records of heaven, were inwardly
nourished by the weekly "feast of fat things"
provided for them, and had their lives redeemed
from sordid tedium by the inspiring motives and
splendid visions exhibited to their view.   How
could they do other than throng Gilcomston
Chapel?   If it had no loveliness in itself, yet
within its walls the beauty of holiness was
revealed to their souls, and aspiration was kindled
within them as they were made to feel that the
higher life by which they became sharers of the
Divine was a possible possession to craftsman
and peasant, to the poor and illiterate, and even
to the vicious and abandoned.   To many who,
during the week, were tied from early morn till

late at night to the loom and the lapstone, and
to whose minds the Gilcomston sermons introduced an ideal element, by providing material
for thought and discussion, which lifted them
above their monotonous and toilsome drudgery,
but did not unfit them for their duty—to many
such the lines of Herbert were indeed true:—

> " The week were dark but for thy light:
> Thy torch doth show the way."

Gilcomston Chapel was a kind of university
for the multitude, the place where ideas were
propagated, where life was placed in its proper
perspective, where truth and righteousness were
shown to be more than bread, and where eternal
and immutable principle was held up against the
most specious and prosperous expediency. Above
all, sitting in that chapel, men were made to feel
that it was indeed the house of God; for if they
went to it in a right spirit, what was best in
them rose to the surface, what was mean and
earthly was rebuked; and heaven becoming an
experimental reality, they, on leaving the place
for their homes, felt constrained to try again,
with the help of Him of whom they had heard,
to live according to the " pattern shown to them
on the mount."

CHAPTER XI.

OLD MACHAR AND GILCOMSTON AT WAR.

GILCOMSTON CHURCH was what is called a "Chapel of Ease," *i.e.*, a place of worship erected for the ease or convenience of those residing at a distance from the Parish Church. Its minister had not the status nor the emoluments of the parish dignitary. His position was very much that of an assistant and subordinate, to whom, owing to the largeness of the parish, preaching and certain other sacred functions were delegated; and Dr. Kidd was, therefore, ecclesiastically subject to the control of the ministers and Kirk Session of Old Machar.

The seat of the Old Machar ecclesiastical authority was in Old Aberdeen, and it and Gilcomston, in the spirit or genius possessed by each, were much farther apart than could be measured by the mile or two which lay between the two parts of the parish. Old Aberdeen is little more than a Cathedral and a University, with the needful adjoining dwellings, and, as might be expected, was, in those days, largely dominated by the past. Gilcomston, on the other hand, was the home and rendezvous of new ideas, which came flocking to it as doves to their

windows.   Old Aberdeen, weather-worn, still,
suffused with hoary associations, has an air of
academic dignity and cloistered repose; a de-
licious calm pervades its streets, which acts as
medicine to the spirit of him who escapes from
the din and turmoil of the city; but it is no
place for the innovator. It is easy to be believed
how those who dwelt in its ivy-clothed houses,
with their moss-encrusted walls, should have had
their serenity as much ruffled by the entrance of
a phenomenon like that of Dr. Kidd as if a bomb
had come tumbling and spluttering into the
quiet and grass-grown lanes of that venerable
suburb.

Those staid and formal gentlemen of the
Aulton found Dr. Kidd to be as lively a subject as the proverbial " Tartar " who has been
" caught," and was about as docile in their hands
as Samson was among the Philistines.   There
could not fail to be abiding aloofness and not
infrequent collision between men whose habits
of thought and views of public duty differed so
much as those of Old Machar and him of Gilcomston.   Dr. Kidd would not put his " new wine "
into their " old bottles," and for a time they were
equally determined to smash his " bottles " one
by one as they came into use.

Amongst the many unauthorised innovations
and " uncanonical " arrangements which Dr.
Kidd had introduced at Gilcomston, was a stated

Sabbath evening service, in addition to those of the forenoon and afternoon. This was the most popular and generally the most effective service of the day, the Doctor obtaining the use of himself, and "coming out" in most characteristic fashion at this, the last opportunity of the day for the deft swordsman piercing the hearts and consciences of his hearers. Moreover, this diet of worship, by the comparatively large collections that were taken, contributed very materially in swelling the sum raised by the church for the support of the poor in the parish. It had, however, the drawback of being an unprecedented course of procedure, and in those days when evening services were quite unheard of in this part of the country, except among a few straggling dissenters, the novelty must have shocked the ecclesiastical susceptibilities of those old-world sticklers for established form and usage.

In due time the decree came forth from Old Machar that the evening lecture must be discontinued. How did Dr. Kidd meet this prohibition? With defiance? Nay, verily; he was too law-abiding a man to do that. A smaller and weaker man with the same burning fire of earnestness in his bosom might have adopted that course, which would have brought him under ecclesiastical censure, and created no end of troublesome controversy. The Doctor desired to avoid that, and yet get on with his work in his own way. He, with his Irish resource and nimbleness of mind, fell upon an expedient which technically yielded the point to his ecclesiastical superiors, and yet left him in possession of the substantial fruits of victory. According to the strictly legal view of the duty of a minister of the Church of Scotland, he had no right to preach except in the pulpit, or rather, when he held forth in any other place, the service he conducted was not supposed to be "canonical." Taking advantage of that convenient loophole, the Doctor, after the commandment had gone forth, and the people were wondering what he would do when Sabbath evening came, quietly stepped into the precentor's desk and went on as formerly, the only difference being that the people in certain parts of the back gallery had to screw their heads round a great deal more than was comfortable to obtain a good view of the preacher. The authorities in the Old Town, foiled, beaten, in a way so ingenious as to make further action on their part most ungracious, if not impossible, like men not altogether destitute of good sense, quietly submitted to the inevitable, and gave the incorrigible man permission to go on with his evening service in the old way. The precentor's desk had served its temporary purpose.

Some time after, Old Machar and Gilcomston had another encounter, in which different

tactics were pursued, but with a success quite as
brilliant. In the year 1820, and for several years
before that, the country was greatly excited
over King George the Fourth's treatment of his
consort, Queen Caroline. The people, having
less pertaining to worldly position to hamper the
free action of the generous impulses of the
human heart, generally took the Queen's side.
Pitying the woman, firmly persuaded of her
innocence, and indignant at the mean and foul
injustice she was receiving at the hands of the
unworthy wearer of the purple, they came nobly
out as the Queen's party. There were not wanting men of conspicuous place and talent, such
as Brougham, who gave voice to the sympathy
of the people for Queen Caroline, amongst whom
also were many dissenting ministers, Dr. Kidd
being one of the few among the State clergy
who took that side. Praying as he had been
accustomed to do for the Queen, he was summoned
to appear before his ecclesiastical superiors to
answer for his conduct in that respect.

Going to St. Mary's Chapel, in which the
members of the Presbytery were assembled, Dr.
Kidd stood before them, and said—" Gentlemen,
to what am I indebted for the honour of this
invitation to wait upon you?" Cowed by the
calm, leonine aspect of the man whom they were
met to reprimand, and knowing from experience
that to come to close quarters with him was

rather a lively enterprise, there was considerable diffidence in breaking to him the nature of the business on hand. There was not any competition among the reverend gentlemen for the honour of bearding the lion who, at their bidding, had come into their own den. Indeed, the members of Presbytery, now that they stood face to face with the accused, were ashamed of themselves, and the task which the powers that be had laid upon them: and each was looking to the other to say the needful word.

The Doctor, becoming impatient, again said —"Gentlemen, you have summoned me to your bar; I am a busy man, and have no time to wait; will you please tell me what is wanted with me?" At last he was told that he had disregarded the instruction received, and, in violation of it, had prayed for the Queen. "Why," he asked, "should the Queen not be prayed for?" One of them answered—"Because she is a bad woman." "Then," replied the Doctor, with flashing eyes and indignant tones, "she has the more need to be prayed for. I have prayed for the Queen; I will pray for the Queen;" and then, looking from one to the other of the leading members of the Court, added, "and I'll pray for you, and you, and for any other sinner out of hell!" And, bidding them "good morning," he marched off, leaving the would-be censors in much about the same frame of mind as were responsible actors in the Diet of Worms, when Martin Luther, by the sheer grandeur of his moral resolution, left them discomfited and crestfallen.

Next Sabbath in Gilcomston Church, one of the waves which succeed the tempest, after it has begun to calm down, were to be seen. A member of the congregation, on presenting his child for baptism, handed up to the minister the paper containing the baptismal name. On opening and reading it, the Doctor looked up and took a step back, evidently surprised. He asked the father to repeat the child's name, which was done audibly—" Caroline Brunswick Queen." The child was baptised accordingly.

This little incident was the occasion of much talk and some misrepresentation. The Doctor wrote a letter to the *Chronicle* newspaper, declaring himself, against the aspersions of enemies, to be a loyal subject, but one who claimed the right of independent judgment in the great controversy which the nation had taken up. He also explained the circumstances in which the name of the child had been given in church, he being no party to the choice, but merely, according to practice, pronouncing audibly what the parents had agreed upon, and put upon paper. It is said that the unfortunate Queen took notice of the child, and sent the parents a present.

I

Anticipating what belongs to a later development in our narrative, it may be said that the General Assembly, in the last year of Dr. Kidd's life, dealt with the case of ministers of chapels of ease, and a very considerable measure of relief was passed, which removed most of the disabilities, protected the independence, and generally improved the status of ministers situated like Dr. Kidd. As was to be expected, there was great rejoicing over this ecclesiastical emancipation on the part of Dr. Kidd and one or two other brethren in the North, who were now released by the formal enactment of the Church from the petty restraints and occasional persecutions to which they had been subjected. The Rev. Andrew Gray of Woodside, one of those from whom the ecclesiastical yoke was now taken, met Dr. Kidd after the happy deliverance, and in their mutual congratulations, Mr. Gray said, when the news reached him, he could not help repeating the lines in the 126th Psalm : —

> " When Zion's bondage God turned back,
>   As men that dreamed were we ;
>   Then fill'd with laughter was our mouth,
>   Our tongue with melody."

"Ah!" replied Dr. Kidd, "that's not it, man ; here's the right thing," and he repeated part of the 129th Psalm : —

> " The plowers plow'd upon my back ;
>   They long their furrows drew.
>   The righteous Lord did cut the cords
>   Of the ungodly crew."

CHAPTER XII.

PERSECUTIONS.

DR. KIDD, during the whole of his career in Aberdeen, except, perhaps, towards the close, never ran any risk of incurring that "woe" which is passed upon those of whom all men speak well. A man of his pronounced character and militant spirit, not to say fiery temper, generally succeeds in placing himself beyond those temptations which beset the universal favourite. Men full of driving energy, like Luther and Knox, have earned the gratitude of posterity on other grounds than that of inoffensiveness. The rushing stream has much to recommend it; but it cannot be said that it has the noiseless placidity of the lake or standing pool.

We are so unreasonable in the combinations of character we expect. When we are favoured with a Paul or a Peter, we are disappointed if he does not add to his native properties those of a John. We forget that men are but fragments of the ideal humanity. Each one has his own phase of excellency to exhibit, his own function as a member of the body to fulfil, and no one has in himself all that the others have. If we are to have a man amongst us to do the work of a Dr. Kidd, we must not, at the same time, look to him for those qualities which belong to an opposite temperament and different order of abilities. The hatchet has its place in carpentry as well as the plane. In husbandry we need the harrow as well as the hoe. There were many men in England more amiable than Oliver Cromwell; but was it not worth while to have the Protectorate, though in it grace was less conspicuous than strength?

A man who feels himself called upon to take an aggressive attitude in relation to the evils of his time, is not likely to be in danger of undue popularity. Evil always has its "vested interests" in the heart and habit, and the preacher of righteousness is to it what heaven's light is to the diseased eye—an irritation and an offence. It must be owned that Dr. Kidd sometimes needlessly aggravated, as well as justly rebuked, by the impetuosity of his manner and the violence of his language. A member of his congregation was deploring some recent outburst of Dr. Kidd's, when the person to whom he was speaking remarked, "It is a great mercy for us he has such faults." "Why," replied the other, "when it hurts him in the estimation of others, and injures the cause he loves?" "Well," was the decisive rejoinder, "if it were not for these faults we would just worship him!"

But there was no malice in his invective, no

bitterness in his severity. He had a quick, not a bad temper. His rebuke was the outburst of a warm, ingenuous nature, intensely in love with what was right, and resolved to do the very utmost on its behalf. He was a born leader of men, and his ministerial office, which he magnified so much, gave him a sense of responsibility as a guardian and champion of down-trodden goodness; and his fiery remonstrances had no more of the vindictive in them than has the chastisement administered by a loving and conscientious parent. He was so intent upon striking the iron while it was hot, that he might put it into right shape, that he did not notice where the sparks went. That kind of temperament which ignites easily when joined, as in his case, to a thoroughly unselfish and aspiring spirit, is by no means the worst you can meet. When a man is angry and shows it, you are aware that he is offended, and you know what you have to do in order that things may be put right. But when one is offended, and does not show it, you are fighting an enemy in the dark. Righteous anger is like a bad odour—it is one of nature's danger signals hoisted, and seeing it you know where you are and what you have to do. But to be the object of a displeasure which does not make itself audible or visible, and watches you in sullen silence, as under a mask or behind a hedge, is to be in the hands of one who has in

him more of the fiend than the man.   Better by
far the boiling over and scalding anger of an
open, transparent, straightforward nature like
Dr. Kidd's.   Or, to change the figure; the
plumping shower of big raindrops, or even
thumping hailstones, that is soon over and is
succeeded by sunshine, is much to be preferred
to the perpetual drizzle which is so noiseless and
unobtrusive, and yet so blots out the brightness
and tries the patience.

Still, Dr. Kidd himself would have been the
last man to attempt to justify all that he said
and did in public.   Mrs. H. Oswald says:—
"He had a horror of being held up to posterity,
as many of his contemporaries were, as possessing
a character of faultless beauty: he often laughed
as he read of those, declaring he hoped no one
would ever write so of him."   He himself knew
that he often gave a "handle" to his enemies by
his hasty and indiscreet words.   His excesses in
extemporaneous speech—his great trouble in
speaking not being omission but commission—
were enough to damage most seriously, if not
utterly to ruin, a man who had not the extraordinary staying power of an exceptionally
strong and noble character.   Sir Walter Scott,
quoting a Scottish proverb in his journal, says:—
" Hain your reputation, tyne your reputation," *

---

* To *hain* anything is, anglice, to deal very carefully,
penuriously with it—*tyne*, to lose.   Scott used to say, " hain
a pen (a quill) and tyne a pen."

i.e., to be very careful and timorous about reputation is the way to lose it. Is it not he also who testifies:—"I never knew name nor fame burn brighter for over chary keeping?" Dr. Kidd did not "hain" his reputation, but ever tried, amidst many shortcomings, to be consistent with the principles which his conscience approved.

But after discounting all the ill-will he provoked that was due to his occasional asperity of manner and intemperance of speech in the presence of wrong, we are left face to face with the undeniable fact that he, at the outset of his career, suffered much for righteousness' sake. There can be no doubt that the concocters of the atrocious plots of which we are about to speak were "sons of Belial," "lewd fellows of the baser sort," who, alas! are seldom entirely absent from any community in this world. There is no difficulty in apprehending why such foul conspiracies should have been entered into at the beginning rather than at the end of his career in Aberdeen. Persecution is usually cowardly as well as cruel. It is not so ready to strike a man when he, by patient continuance in well-doing, has succeeded in establishing himself in the confidence of all worthy fellow-citizens, and would-be gainsayers are shamed into silence. Everything that is good in this world has to work its way to respectful toleration, not to say acceptance, through opposition and trial. It was so with Christianity itself. It was persecuted till it proved itself to be something that was not to be put down. In like manner this faithful man, whose testimony against wickedness was inconveniently emphatic and uncompromising, was battered and bruised in reputation, till in the course of years public opinion in his favour became so strong that it was impolitic, and also seen to be useless, to continue such manifestations of malice.

It would be nothing short of a scandalous breach of charity to affirm, or even insinuate, that Dr. Kidd's ecclesiastical opponents were in any way implicated in those attempts to blacken his character. But, considering his relations to some of his contemporaries, with whom he had little in common, it is not so very surprising, human nature being what it is, that one or two of them should have given too ready an ear to some of the stories which were afloat in the town about him. Where there is no sympathy, suspicion easily creeps in. When we have a prejudice against a man we are not so prompt as we might be to repel the tale-bearer, and to defend the reputation of the absent against foul aspersions.

There is before me as I write a huge petition, five yards long, containing in six parallel columns the signatures of 1,520 members and

adherents of Gilcomston Chapel, addressed,
" Unto the Very Reverend the Presbytery of
Aberdeen." It bears the date of January, 1807,
and in the preamble it is stated that " for some
time past we have been deeply penetrated with
sorrow and concern on account of the severe and
unjust calumny so cruelly and so industriously
circulated against our dear beloved Pastor, Professor James Kidd, and having been fully convinced from the very first of his innocence, and
knowing the purity of his moral character, and
the public in general being of the same mind
with ourselves, we waited with much impatience
and anxiety to hear of your decision on the
affair, as it came before you on the twenty-
fourth of December last." Then it goes on to
say that, " much gratified and rejoiced on
account of this decision," they wish to express
their " high approbation and heartfelt satisfaction with the tenor of the minute by which our
worthy Pastor was most deservedly and justly
relieved from the shocking and cruel, calumnious
charges presented to the Very Reverend the
Presbytery against him on the third of December
last."

But Dr. Kidd's people in that petition go
further. The tables are now completely turned,
and the accused becomes the accuser. They
express their very natural indignation at the
conduct of those members of the Presbytery who

lent such a ready ear to the foul lies of an
abandoned woman, who was known to have been
in the criminal court, and was the tool of wicked
men who thought they would silence the
strenuous voice of this fearless and scathing
preacher of righteousness.

The following is an extract from the Presbytery records of Aberdeen, with which we have
been favoured by the Rev. J. Catto, Fintray:—

"DIVINITY HALL,
"ABERDEEN, 24th Dec., 1806.

"The Presbytery met, and, after prayer, sederunt
—Dr. Sherrefs, Moderator; Dr. Mitchell, Clerk; Dr.
Cruden; Messrs. Morrison, Leslie, Dr. Hogg, Dr.
Brown, Dr. Gerrard, Paul, Ross, Dr. Gordon,
Walker. With regard to the papers given in at last
meeting with respect to Mr. Kidd, the Presbytery,
having heard their Committee which was appointed
to converse with Mr. Kidd on that matter, and having
had several papers laid before them by the Committee,
the Presbytery find no ground of accusation against
Mr. Kidd."

So the bottom was completely knocked out
of the infamous conspiracy, and it is to the
credit of most of the Moderate clergy in the city
that they aided in bringing about that result.
But what can be said of the Gilcomston people
at this trying crisis? Their whole-hearted and
unconquerable belief in the integrity of their

minister, their tender concern for his reputation, and the bold stand they took in his defence are beautiful to behold. Such a demonstration shows the strength of the hold he had already, at this early date, taken of Aberdeen. John Wesley, after visiting Bon-Accord, said that its people were "swift to hear, slow to speak, but not slow to wrath." Certainly this, the most Scottish part of Scotland, may well be compared to a burning mountain covered with snow. In 1807 the snow melted as the lava came forth, which did not fail to scorch some in places where the scars were likely to remain to the day of their death.

There is a quaint and touching prayer still remembered, as having been prayed by one of the Gilcomston members, at a meeting which was held when this great trouble was upon them and their minister. It was succinct, and to the point:—"O Lord, Thou hast said we shall hae tribulation in the world, but in Thee we shall hae peace. Noo, Lord, Thou hast been faithful in the first pairt o' Thy promise; we pray Thee that Thou wouldst fulfil the second pairt to Thy servants."

Farther on in his life another diabolical attempt was made to damage Dr. Kidd in public estimation, the recital of which should open the eyes of those who are inclined to disbelieve in the existence of evil spirits. It is almost in-

credible, but it is too true, as the account comes
from a most trustworthy source. One morning
about two o'clock, two men came knocking
loudly at the door of Dr. Kidd's house. When
it was opened by the servant, they said they had
come from a poor dying woman who implored
Dr. Kidd, through them, to see her before she
died, as she had something on her mind she
could tell to no one but himself. Like himself,
the simple-hearted man that he was, he rose immediately, nothing surprised, as he had so often
before been the recipient of such confessions.
The men took him to the Gallowgate, and into
one of its low courts, where was a stair leading
down to a cellar. On reaching the top of the
stair they tripped him up, so that he fell head-
long, and lay stunned for some time, while the
scoundrels had some persons brought to witness
his emerging from a place of ill-fame! After
that experience he always had a deacon or elder
to accompany him when called in this way.
Could not the words of the Psalmist be used by
this man of God as describing his own case:—
"False witnesses did rise up; they laid to my
charge things that I knew not. They rewarded
me evil for good to the spoiling of my soul. But
as for me, when they were sick, my clothing was
sackcloth, I humbled myself with fasting. I
behaved myself as though he had been my friend
and brother?"

CHAPTER XIII.

PERSONAL HABITS.

DR. KIDD's personal appearance was striking, and indicated exceptional physical strength. He was a big man, and no stranger could pass him on the street without looking at him. He was not remarkably tall, not more than five feet ten inches in height; but he had a body of massive build, a large head, broad chest, with a strong, deep voice, which, when occasion required, could peal forth majestic tones.

To the end he continued to wear the style of dress that was common in his early days—knee breeches and black silk stockings. One of his best-informed relatives says that he was particular about the latter; but, as he grew old, he was attacked with gout, and was obliged to use woollen ones beneath the silk for the sake of warmth. His greatcoat had always to be made of the same pattern, loose, long, blue, resplendent with brass buttons, and with very wide sleeves, that in cold weather he might slip his gloveless hands into them, very much as a lady does with a muff. No one could ever accuse him of being a clerical dandy. Indeed, he was often so much absorbed in other things that dress, as something that is meant to please the eye as well as clothe the body, received from him but scant attention.

Dr. Kidd's unconquerable tenacity of purpose is made abundantly evident in the habits he was at pains to form, and which, with an almost unvarying constancy, he clung to till the end of his days. Some of these throw light upon his career, and help to account for the prodigious amount of work of various kinds which he was able to do. One of the habits was early rising. He had a very keen appreciation of the value of time as an indispensable factor in the attainment of human excellency. Time was to him what gold is to the miser. He therefore allowed himself no more sleep than what nature absolutely required, and in the hours he chose for that part of his duty, he followed the example of the other living creatures which share the earth with man rather than depraved human custom. When no public engagements interfered, he usually had worship, and prepared to go to bed at eight or nine o'clock, and rose at three o'clock. "Mary," he would say—no matter what the servant's name was, every one that came to the house was "Mary" to him—"bring two or three bits of coal and lay them ready for me before you go to bed." In his old age he indulged himself so far as to take two hours longer in the morning; but during the most of his life, as sure as the clock struck three, he was up and at his work. It could not be said of him, " He loses half an hour in the morning and runs after it all day long without being able to overtake it."

He gave an amusing account to his friends of the hard struggles he had with the body before it was, in this respect, brought in subjection to the will. In America he engaged a watchman not only to " knock him up," but to get him up. The terms of the contract were that the person hired was not to receive a single cent unless he succeeded in putting the would-be sleeper upon his feet. Who can deny, in the face of the facts before us, that human life is a contradiction and paradox? James Kidd resolved to rise at three o'clock, and yet he was often unwilling to move. He wished the unwelcome sound and its author were a thousand miles away when he was roused out of a profound slumber, and answered, hoping the man would mercifully go away and leave him in bed just for another half-hour. But no ; the inexorable Yankee, determined not to lose his fee, would come into the room, shake the sleeper, and not leave the bedside till the horizontal position was changed for the perpendicular—and Mr. Kidd could not complain, for he himself had dictated the terms and prescribed the treatment. So, it appears, James Kidd had his own share of the conflict between duty and inclination. Virtue was not an easy-going and inborn instinct to him any more than it is to the rest of us.

Dr. Kidd's grandson, Mr. Henry Oswald, afterwards one of the magistrates of Aberdeen, who, when a boy, was for some time resident in the minister's house, has left amongst his papers a most vivid account of the impression made upon his mind by Dr. Kidd's heroic devotion to duty in the early morn :—" In the darkness of a cold winter morning I have once and again heard him rising while the rest of the household was hushed in slumber. I listened while he (Dr. Kidd) patiently lit his fire, not with the ready help of lucifer matches, but with flint and steel eliciting a spark (how little we moderns prize our luxuries !) ; then he began to breathe out his soul in the most earnest tones at the throne of grace ; the utterances of his devout heart were not audible to me, who was in an adjoining room, but, youngster as I was, I felt awed as I heard the sound of prayer that often became wrestling, and I knew that the man I revered was doing business with God." He held with Martin Luther that to have prayed well was to have studied well.

Then he began his work for the day as a student, which, generally speaking, was well advanced by breakfast time. Marvellously nimble as were the movements of his mind, and ready as he was to " pick up " and take in, he was not a quick reader. His method, which was very slow, but very thorough, is indicated in the counsel he once gave to a young relative on reading and study:—" The best way to profit by any book is to read the title page and chapter of contents; and, before taking a step further, close the book, and then ask yourself—'What do I know of the subject that is about to be laid before me in this book?' Ascertain your own views, and the extent of your knowledge already in hand, before you begin to read. Then open the book, and, in reading, compare your own ideas with those of the author—test their accuracy—and thus proceeding, chapter by chapter, the book, or as much of it as came home to you, will become a real inward possession."

What he advised he did. The tradition has come down that, when Dr. Kidd began to preach he consulted all the most celebrated preachers to whom he had access, as to the best methods of pulpit delivery. On collecting the opinions he had elicited as to the most effective elocution for the preacher, he shut himself up in a room to ponder and digest what he had heard and read, and, before leaving it, he made up his mind as to the line of action he should adopt as a public speaker. He ever gave heed to the outward testimony; but not the less resolute was he to receive the inward witness.

When there were young people in the house

K

he called them into his study at half-past six
o'clock to read a chapter of the Bible to him.
At seven o'clock they had family worship "so
regularly," writes Mr. Oswald, "that I do not
remember of its ever being omitted." Then came
breakfast. Mr. Oswald, in his memoranda, goes
on to say:—"There was a simplicity in his
diet very unusual in the present day." By
breakfast time, the work for the day indoors
might be said to be done. His mind was now
free to attend to the duties which lay outside his
home. He never appeared to be in a hurry.
"He had a time for every work, and a work for
every time," he was accustomed to say, "else he
could not have got through so much work."

In his prime he spent part of each day in
visitation, and in passing through the town he
usually walked with deliberation on the middle
of the street. In perambulating his parish there
was a double process of thought going on in his
mind. He was adapting himself to the circumstances of his people as a wide-awake observer
and ready helper, but he was also taking note of
what afforded him material for his pulpit work.
A visitor once asked the servant of Wordsworth,
the poet, in what part of the house was her
master's study. Pointing to a room, she said—
"His books are in there; but his study is out in
the fields." So it could be said that while Dr.
Kidd had a well-used study in Chapel Street, he

had another all over Gilcomston. Sir Walter
Scott, who also did the principal part of his work
in the morning, has left it on record that, in his
opinion, it is a distinct advantage to a literary
man to keep himself in the current of the world's
affairs, and not shut himself up among books.
Dr. Kidd felt too, as a minister, that, while he
must be abreast of the literature of the day, he
must also be in close touch with the people
around him.

His breadth of outlook and interest, and the
many-sidedness of his character, were evidenced
in the extensive correspondence he was able,
amidst his multifarious public duties, to keep
up with good and able men in different parts of
the world. Sir George Sinclair, Dr. Macdonald
of Ferintosh, and other Highland clergymen
were among his correspondents in Scotland.
Other eminent men in England and America ex-
changed letters with him. Most of the epistles
have disappeared during the fifty-eight years
which have elapsed since his death. Some have
survived the upturnings of that long period,
which will be found in these pages. There is
one from Dr. Robert Morrison, who may be
called the founder of Protestant missions in
China, that incidentally reveals some of the
things which were in Dr. Kidd's mind at this
stage in his career:—

"CANTON, 6th January, 1816.

"REV. AND DEAR SIR,—By the arrival of the ship of this season, I had the pleasure to receive your kind letter of 17th December, 1814. I thank you for your prospectuses of your intended publication, which I have no doubt I shall have much pleasure in perusing, should my life be spared to receive it. China is at present in a very unsettled state. . . . We must pray, and wait for better days. I am going on with the translation of the Book of Psalms. In compliance with your request, I send a few Chinese books, and have desired my friends in England to send you a copy of the first number of my Chinese Dictionary, which I send to England this season. My Grammar is, I believe, finished, but I have not yet received from Bengal any copies. My Grammar has been in Bengal since 1812. From the books which have been published, you may acquire some knowledge of Chinese, but I think it is not practicable to learn to read it generally. Whether language, or rather letters, be of Divine origin or not, I cannot say. The idea that they were superior to human invention seems to have struck the Chinese; but the idea is not general. It is a question which cannot, I think, be decided, and therefore it is in vain to discuss it.

"My college friend, Milne, is at Malacca, doing well. We intend that to be the seat of the Mission for the Extra-Ganges countries—China, Japan, Java, &c. Moral changes are commonly effected by slow degrees. 3,300 years had passed away before the account of the Creation, which Moses wrote, reached

China in the language of the people who inhabit these lands. Who can tell how long the New Testament may be in producing the desired effect! God alone knows. It is a source of comfort to the mind to be an instrument in God's hands in promoting, in some degree, the knowledge of His name amongst our fellow-creatures.

" To a person standing on the eastern verge of the Asiatic Continent, and who hears or knows little of Europe but of its perpetual wars, it presents a melancholy spectacle. European nations appear little better than a few uncivilised States, filled with endless rancour against each other, unwilling to listen to reason, and yet unable to conquer each other. It is lamentable that religion, which does so much for you who inhabit the western regions of the globe, does not do more. I hope Europe will be benefited by her efforts to improve others. The comparative general intercourse of all nations which has taken place during the last 200 years, appears to me to indicate that better days are drawing nigh. Come, Lord Jesus: come quickly!—I remain, rev. and dear sir, yours sincerely,

"R. MORRISON.

" The Rev. James Kidd."

The next letter is from the college friend alluded to by Mr. Morrison, the famous W. Milne, who went to China from the North of Scotland: —

" A. C. COLLEGE, MALACCA,
"4th December, 1821.

"MY VERY DEAR SIR,—In reply to your kind
note of 12th December, 1820, I must be very brief,
as I very lately wrote you. I rejoice to hear of your
full congregations—your discourses on Ezekiel must
be both curious and edifying. Alas ! *we* cultivate an
overgrown field and an unpropitious soil. Still we
faint not. We want to be more thoroughly mixed
with the natives, and divested of European prejudices,
ere we can do them much real good—there is much
in the Catholic Missions worthy of imitation in these
respects. But it is not an easy thing to be a missionary for *ten* years—how much more difficult to keep
the spirit of the great work alive *through life !* Pray
for us, and ask the continued prayers of your people
for us. I hardly think the nations about us are likely
to be converted without the persecution and martyr-
dom of some missionaries. These, I think, may
almost be calculated upon with certainty ere much
good be done. Here we go on as usual like others.
Ah ! my reverend friend ! a *faithful* man—and one
who will *not* ' *seek his own things*'—is a rare jewel,
and abroad peculiarly so. Depraved nature has a
powerful hold of us. When my little Chinese work,
called ' The Portals of the Church,' is finished, I will
try to send you a copy. Remember me to your own
family and any other friends with whom you know
me to be acquainted. Can you do anything for our

college among your friends? However small the aid, it would be accepted.—I am, my dear sir, yours ever,

"W. MILNE.

"Rev. James Kidd, D.D."

"P.S.—Our neighbours, the Siamese, are at war with Burmah, and there are some internal commotions in Cochin China and China. 'The Lord reigneth.'"

CHAPTER XIV.

CONTEMPORARIES IN ABERDEEN.

BOSWELL, in giving an account of the visit which Dr. Johnson paid to Aberdeen, twenty or thirty years before the period of which we are writing, reports:—"We sat contentedly at our inn, and Dr. Johnson then became merry, and observed how little we had either heard or said at Aberdeen—that the Aberdonians had not started a single mawkin [*i.e.*, hare] for us to pursue." In the last decade of that century, Aberdeen would have given a better account of itself, and stood less in awe of the Jupiter-like lexicographer. The men whom we, in the opening part of this chapter, are about to introduce, brought fame to themselves and to the city; but they were comparatively young when this gruff and overbearing, though delightful man of letters, appeared amongst them, and modesty was then justly held to be a virtue, more especially in the presence of one who was not only old, but oracular.

The accomplished and erudite Dr. George Campbell, Principal of Marischal College, passed from this scene three years after Dr. Kidd began his work in Aberdeen. Principal Campbell, " the

Paley of Scotland," did much to shed lustre upon the city by his able "Treatise on Miracles," his "Ecclesiastical History," and "Philosophy of Rhetoric," and other works which commanded general attention at the time, and for long were standard works in their several departments. We know that he met the young Professor of Hebrew, and doubtless that prince of polished Moderates had his own opinion of the energetic and unconventional Irishman, who, like a stranded boulder belonging to far-away formations, had found his way to this northern land. About the same time, Thomas Reid, the founder of the Scottish School of Philosophy, died. He was a true Aberdonian, though he had spent the last thirty years of his life in professorial work in Glasgow. James Beattie, the author of the famous "Essay on Truth," which was intended as an antidote to Hume's scaring scepticism, passed away in 1803. His "Minstrel" is likely to have a much longer lease of life than his "Essay," as dialectics and metaphysics do not usually survive the generation for whose benefit they saw the light, but what has in it the soul of true poetry may live as long as humanity itself. Dr. Gerard and Dr. Lawrence Brown were also among the more conspicuous of Dr. Kidd's ecclesiastical contemporaries.

The more notable of Dr. Kidd's clerical townsmen in the Established Church of his own age were mostly of the Moderate school. That Moderatism which was at its height, but near the close of its predominance, when Dr. Kidd appeared, is a strange chapter in the ecclesiastical history of Scotland. Divested of its national colouring, it was, however, nothing more than a particular example of that tendency in religion beset with earthly conditions to go down. Many of the men of that school, under the respectable name of Moderatism, cloaked nothing more worthy than commonplace Laodicean indifference to the spiritual needs of their fellows, and the solemn responsibilities of the office which they had assumed.

Others more reputable were what they were by keeping in the background what should have been placed in the forefront of their preaching. The intellectual framework and the ethical contents of Christianity were the principal themes of their discourse, and the doctrines of grace, which are the distinguishing characteristic of the religion of Jesus, were presented in a vague, general fashion, which had little effect upon heart and conscience. "Religion is the banquet of the spirit, not the feast of the mind; and therefore danger is ever present when men begin to listen to the sermon as a manifestation of intellectual force, and not for its spiritual power."

Philosophy, literature, and intellectual cul-

ture generally in Scotland, it must be frankly
owned, were greatly furthered by the best of the
men who were ranked among the Moderates.
They did a great deal to maintain elegance of
manners and classic refinement of taste. But an
icicle, however clear and shapely, is out of place
in the pulpit. Much as chasteness of style and
beauty of form are to be admired, the kingdom
of heaven, in its aims and ends, cannot be reduced to the narrow limits of such a ministra-
tion. What might be fitting enough in the
academy or in the professor's chair, was intolerable in the pulpit, which is nothing at all if it
is not the symbol of a doctrine as high as heaven,
as deep as eternity, and as intense as life itself.

It has been pithily said that "the thoughts
of men through all the ages have oscillated between two extremes, and there is and can be no
other, viz., between salvation by self and salvation by Christ. In proportion as they have been
guided by speculation, they have gravitated to
salvation by self; to the extent, however, they
have submitted their hearts to the teaching of
Scripture, they have believed in salvation by
Christ." But seeing the Moderates, as well as
the Evangelicals, had signed the Confession of
Faith, which was professedly based upon the
statements of Scripture, how came it that, as intelligent and honest men, they could take any
other course than give prominence to the doc-

trines of Redemption? The explanation is to be
found in the fact, not unknown to the experience
of most, that what is not vital to us is easily
ignored or overshadowed. The specially spiritual
parts of the creed were treated as dead dogma or
mysteries not to be handled too freely. The
Moderates had as their distinctive note—out-
wardness. Their religion was very much a creed
to which the understanding gave an assent, and
a code of morals that regulated the conduct; but
they to a great extent ignored, if they did not
slight, spirituality of mind, which is to the other
parts of religion what the soul is to the body.

History abundantly shows that whenever
this Moderatism gained the ascendancy in the
Church of Scotland, division was the inevitable
result. Behind all the ecclesiastical disputes
which agitated the Church and led to secession
after secession, there was the deeper difference
of doctrine and life. There were at least two
congregations in Aberdeen before Dr. Kidd's
time belonging to some of the religious communities which had the general designation of
Seceders. Perhaps the most prominent divine
of that order, who was a contemporary of Dr.
Kidd, was James Templeton. He was ordained
minister of what is now Belmont Street U.P.
Church in 1801, and died in 1840. He was a
man of quiet power and singular shrewdness of
observation. His mother wit, spiritual fervour,

homely illustrations, and unabashed vernacular gave him acceptance with the people, though on a much more limited scale than that which Dr. Kidd attained. Some of his choice sentences still remembered, must have had, to a Scottish audience, the effect of strokes of genius. One Sabbath, speaking to persons who complained that their burdens in life were exceptionally heavy, he said—" Suppose now you were to take all your separate burdens to the Castlegate and drop them doon there, and, after examinin' them and comparin' them one with another, I am thinkin' you wouldna be willin' to exchange with any when you really saw what they were; but, pickin' up your bit bundlie, each one of you wad gang awa' hame mair contentit than when you went to the Castlegate."

On another occasion he was alluding to the unwillingness which even good people sometimes had to die. " It just reminds me," he said, " of what happened when I left the auld hoose. When a' the furniture was oot, and a' the rest had gane to the new ane, I couldna leave; I paced up and doon the room in which my children were born; I gazed upon the wa's of the chamber where I studied and wrestled with God, and I couldna tear myself away. But Betty, the servant, came, and she said, '*Come awa', sir, come awa'; the time's up, and the ither hoose is far better than this.*'"

In 1797, just four years after Dr. Kidd arrived in Aberdeen, a few Christians solemnly formed themselves into a fellowship, having the following sentence as part of their first minute: —"Most churches or parties are remarkably strict in demanding assent and subscription to human creeds and confessions, remarkably lax in inquiries into the knowledge, Christian experience, and moral character of such as desire admission, remarkably languid and indifferent about the one thing needful, and remarkably zealous about some things needless." This was the "confession" of what became George Street (or the Loch Kirk), afterwards Belmont Congregational Church, and of which John Philip was pastor from 1804 till 1818. He was a man of cultured mind and catholic sympathy, whose persuasive eloquence drew large congregations to his ministry.

A conversation Dr. Philip had with an infidel had something to do with his leaving Aberdeen and going to Africa to take charge of the Cape Mission of the London Missionary Society. This sceptic, after being foiled in his assault upon Dr. Philip's faith, taunted him with being inconsistent. "You profess to believe that untold millions are perishing in ignorance, and yet you are living in comparative ease and comfort addressing a few of your fellow-creatures." This, along with other thoughts, so worked upon his

mind that he gave himself to what proved to be
a most distinguished course of service as a
superintendent of missions in South Africa.   His
immediate successor, Rev. Alexander Thomson,
a man of saintly character and simple-hearted
devotion, was for fourteen years on terms of
intimate friendship with Dr. Kidd.

Another contemporary, and also a fellow-
countryman of Dr. Kidd's, was the Rev. John
Brown, of St. Paul's Episcopal Church.   He was
a man whose character was full of healthy
human interest, and made you think, when you
saw him, not so much of the professional clergyman as of the country gentleman who had devoted himself to ministerial duty.   He was
utterly free from morbid taint or sanctimonious
mannerism.   A truly saintly man, as meaning a
sane, sound-hearted Christian, he was far removed from the "saint" of the mediæval and
conventional pattern.   This evangelical Episco-
palian of the old school was no thin-blooded,
sour-faced ecclesiastic, no attenuated, emascu-
lated ascetic, but a man who was conscious of
the fact that God had given him a body and
placed him in a beautiful world, and was not the
less conscious of the power of the glorious gospel
of Jesus Christ.

Going to church one Sabbath morning from
his house, which was in Old Aberdeen, he saw a
building on fire in the Spital.   Like a "muscular"

Christian and a cleric who had a human heart beating in his bosom, he doffed his coat at once, and, with pail in hand, joined in the effort to extinguish the flames, feeling that this was the ministry which he, in the Providence of God, was at present called to exercise. He came out of the fire with soiled clothes and dirty hands and face, but with the added respect of all who do not deem that service in the spiritual sphere should unfit a man for grappling with any crisis or emergency which may arise in the present world.

He was not less pronounced in his own appointed sphere of duty. An eloquent preacher—he was an Irishman—he attracted large congregations at the evening service. But he has made his mark in Aberdeen as a religious teacher chiefly by his Bible class. He was at great pains to instruct the younger people of his congregation in Scriptural doctrine, and to bring them to an experimental knowledge of Jesus Christ. There are persons still alive who honour his memory as that of their spiritual father.

Another of Dr. Kidd's ecclesiastical contemporaries was Priest Gordon, to whom there is a monument in front of the school endowed with his money in Constitution Street. He was a genuine Aberdonian, and a simple-minded, good man, with whom Dr. Kidd was ever on most friendly terms, however much they might differ on doctrinal subjects. Dean Ramsay, in his "Reminiscences of Scottish Life and Character," speaks of Priest Gordon as a man beloved by all, rich and poor. He was a sort of chaplain to Menzies of Pitfodels, and visited in many of the county families round Aberdeen. "I remember once," writes the Dean, "his being at Banchory Lodge, and thus apologising to my aunt for going out of the room—'I beg your pardon, Mrs. Forbes, for leaving you, but I maun just gae doun to the garden and say mi bit wordies,' these 'bit wordies' being, in fact, the portion of the Breviary which he was bound to recite."

Priest Gordon thus admonished his congregation one day, as was related by Miss Farquharson of Ballogie to Mrs. Johnstone of Belhelvie: —"I canna get ye to come in time. I gaed ye tae half-past awleven, an' ye're nae here in time! An' gin I gaed ye tae *twal*, ye wudna be here!"

As Dr. Kidd was passing along Castle Street one day, Priest Gordon met him, and said— "What is this I hear? You have been preaching against the Holy Virgin Mary." "Well, sir," replied the Doctor, "I have only been telling the Bible truth of her; she was a saint; but only in the same sense as my mother was a saint." "I dinna ken, Doctor," said Gordon, "*aboot the mithers, but I ken there's an awfu' differ in the sons!*"

L

CHAPTER XV.

SHEPHERDING.

Dr. Kidd had occasion to call one day at the office of a lawyer in town, who was reputed to have a good knowledge of the law, and was, moreover, by no means backward in his appreciation of the profits. He was engaged at the time with a client, and as soon as the figure of the Doctor crossed the threshold, he was hailed familiarly, and in rather a bantering fashion: "Come awa', Doctor; come awa'; there's ane o' your flock here, tho' I dinna ken whether he's a sheep or a goat." "Well," rejoined the minister, somewhat testily, "if he be long in your hands you'll know well before you be done with him; for if he be a sheep he has come to a place where he will soon be shorn."

That sharp-witted "man of business," who had met his match for once, Greek meeting Greek, was as truthful as he was sarcastic—more so, perhaps, than he meant to be at the time; for those who attended Gilcomston Chapel were a flock who had a most devoted shepherd or pastor.

Dr. Kidd was one of that type of men who must bring themselves into accord and sympathy

with the requirements of their environment,
He, being what he was, could not hold himself
aloof from the responsibilities and possibilities
of his pastoral position. They and he had to
be at one: he must be closely and persistently
identified with all that properly belonged to his
calling. One of the most beautiful and touching
reminiscences of Dr. Kidd, which perhaps more
than any other comes with a fond familiarity to
the popular mind, was the extraordinary attraction which the children of the town and he had
for each other. They stood in awe of him, but
it was awe with which affection was mingled,
and it did not repel. It need not surprise anyone who has the slightest knowledge of the
heart of man, and the strange combinations to be
found in human character, to be told that this
" son of thunder " was as gentle as a woman in
his treatment of children. The big-souled man
had so much of the child in himself that he and
children were at home in each other's company;
and in nothing was his Christ-like character
more conspicuous than in his solicitude for the
welfare of the rising generation. Why have not
some of the many eminent artists whom Aberdeen has sent out taken the oft-described scene
of Dr. Kidd blessing the children on the streets
of Aberdeen as the subject of a historic paint-
ing? Nothing certainly could be handed down
to the future more worthy of perpetual local

remembrance than the picture of this venerable man, with a group of children who have stopped before him, or are standing up against the wall, with uncovered heads, that his hand might be placed upon each of them in turn, as he said— "God bless you; be good; be all good, my children," and then took a raisin or a "sweetie" out of his capacious waistcoat pocket, and gave to each one as long as the supplies lasted.

There are old men and women yet alive in Aberdeen whose eyes sparkle with pleasure as they recall the fact that the hands of this man of God were placed upon their heads, and it is confessed that so eager were some of them to get as much as they could of this good thing that by diving down some side streets they were able to reappear at a later stage and come in for a second imposition of holy hands; though that was rather a dangerous trick to play, as the Doctor had sharp vision, and more than one boy met with the rebuff—"Go away, you rogue; you are not Benjamin, to get a double portion."

An instance of Dr. Kidd's genuine kindness of heart and love of children has been told us by an elderly lady, a townswoman, who can quite well recollect the time when the bairns were in the habit of ranging themselves up in front of the good man for the purpose of having their heads "clappit" by him. We give the incident as nearly as possible in her own words:—"It's mair

nor sixty years ago, an' I maun hae been about
four year auld. I was wi' some o' the bairns
playin' at the en' o' Huntly Street on a fine day
in the beginnin' o' simmer. It was jist in fae
faur the Roman Catholic Cathedral stan's noo,
an' the hooses up that side war bein' bigget.
The muckler anes war a' rinnin' barefit; an' ye
wudna hin'er me to tak' aff my stockin's an'
sheen to be like them. But, weary me, the
masons' chips war mair nor my saft soles could
stan' to gyang upon; an' there I was greetin'
helpless, fan Dr. Kidd comes by. So he looks a
minute, an' gatherin' up my hose an' sheen, sits
down on a big steen wi' me on his knee to pit
them on again. An' jist fan he was about deen,
somebody that kent him cam' past an' stoppit to
speak. An' I could never forget hoo the doctor,
aifter divin 's han' deep doun in o' a muckle
pouch in 's coat, gied me an almon' sweetie as he
set me doon, an' said to the body aside him,
' Little makes the sorry heart glad.' ''

No one was better fitted than the Doctor to
make himself interesting to boys. On passing
down Chapel Street he saw a number of youths,
on the day of some public celebration, doing
their best to make an old key serve the purpose
of a cannon. They were not very skilful in
handling the extemporised fire-arm. Seeing
they were in a difficulty, he stopped and did his
best to take them out of it. As he was working

away at the old key a friend came up and said, in some astonishment, " Dr. Kidd, what is this you are about?" Looking up, he replied, with fun lurking in his Irish eyes—" I'm teaching the young idea how to shoot!"

But while in full sympathy with the young people in all their recreations and innocent amusements, he never forgot the one thing needful. On going to church one Sabbath evening in winter, he overheard a number of youths asking each other where they were to spend the rest of the day. One of them, not knowing that the Doctor was within earshot, said—" Let us go to hear Dr. Kidd; we'll get some fun." After entering the pulpit, the minister spied them sitting together in one of the side galleries. Towards the close of his sermon he became more than usually solemn and earnest, and after uttering some terrible sentences against those who trifled with sacred things, and treated lightly the great matter of personal salvation, he turned round, and, looking the youths straight in the face, exclaimed—" There's fun to you—you who have come here for fun; may God bless what I have said, and make it serious fun to you."

Factory workers, in Dr. Kidd's time, had to work from twelve to fourteen hours a day. While preaching a sermon to factory girls one evening, he expressed a sincere desire to see their condition improved, but warned them that

it could be accomplished mainly by their own
exertions and attention to religious instruction.
He said, having to be so early at work at the
factory, they might not always find time to say
their prayers; "but," he added, "in that case, I
must ask you just to do as I often have to do—
to say your prayers on your way to your work.
I can quite sympathise with you, because I have
to work myself every day as many hours as
you."

His ministry was carried on amongst old and
young, in the street and market place, as well as
in the church. In season and out of season he
was ever engaged in his Master's service. Members of his church who were irregular in their
attendance were not as anxious to catch his eye
on the street as budding orators in the House of
Commons are to obtain the notice of the Speaker,
but rather gave the Doctor a wide berth when
he shot up above their horizon. One day an incorrigible defaulter was unexpectedly caught and
attacked for being absent from church without
sufficient reason. Put at bay, the man's temper
rose, and he gave as much as he got from the
minister. "There is no preaching in hell," said
the Doctor. "I kenna," said the hardened and
brazen-faced sinner. And then, as a parting
shot, added—"I doot it's nae for want o' ministers; but ye ken there are nae stipends there!"

But most of the persons the Doctor exhorted

and rebuked were so overawed when standing in his presence as to leave him victor and possessor of the field. He noticed a young woman, overcome by the close atmosphere of the well-filled building, sleeping in church on Sabbath, and by her nodding head giving visible indication of the same. Next day he called at her father's house, and enquired of her what was wrong, and why he was sent for. "Oh, Doctor, there's nothing wrong," was the reply; "we are all well, and we did not send for you." "But if you did not want me," replied her minister, with a roguish twinkle in his eye, "why did you nod for me yesterday?"

It is to be quite easily understood how a man of his fervid temperament, doing his best to impress the people before him, should be much annoyed when his eye detected some who, by their own act, voluntarily or involuntarily, had placed themselves for the time beyond the reach of his best efforts. It is also not beyond comprehension how, in a building ill-ventilated and packed with human beings, there should occasionally have been some overcome by sleep, especially among those whose occupations kept them in the open air during the week. But while many good things were to be had in Gilcomston Chapel, it was the last place to go to for a good, comfortable sleep. It is a wonder anyone had the hardihood to attempt it, knowing as

he did, from abundant evidence in the past, what
terrible risks a man ran when he so indulged.
In the twinkling of an eye he might become the
observed of all observers, and have caustic words
addressed to him which would cover him with
ridicule for a lifetime. Verily, it was strange
indeed that Morpheus should have had votaries
in a church, the pulpit of which was so wide-
awake and so eagle-eyed. The atmosphere must
have been very oppressive, and the drowsiness
overpowering, before one could have slept in
such circumstances. Here are some of the choice
sentences, still remembered, that fell from his
lips in dealing with sleepers :—" Wake up, sir ;
wake up ; there will be no sleeping in hell."
"You, sir, No. 3 in the second seat from the
front in the top loft, what are you asleep for?
Put your thumb into him—his next neighbour."
On one occasion his eye caught a man asleep
whom he knew, and whose wife was seated
beside him. The minister called to the latter,
"Go home, Betty, and bring John's nightcap."
John somehow heard those words, which were
more pointed than pleasant, and the nightcap
was not required.

The Doctor was very regular and strict in his
district visitation. He felt that, as a shepherd,
he ought to know his flock one by one, and he
was at pains, at least as long as he had strength
for it, to come into close personal contact with

them. He questioned all, young and old, on points of doctrine, and would reprove very severely, if he did not receive a satisfactory answer. Hence it was no uncommon thing to see even old men and women perusing the Shorter Catechism before the minister came round. In the afternoon or evening of the days of his visitations he usually had a service in some place in the neighbourhood. Besides being a frequent visitor at the various schools and classes in connection with the church, he had a special service for the young on New Year's day, when they marched to Gilcomston Chapel, to be addressed by the minister, who could speak to children so well because he loved them so much.

No one in Aberdeen was better fitted, from his commanding presence, to obey the instructions:—"Go out into the highways and hedges and compel them to come in, that my house may be filled." When the circumstances of a busy life favoured it, he sometimes gave a literal obedience to that command. On going to church on a Sabbath morning, he met a young man who was evidently setting his face in a direction that was not likely to lead him to any church. "Come with me," said the Doctor. The man was overawed by the Doctor's manner, but mustered courage to explain—"O, Doctor, I could not go into church with these clothes;

besides, I haven't a seat." "Come with me, sir,
and I'll find you a seat," was all the answer he
got. The man, powerless as a sheep with its
shepherd, went with him to the church: they
walked in together along the passage, till they
came to the minister's seat, when the Doctor,
pushing the man in beside Mrs. Kidd, shut the
pew door and went straight up to the pulpit.

On another Sabbath morning he met three
young men whom he knew to be communicants
in his church, and asked them where they were
going. After some hesitation they admitted
that they were intending to spend the Sabbath
with a farmer in Skene. "No, no," said the
Doctor, "come away back, and if I do not give
you more to think and talk about during the
week than you would get at Skene I shall give
you leave in future." He brought them back,
and put them into the church.

When his sympathies were enlisted, Dr. Kidd
threw himself with an uncalculating spirit and
unmeasured devotion into the case of any who
needed his assistance. What, above all things,
endeared him to the people was his warm-
hearted espousal of their cause, and his readiness
to put himself to any pains in order to serve in
times of deepest need. The worst criminal in
the town was made to feel that, while this
minister could be an austere monitor, yet, when
a man's back was at the wall, he was a brother

and a friend. He undertook the spiritual care and direction of unhappy convicts before they underwent the last dread sentence, though it does not appear that he was a paid chaplain or held any official position in connection with the prison. He spared no pains to bring them to a proper frame of mind, going with them to the scaffold, and standing alongside of them as they were about to be ushered into the presence of their Maker. Who can doubt that the sight of this venerable man of God, coming as near to the lowest as his Master himself was willing to do, had much to do with the deep and abiding impression which he has left upon the popular mind? All, too, was so ingenuous and whole-hearted, nothing being done for effect and popularity. One night he came straight from the condemned cell to a meeting of workers connected with his own church, and, bursting into tears, he began to tell them of the interview he had just had with the unhappy criminal. "All that she needs," said he, "is the grace of God," and adding, somewhat bitterly, "she will never get that at the end of a cart rope!"

The further down a man was, Dr. Kidd came the more closely to him, realising that in his deepest degradation the drunken wretch before him was a brother man, who stood in special need of a helping hand. Principal Brown tells us he once saw Dr. Kidd handling a case of that

kind in a street in Aberdeen. A man who made
a religious profession was seen in a state of helpless intoxication, and the laughing-stock of a
crowd. As Dr. Kidd came up he noticed one man
making himself conspicuous by his loud jeering
at this church member in such a scandalous condition. Staring the mocker in the face, and
holding up his staff or umbrella, he cried out in
the hearing of the crowd, who were awed by his
commanding look, "Many walk, of whom I have
told you often, and now tell you—not *laughing*,
sir, not *laughing*, but weeping : weeping that
they are the enemies of the Cross of Christ."

In those days, sheep-stealing was visited with
capital punishment, and the Doctor, deeply interested in a man who had been convicted of
that crime, and was in a few days to suffer the
extreme penalty of the law, hired a horse, and
rode to the Duke of Gordon's house to plead for
the life of the doomed man. The Duke declined
to take any action, saying—"We must just
allow justice to strike." "What," replied the
Doctor, and, doubtless, pricking the Duke's conscience with his look and word—"what will become of this licentious generation if all that is to
be done for it is that 'Justice should strike?'"

CHAPTER XVI.

BAPTISMS AND MARRIAGES.

BAPTISMS and marriages were not mere formal celebrations or ceremonial occasions with Dr. Kidd; they were to him pastoral acts, into which he put a great deal of the best feeling of his nature. He regarded the administration of those ordinances as so many sacred and tender links to himself, and to the cause he represented. By baptism the child was solemnly committed and dedicated to God, and by marriage, the giving away of two human beings to each other was publicly ratified; but, at the same time, he himself, as entrusted with pastoral responsibility, was felt to be brought by such acts into intimate personal relations with the persons baptised and married. The child baptised in Gilcomston became, in a sense, his child, whom he, as well as the parents, was bound to guard and care for as a real "godfather." A person whom he married was, by that act, joined to him, as well as to his or her "partner in life," and a special claim upon his sympathy was recognised as one of the consequences which flowed out of the act. He remembered and prayed for them as part of the host he was specially answerable for, and whose onward progress he ought to spare no pains to further.

The local newspapers in 1832 gave a most striking illustration of the close identification of Dr. Kidd with any who had participated with him in the exercise of those Christian privileges. George Mathieson, a shoemaker in Holburn Street, had, in a passion, killed a man dwelling in the Hardgate. The latter had gone to Mathieson's shop and quarrelled with him, when in a moment of hot blood, Mathieson took up a knife, used in his trade, and stabbed him, so that he survived but a few hours. When the trial took place, Dr. Kidd was seated on the bench, at the left hand of the judge, and said—" The prisoner is a member of my congregation ; I married his father and mother; I baptised himself; I admitted him to the Lord's Table ; I married him ; I baptised two children to him ; and as one of my own people I cleave to him still; and I appear here where I stand this day to countenance him ; and I told him last night that, if it would be of any use to him, I would appear in that box with him to-day." This he said under strong and visible emotion. The criminal, however, was sentenced to execution, which was afterwards commuted to banishment mainly through the exertions of Dr. Kidd.

"I cleave to him still," said the Doctor, alluding to a man whose hands were imbrued in

the blood of another, and offered to take his
stand beside him in the dock if it would do him
any good—was that not divine like, the act of a
man who was worthy to be called the under-
shepherd of Him who laid down His life for His
sheep? What was the severity of such a man
but intense love, forced to wear a severe aspect
by the perversity of those whom he rebuked?
He was cleaving to others even when his correction was of the sharpest. Just because he had
so much fatherly feeling, and cared so much for
his people, he did not spare them.

When Dr. Kidd came to Aberdeen he found
much ignorance, mingled with superstition,
among the people on the subject of baptism.
Parents would come to him saying they wanted
him to "gie their bairnie a name." "If that is
all you want, my friends," he would answer,
"you can do it yourselves better than I can ; you
don't require me." For many years he instructed
them carefully on the solemn nature of baptism,
and during that time refrained from pronouncing a name at all, so as, if possible, to eradicate
low and erroneous notions of baptism from their
minds. Private baptisms he discouraged by saying "they were intended only for children that
were fatherless or bastards!" When forced by
circumstances to baptise in the house, he insisted
on as large a gathering of friends and neighbours
as could be got, and he turned it into an occasion

for enlightening the minds of all present on the nature of baptism, its significance, and its obligations.

Dr. Kidd was also at pains to make it clear that, while infant baptism had its place as an ordinance of the Church, it produced no inward or moral change. A member of his congregation came and said—"My child is very weakly, and my wife is anxious it should be baptised before it dies." The Doctor turned upon him and said—"What kind of mother can your wife be, to suppose that a little water put by me upon its face would make it more sure of heaven?" In his "Catechism for assisting the young preparing to approach the Lord's Table for the first time," he denies most stoutly that baptism washes away sin:—"If you take an infant that has been washed in baptism, as clean as it can be washed, by an ecclesiastic pretending that he can thus wash away original sin, and take another infant who has been baptised by another minister who did *not* pretend to wash away original sin by the dispensation of the ordinance, and let both these infants suck the same breasts, be dandled upon the same knees, rocked in the same cradle, and brought up in the same nursery—it will be found that the one will become, as soon as the other, a liar, a Sabbath-breaker, disobedient to his parents, and a partaker in every sin peculiar to youth."

M

Through the kindness of the clerk of Gilcomston Kirk Session, we have obtained access to a baptismal register which was kept by Dr. Kidd during his pastorate of Gilcomston Church. In that private register there are four thousand one hundred and fifty-six entries of baptisms performed by himself.

Some of the entries have touches of pathos and human interest:—"M—— B——, a foundling, was baptised in the schoolhouse, the elders standing as sponsors, who gave her the above name." "A soldier (he now in Egypt), the mother living in Windmill Brae, had a daughter baptised in her mother's house; held up by the mother." "16th January, 1825.—James ——, a young man brought up in the Anabaptist persuasion, presented himself for baptism, and was baptised in the presence of the congregation, by his own name James."

On looking over the register, the reader is struck with the number of children whose fathers were soldiers, showing that the North gave, at that time, a very liberal share of its population to recruit the army. Amongst the trades mentioned the "weaver" is in the majority.

For a year or two after beginning to keep a register, the Doctor uttered, in writing, a short prayer on behalf of every child whose name he entered:—"May the God of all mercy be gracious to her, and bless her with all spiritual

blessing in heavenly places, in Christ Jesus:"
"May the Lord of all grace bless the lad, and
may he be a blessing to his parents and friends,
and to the Church of the living God:" "May
the Lord write his name in the Book of Life,
and preserve him from the evils that are in the
world, for Christ's sake:" "O, that God, in his
abundant mercy, may bless and preserve her to
Himself for ever, for Christ's sake." The last
benediction we quote is very brief, and yet how
comprehensive—"May he live before God
always."

There are sometimes circumstances attending
baptisms in church which try the nerves of the
most self-possessed ministers, and the Doctor,
who was not endowed with a super-abundant
measure of patience at any time, was now and
again sorely tried by screaming babes and *mal-
adroit* parents. One Sabbath there were four
or five children brought before him, but there
was a difference of opinion amongst the parents
as to which was to be presented first. The
father of a girl persisted in going first, notwithstanding the protests of those who had boys
with them. Most direful consequences were
predicted in those days if a female were to take
precedence of a male on such an occasion.
"What superstition is this?" thundered out the
Doctor. The difficulties of the situation were
not yet safely weathered. The line the father,

who now came forward, handed to the Doctor had a string of names upon it—"William Francis Joseph"—or something like that. "What fiddle-faddle is this?" said the irate minister, and proceeded to baptise the child "William."

A little narrative, given to us at first hand, and which starts with an incident connected with Dr. Kidd's ministry, carries with it not a little of the pathetic. It was in the latter part of the summer of 1826, at an evening service in Gilcomston Chapel, that a young woman appeared for the purpose of having two infants, twins, boy and girl, baptised. She and some of her friends had taken their places in the seats provided for baptisms, but no male parent put in an appearance. When the time for the minister to perform the ceremony was come, Dr. Kidd was in a dilemma; but by-and-bye he ordered the mother of the children, a young creature, evidently in delicate health, to stand up, which she did, although from agitation and want of physical strength one of the kindly women who were at hand had partially to support her. Dr. Kidd, whose temper had been sorely tried, spoke rather sharply to her. He asked several questions, one of these being whether she, or anyone else, knew if the father of the children was in the church or not. The poor young mother could only answer, "He promised to be here, sir." "Well, if I knew where he was I should soon make him shift his position," said Dr. Kidd. And then after further giving vent to his feelings he baptised the children. In giving the male child his name, he said, in the untempered excitement of his indignation, "If that child grows up to be a man, and if he were to meet his unworthy father in the street, I would consider it no sin if he were to take up a brick and knock that father down dead." It was not to be thus, however. For although that same unworthy father was present in the church, skulking out of sight, as he could among the large congregation, and heard what was said of him, it was not until the infant boy had grown to manhood, after his weakly and ill-used mother had long filled an early grave, and himself was now a married man, that he sought out his father, and with difficulty discovered him living in Musselburgh, and now the husband of another woman. "And when I confronted him as his son—the son of a mother he had betrayed and basely deserted—he had not a word to say," added our interlocutor, who, with a lively recollection of Dr. Kidd's words to himself and other youngsters in passing—"Be all good: be all good"—has through life striven to fill his humble place honourably and well, as all will testify who know him.

The Doctor was strongly impressed with the risks and hardships which the wives of soldiers and sailors had to endure. It did not put him into a good humour to be asked to officiate in connection with the marriage of any of the young women of his congregation to a sailor; but when a soldier made his appearance on such an errand, he was treated with scant civility. A redcoat came to his house one day on business of that kind, against whom the Doctor had probably some other objection besides his calling. He looked sternly at the soldier and said, "Marry you! No; better take your musket and shoot the woman!" And he turned away from the man, muttering to himself, "I'll not marry you."

A question that the Doctor often put to the bridegroom, immediately after the ceremony was over, was—"What makes a good husband?" The answer expected was, "The grace of God," to which the minister sometimes added, "Yes, and keeping out of debt." A young man, wanting to be fully primed before he had to submit to the fiery ordeal of the Doctor's questioning, got the whole thing up in parrot-like fashion. The usual question being put: "What makes a good husband?" the young fellow glibly blurted out: "The grace of God, sir, and keeping out of debt." The Doctor gave him a curious look, and then, with a comical twinkle, added, "I see, sir, you have been ploughing with my heifer."

CHAPTER XVII.

THE MINISTER-MAGISTRATE.

NEVER since the time when that part of modern civilisation, a police force, was introduced, has Aberdeen had one that was more efficient and cost so little, as that which was rolled into the bulky figure of Dr. Kidd. He was literally a terror to evildoers, and a praise to them that do well. His baton of office, or sword of state, as a minister-magistrate, was not unfrequently a big, old-fashioned umbrella. Adapting the language of Scripture, and without a particle of irreverence, it could be said of him—He beareth not the umbrella in vain! It was a very handy weapon, as he could soften or harden the blow according to the part of the umbrella he used. When the offence was not very grievous, the cotton flaps were allowed to come down upon the shoulders of the culprit. Bùt, if roused to indignation, woe betide the offender. That umbrella, commonplace enough in itself, became a symbol of awful portent when held by Dr. Kidd in the presence of evildoing.

If he saw any young Aberdeen savages using their strength to disfigure each other with their fists, his blood was up at once, and, throwing himself into the fray, making no unsparing use of his umbrella all round, he compelled the young combatants to desist from their brutal sport. But he liked to see young people engaging in athletic and harmless exercise, such as snowballing. When passing through the College grounds as the students were enjoying that most exhilarating forthputting of energy, which only juvenile superfluity of that article and a snowy day make possible, he would say to them, as they proclaimed a truce to let him pass— " Heave away, boys; heave away, boys! Never mind me."

His strong affection for children made him dangerously angry when he saw a mother at the street door unmercifully beating her child, or heard her calling down heaven's imprecations upon it. He made for the wretched woman at once, and she, knowing that there was an avenging fury at her heels, ran speedily up the stairs, and did not feel herself to be safe till she had a locked door between her and the Doctor.

But the wives and mothers in the Denburn and other parts knew they had no truer friend than Dr. Kidd. If any of them had husbands who were addicted to excess in drinking, they knew they could ever count upon the sympathy and helpful co-operation of their minister. He has been seen driving a drunken man along Skene Street heaping epithets upon him and making him feel the weight of his umbrella occasionally; but all the while putting himself to the trouble of conducting the unhappy drunkard to his own home and wife.

Drunkenness was a vice too common among all classes in those days, and one class in Aberdeen, quite as notorious in this respect as any other, was that known as *hecklers* or flax dressers. On passing what were then called the Steps of Gilcomston, the Doctor, in the early days of his ministry, observed two of that trade, members of his congregation, far gone in intoxication, and fighting at the side of the burn. He came up to them, seized them both by the nape of the neck, knocked their heads together, dipped them in the water, and then left them to their own cool reflections.

To Aberdeen, generally, Dr. Kidd came to be a kind of visible and incarnate conscience, an embodiment of righteousness, the ten commandments on two legs. All were made to feel it, high and low. A gentleman who had returned from the West Indies to Aberdeen, bringing with him a considerable sum of money and a black man, had a call one day from Dr. Kidd. The occasion of the visit was a rumour in the town that this person was doing an unlawful thing, viz., keeping a slave in this free country, and treating him with cruelty. The question was pointedly put whether the coloured person under his roof was held as a slave. The man of fortune at first stood upon his dignity, and demanded to know Dr. Kidd's right to interfere. But the interference of Dr. Kidd led to the authorities stepping in, and the slave was made a free man.

Walking along Union Street, he saw a soldier, in a mood for practical joking at the expense of others, knock a basket of rolls off the head of a baker's boy. The soldier stood laughing at the plight of the poor lad as he was collecting the scattered and soiled rolls. But the laughter of this man, who was a disgrace to his uniform, was soon brought to an end when he was collared and shaken by Dr. Kidd, and ordered to assist the boy in picking up the bread, the big burly ministerial figure, moved with indignation, standing over him as he did so. "Now, sir," he said, when every roll was in its place, "put the basket upon the boy's head," which the red-coated poltroon submissively did. Having dismissed him with the exhortation, "Never again be such a coward in soldier's clothes as to lord it over the weak," the Doctor left him to profit by the lesson he had received from one who probably did more for him than the drill sergeant had done.

In the outskirts of the town, the Doctor, as unexpectedly to himself as to them, came upon a number of low fellows who had everything in readiness for a cock fight. He soon set the cocks at liberty, and scattered the men, calling them

cruel and cowardly ruffians. One of the boldest
of them had the hardihood to mutter, as he
looked over his shoulder at the minister from a
convenient distance, that the only thing which
saved him from getting the drubbing he deserved
for his meddlesomeness was his black coat. Upon
hearing that taunt, which he at once took as a
challenge, the Doctor exclaimed—"If that's all
that stands in your way, we'll soon get rid of it,"
and throwing his coat off on the road, he faced
the man in his shirt sleeves, ready if need be for
a pugilistic encounter. It was an application of
the scriptural maxim—"Answer a fool according
to his folly," which it would not be convenient
for every minister to try, but it answered in this
case, for the fellow slunk off, probably as much
overcome with astonishment as fear at the
spectacle, with these stinging words following
him—"Didn't I say you were cowards?"

Walking along the country road that then
went out westwards, and is now called Carden
Place, on a Sabbath morning, he came upon a
professional bird-catcher with his limed twigs
and lines in full operation, and the cages standing at the foot of the garden wall containing a
few linnets that had been caught. Fired with
holy indignation at this man, who was profaning
the day and outraging nature's quiet, he liberated
the birds, smashed the cages, tore away the
nefarious apparatus, and chased the scoundrel

till he himself was out of breath, and could run no further.

It may be said that his conduct in checking evil was often high-handed, and had more law than gospel in it. But the people bore it all patiently because of their strong conviction that Dr. Kidd was generally in the right, or, at least, was anxious to be on the side of right; and, moreover, they ever felt that he had boundless stores of mercy and good nature when any one turned from the wrong way. Those, too, were simpler times, and his position was exceptionally strong. No man could have been more favourably situated for exercising the virtues of a benevolent despotism. He took full advantage of his opportunity, and occasionally strained his prerogative by his outbreaks of moral vehemence. But when the popular judgment felt that the minister had by language or act overstepped the bounds of propriety, there was always the reserve consideration to fall back upon that it was Dr. Kidd.

He did not like to see people loitering about the church door previous to service, and again and again he had to remonstrate with them for not going in at once and taking their place in God's house, waiting for worship to begin. One day he came upon a group who were having their "crack" at the kirk door. "What devil's committee are you holding here? Get in, get in," he exclaimed, as he chased them in before him.

It was customary in olden times to make intimation at the church door, as the people were retiring, of public sales, etc. This practice was highly obnoxious to Dr. Kidd, and he had without effect made it the occasion of public rebuke. One Sabbath, after the forenoon service, the public "crier" was at his post as usual, shouting at the top of his voice notices which, to say the least of them, were somewhat incongruous in view of the engagements from which the people were retiring. The Doctor, happening to come out of church a little earlier than usual, saw and heard the man persisting in his forbidden practice. Advancing from the church door, the Doctor with a bound cleared his way among the people in the direction of the obnoxious official, and called out—"You child of the devil, go home to your master you serve, and not destroy God's message to my people." Rather an unseemly altercation ensued, but the Doctor's action, which some might consider to be undignified and violent, led to the objectionable practice being abolished.

When vaccination was introduced in Aberdeen, there existed a strong popular prejudice against it and a corresponding reluctance on the part of parents to allow their children to undergo that operation. It "*went over*" the medical men of

Aberdeen to disabuse people's minds of the fear that it "would do more harm than good." This having come to Dr. Kidd's knowledge, he was determined that it should not go over *him.* He accordingly took up the subject with characteristic energy, and at once set himself to acquire as much knowledge and information regarding it as he could from the local medical men and other available sources. In this way he soon mastered the theory of vaccination, but would not rest content until he had mastered the practice also; and having found a willing coadjutor in the person of a medical friend, he was soon able to perform the operation himself. Thus equipped, he frequently from the pulpit enforced on parents the duty of having their children vaccinated, and of giving them the benefit of that invaluable discovery. On one of these occasions he said—— "If you mothers have any scruples about taking your children to a doctor, bring them to me, at my house, any week day morning, between nine and ten o'clock, and I'll vaccinate them to you myself. You don't seem afraid to entrust the *souls* of your children to my care, and surely you won't have any fear to entrust me with their *bodies.*" This appeal had a wonderful effect, and many mothers came to his house with their children at the daily appointed time. The result came to be that the prejudice against vaccination gradually subsided, and Dr. Kidd was soon able

to discontinue his own amateur labours in favour
of the medical men of the city, who, ere long,
had as much work of that kind on their hands as
they were well able to overtake. His personal
ascendancy once more asserted itself, though
even he had a stiff fight before he overcame the
stubbornness and fears of the people. They had
such faith in the man that they at last submitted, when their own judgment was uncon-
vinced, and their own inclination was decidedly
hostile. What power there is in character!
How much it can carry with it!

CHAPTER XVIII.

THEOLOGICAL AUTHORSHIP.

It is not often such a union of the oratorical temperament and the faculty that makes the scholastic divine exists, as it did in Dr. Kidd. The most illiterate artisan or fishwife in Aberdeen had no difficulty in following Dr. Kidd— unless when he took wings and flew into the region of unfulfilled prophecy; and he, at the same time, could write so as to stir the admiration of metaphysical theologians. The late Dr. Candlish was so impressed with the acumen and grasp displayed by Dr. Kidd in his treatise on the "Eternal Sonship of Christ," that he put himself to the trouble of writing an elaborate Introduction to it when a new edition was published in 1872. In the last sentence of his tribute to the memory of the Aberdeen Doctor, he speaks of him "as entitled to rank amongst the profoundest and most original thinkers of his age." It is to be regretted that the University of our city did not honour itself by conferring upon such a man one of those marks of distinction which would have been an outward and permanent memorial of its own sagacity as well as of his worth. His degree of D.D. came from New Jersey, U.S., in 1819.*

Dr. Kidd's early works had doubtless something to do with the mark of distinction which came to him from the other side of the Atlantic. He had betaken himself to the field of theological literature, and challenged the attention of the world as an author, as much, perhaps, for the relief of his own mind as for the enlightenment of those whom his pen could influence. Aspects of Divine truth had appeared to him in his profounder moods and moments of clearer vision, which demanded a presentation such as he would not be justified in giving before the miscellaneous audience that met him on Sabbath. So he resolved to bring his contributions to the discussion of those sublime and mysterious verities which for many centuries had exercised the subtlest intellects and most consecrated hearts in

---

* PRINCETON, NEW JERSEY, 8th April, 1819.

"The Rev. James Kidd, Professor of Oriental Languages in the Marischal College and University of Aberdeen.

"SIR,—It is my official duty, which I find a pleasure in performing, to make known to you that the Degree of Doctor in Divinity was conferred on you in September last by the Trustees of the College of New Jersey. I wait only for a favourable opportunity to transmit to you the usual Diploma.—With great respect, I am, reverend sir, your obedient servant,

"ASHBEL GREEN,
"President of the College of New Jersey."

N

Europe. Columba in Iona had some spare hours
for the contemplation of themes which lay apart
from the practical urgency of his work as a
herald of the cross; and why should not he,
another Irishman in another part of Scotland,
turn aside for a little into the sacred region of
scientific theology?

His first work on the Trinity, published in
1815, bore this title—"An Essay on the Doctrine
of the Trinity, attempting to prove it by Reason
and Demonstration, founded upon Duration and
Space, and upon some of the Divine Perfections,
some of the Powers of the Human Soul, the
Language of Scripture, and tradition among all
Nations." Before the preface there is an
"Address to the Elders and Members of the
Congregation who worship in the Chapel of
Ease, Gilcomston, by Aberdeen." We give a
part of it:—

"From the day in which the good providence of
God brought us together in the relation of pastor and
people, it has been my constant aim and effort to
instruct you as particularly as possible in the doctrine
of the Trinity, or of the Father and the Son and the
Holy Ghost, whose thrice holy name you bear in
baptism as the foundation of all the doctrines of
revelation, of all true religion, and of all faith and
practice according to the scriptures. As this doctrine
is the most difficult of all others, it requires great
patience and perseverance to obtain any considerable

knowledge of it, lying so far out of the general comprehension of common capacities, it requires a particular turn of mind and mode of thinking to enter fully
into it. Besides those instructions from the pulpit, in
order to carry forward the knowledge of the subject
in your minds to greater perfection, I have drawn up
the following essay, with much care and as much
perspicuity as the nature of the subject would admit,
for the express purpose that a present and permanent
help might remain among you after I go the way of all
the earth."

Very probably Dr. Kidd, like others who have
handled such high and mysterious subjects, was
better satisfied with the conception that was in
his own mind, than with the "Essay" upon
paper. But Dr. Adam Clarke, no mean authority,
said of this treatise:—"I consider his work to
be a mighty effort of a mighty mind, and should
he even fail in the main argument, his work, I
am sure, will do much good. He has dared
nobly; and if he fail, it must be by the sun's
melting the wax of his pinions through the
sublimity of his flight. I believe there is not a
Socinian in Britain this day that will be able to
demonstrate him to be wrong; and I fear not to
pledge myself to eat the book, though a folio, in
which his chain of argumentation can be fairly
proved to cut the opposite way."

Dr. Kidd's "Dissertation on the Eternal Sonship of Christ" was published in 1822, and

re-published, as we have already mentioned, with
an Introduction by the late Dr. Candlish in 1872.
However disposed the present generation may
be to regard such studies as too remote from the
practical purposes of life, it is well for Christen-
dom that there have been men in the church who
went as far as human thought could go in bringing the understanding up to faith. Should
nothing else be accomplished in grappling with
those questions, and trying to go down to the
roots, and back to the essences of things, the
limitations of reason are made apparent at least,
and that is no small advantage.

As was to be expected in handling such
themes as the Trinity and the Sonship, there is
not much colour in the style; but both books
display clear concatenation of thought, expressed
in graceful and flowing sentences. Even in Dr.
Kidd's days there must have been many who did
not find in the treatises any spiritual nutriment
commensurate with the intellectual toil expended
upon the reading. After the latter was published,
the Doctor did, what is ever hazardous in an
author to do—he challenged the verdict of a
friend whom he happened to meet. "Well, have
you got my book?" "Yes," was the reply, with
a laconic significance, which, however, was lost
upon the Doctor. "What did you think of it?"
persisted the author in his unwise interroga-
tions. Unwilling to give his real opinion, this

persecuted reader took refuge in the additional
observation, which was meant to be conciliatory,
that he had "read it with care." Chased out of
that hiding by the sheer pertinacity of Dr. Kidd,
the truth at last came out—"Weel, doctor, if
you will hae't, I didna feel as if your book
brocht me the length of my pike staff nearer
heaven!"

Several years before the treatises on the
Trinity and the Sonship were written, there
appeared "A Volume of Sermons explaining the
Goodness of God in dispensing the Blessings of
the Covenant of Grace, according to the
Sovereign Purpose of his Redeeming Love."
His other printed works of importance were:—
"A pamphlet on the Rights and Liberties of the
Church against the Usurpation of Patronage;"
"A Catechism for the Young on Approaching
the Communion Table for the First Time;"
"Treatise on Infant Baptism;" and another
volume of sermons or rather skeletons of
"Sermons published posthumously."

Dr. Kidd was just the mould of a man to
have made a magnificent scholastic divine. We
can imagine him setting out, if he had been alive
in the Middle Ages, as another Duns Scotus,
nailing his theses to the door of a University,
and challenging all competent to the task to
debate on high and abstruse themes. While
possessing much of the exuberant warmth of

Peter, he was by no means a stranger to the dialectics of Paul; but Thomas must have been to him an incomprehensible personage.

There is abundant evidence to prove that, if circumstances had been favourable to such a direction of his energies, Dr. Kidd's name might have taken a still more honoured place in the illustrious roll of theological and philosophical writers of which Aberdeen can boast. The writer for the few might have eclipsed the preacher for the many, if it had not been for the impelling temperament, the popular sympathies, the active and earnest spirit of the man, which made him so intent upon doing good to the vast multitude that looked to him for bread, as to leave no more than mere fragments of time for literary pursuits. Who can doubt it was well ordered for Aberdeen? For one man who can wield such a mighty spiritual influence upon a community as he did, you will find a score who can write learned disquisitions. It is to the credit of some ministers of the Gospel that they cannot command the resources, as they do not possess the leisure, of the professional scholar. In each man there is only a certain amount of energy deposited, and if one's soul is aglow with zeal for men he cannot shut himself up in cloistered repose.

Dr. Kidd had the instincts of the true philosopher or theologian, who loves truth for its own sake, and hails with delight any luminous and forcible statement of it, from whatever quarter it may come. In the course of his reading he happened to come upon Drew " On the Soul," and " On the Identity and Resurrection of the Body," and in his warm-hearted, generous way he wrote at once to the author—Mr. Samuel Drew, a remarkable man, and one of rare metaphysical acumen—urging him to become a candidate for "the Burnett Prize" of £1,500, to be awarded after three years, on the judgment chiefly of the professors and ministers of Aberdeen, for the best essay on " The evidence, independently of Revelation, that there is a Being, all-powerful, wise, and good, by whom everything exists." Mr. Drew did not get the prize, but this action on the part of Dr. Kidd led to a life-long friendship between these two kindred spirits. The two men were far apart on many points, the one being an Arminian Methodist and the other a Calvinistic Presbyterian, but they were one in their high-toned love of truth and magnanimous catholicity. Dr. Kidd, like all great souls, could, as by instinct, cleave to the heart and essence of Christianity, and if he found a man identified with that he could tolerate a great many differences on minor points.

Moral Philosophy was one of his favourite subjects of study, and, in addition to his multi-

farious duties, he actually conducted a private
class for a series of years, in which he unfolded
the principles of that science, which is the twin
sister of theology. It is often brought as an
accusation against ministers of the gospel, particularly those of marked evangelical sentiments,
that their range of intellectual interest is extremely narrow. Many of them are deemed to
be worthy of the designation sailors sometimes
give to them of "sky pilots"—good enough for
helping men to steer their course aright for
heaven, but of little or no use when direction is
needed for the affairs of this present life. That
certainly could not be affirmed of Dr. Kidd. He
was the first teacher in the kingdom to adopt as
a text-book the "Lectures on the Philosophy of
the Human Mind" of Dr. Thomas Brown, of
Edinburgh. Bacon said he annexed all knowledge as his province. Dr. Kidd made no such
proud boast; but it is instructive to find him in
his old age turning his attention to all sorts of
subjects of interest to the race.

CHAPTER XIX.

"RABBI" DUNCAN IN DR. KIDD'S HANDS.

As might have been expected, considering the position Dr. Kidd took as a preacher, a great many University students attended his ministry. Besides his pulpit abilities and general force of character, which were attractive to them as to others, his generous instincts and accessibility made him a special favourite with young men. His sympathy was so diffusive and catching, and he put himself to such pains to be of service to any one, that he could not fail to exert a potent influence over students whose faces were set in the right direction. He invited them to his house, conversed with them in an easy, familiar way, and made them feel at home in his society. Persons at a distance, who sent their sons to study in Aberdeen, often put them under the charge of the minister of Gilcomston. Amongst Dr. Kidd's papers is a letter from the well-known Dr. Waugh, written on behalf of a young man in whom the great Wilberforce, of anti-slavery fame, was interested. The letter says:—
" Mr. Wilberforce wishes you will have the goodness to send for him (the student), and make enquiry into the nature of his capacities and the

genius or bent of his mind, and give him your opinion respecting the particular line of life, literary or mechanical, in which it would be advisable to bring him forward."

That was as early as 1804. Several years after that, Dr. Kidd had a difficult case on hand belonging to his own parish. John, who afterwards, on account of his extraordinary familiarity with Hebraistic literature, was called "Rabbi" Duncan, owed much in his early days to the judicious help of Dr. Kidd. This profound and original thinker, who, if he had only written as he thought, and occasionally spoke, would have placed himself in the very front rank of teachers of the queen of sciences, said a few days before his death, "Those specially have had influence upon me . . . " "Dr. Kidd" being one of the few who received this honourable mention. Dr. Duncan said of himself, "I am a philosophical sceptic, who have taken refuge in theology." It was certainly no ordinary distinction to have been helpful in establishing such a penetrating and pure spirit in the truth.

In Principal Brown's memoir of Dr. Duncan, we have some illustrations of this "special influence" for good, which was so gratefully remembered at life's close. John Duncan, as already stated, was a native of Aberdeen, a denizen of Gilcomston, and, like Dr. Kidd himself, had passed from the Secession to the Established Church. He was born in humble circumstances, and had considerable wrestling with unpropitious circumstance before he completed his Academic course; but his struggle to get learning was nothing to what he had to undergo in order to keep his faith. This worthy man, who, in his own way, was as great an oddity as Dr. Kidd himself, was for years weltering in a sea of metaphysical perplexity and speculative doubt. By nature a strange combination of the rationalist and the mystic, and dwelling more than was good for him in a world of abstractions, his mind, in the early days of his career, was often in a very restless and morbid state.

He came under the influence of Dr. Kidd after he had finished his University studies, and, as is not uncommon at that stage of development, he had "rather much of the 'young' man, a great deal more than should be of the 'old' man, and far too little of the 'new' man." Dr. Kidd, with his penetrating insight and masterful manner, was just the person to apply the needed correctives. He had the very abundant means of sharp discipline always at hand in his caustic tongue; and as the chastisement inflicted upon the embryo "Rabbi" came from one whom he was bound to respect for his attainments in theology and genius as a preacher, as well as for his downright sincerity as a man, it was not without salutary effect.

Principal Brown thinks that "the 'special influence' that Dr. Kidd exerted upon the young 'Rabbi' consisted mainly in the oracular, epigrammatic wisdom with which he often surprised and overawed him in conversation, and, not least —but probably most of all—when he snubbed him and made him ashamed of himself."

The author we have just quoted gives an illustrative example of the above, as furnished by an eye-witness :—"Joseph Thorburn* gave a grand tea party in his house, at which, I believe, all the Evangelical ministers of the town were present. John Duncan was seated near me, and I observed that he regularly helped himself to everything as it came round, without, however, partaking of the viands, but planting them in front, so that by the time we had finished, his cup stood in the midst of a circle composed of bread and butter, toast, cookies, and shortbread. All this time he was so engrossed with the topics on which he was descanting that he paid no attention to the process of tea drinking. He spoke loudly, too, and occupied much of the conversation. At last Dr. Kidd, who could stand it no longer, exclaimed—'Hold your tongue, sir; you are gabbling nonsense.' This at once silenced poor John, and struck us all with confusion. In fact, it brought tears into the poor man's eyes, and altogether it was a painful scene, though ludicrous too."

* Then Minister of Union Chapel, Aberdeen.

The young theologian needed to be taken out of himself, and Dr. Kidd, by his oracular manner and sharp rejoinder, was just the man to help him to such a deliverance. He refused, as a rule, to be drawn into discussions by the "young man," as he always called John Duncan, who was soon to become the distinguished Oriental scholar. But in the course of their repeated conversations he would now and again drop a sentence as practical as it was sententious, which came with the effect of a shock, and tended to produce a healthier state of mind. Walking with anyone, the Doctor would reserve himself till they were about to separate, and then give his parting word when the person could not dispute with him about it. In notes of conversations with Dr. Kidd, as quoted by Principal Brown,* Mr. Duncan gives us an excellent example of this method:—"Once I was going out of town several miles to teach, and the Doctor walked a bit with me. I was pouring out my complaint to him—'I had a Socinian heart, a Pelagian heart, an Arminian heart, and all kinds of hearts.' As we were parting, the Doctor says, 'O Lord, I have a Socinian heart, and a Pelagian heart, and an Arminian heart, and every kind of bad heart; but the Son of God loved me, and gave himself for me. Good bye.'"

Who can doubt that the man who could

---

* "Life of John Duncan, LL.D.," by David Brown, D.D., 1872.

handle such a difficult subject as "Rabbi" Duncan so skilfully, though occasionally somewhat roughly, must have been a great power for good among the students generally of Aberdeen. At home with people of every grade of culture, and of no culture at all, this many-sided, big-hearted man could at once become all things to any man that he might win him to Christ. Doubtless, too, the day will declare that many young men who came to study in Aberdeen at the beginning of the present century had their faith fortified and their spirituality kept alive by the words spoken in private, as well as in public, by this man, who lived to do good as he had opportunity. The northern part of Scotland has won fame for itself for the large number of able ministers and missionaries it has sent to all parts of the world. May not the influence of this massive Christian personality, exerted all those years, and coming down percolating through the generations, have something to do with this enviable distinction?

There is one little incident related by Dr. Duncan which throws a flash of light upon the spiritual character of Dr. Kidd, and shows that, amidst all his efforts on behalf of others, he ever felt as a brother man. His boldness and vehemence may have given some the impression that he stood above his fellows on a pedestal of professional superiority. Not so: underneath

the kingly manner there was the humble heart.
Dr. Duncan says :—" He had the habit of using
the words ' My God ' in a way that looked like
profanity. One day I was walking with him
when he did so. As we were parting, I said,
having laid hold of his hand, not daring to look
up into his face, ' Doctor, I think you used the
words " My God " just now.' He said nothing,
but pressed my hand, and if he was kind before
he was doubly kind afterwards." When tempted
to regard Dr. Kidd as an overbearing, arrogant
ecclesiastic, let us think of his treatment of a
young man who, in delicate fashion, ventured to
rebuke him.

In recalling scenes in Gilcomston, Dr.
Duncan told friends that Dr. Kidd was " very
fond of picturing the conversation in hell between the damned souls and damned ministers.
He made the lost people say—' Ha ! you preached
a trash of morality to us, and you never preached
the Gospel, through which alone we could have
any morality.' "

He also tells us—" Dr. Kidd took me once
with him to prison, and made me read a passage
to the prisoner. I, conceited young puppy as I
was, began to expound. Dr. Kidd bore it for a
little, and then said—' Young man, will you hold
your peace and let the Holy Ghost speak ? ' I
expounded no more that night. Once I was
propounding my case to him : he spoke not a

word. ' Dr. Kidd, do you understand my case? '
' I understand it quite well—you are running
before the Holy Ghost!' ' "

Professor Duncan has left on record some
interesting reminiscences of Dr. Kidd's gentle-
ness in dealing with cases where the "son of
consolation" was more needed than the "son of
thunder." Fearless, and even violent, censor of
unrighteousness as he was, he did not " break the
bruised reed nor quench the smoking flax."
There was a serious, good man, as everybody but
himself judged, a hearer of Dr. Kidd's, who was
asked one day—" Well, Thomas, how long have
you been praying?" " For forty years." "And
what have you got?" " I canna say I hae gotten
onything." " I wonder you are not tired, and
don't give up that kind of hopeless work." " Na,
sir, we manna dee that." Well, when Thomas
was dying, the Doctor called and asked (as he
always did when he was going to pray), " What
shall I pray for?" " Give thanks," said
Thomas, " give thanks, give thanks for my
forty years' prayers in a lump."

CHAPTER XX.

LETTERS FROM DR. KIDD.

SOME of the many letters written by Dr. Kidd have been rescued from oblivion, and we insert those which tend to illustrate salient features in his character, or give us glimpses of the times : —

To the MARQUIS OF HUNTLY.

"ABERDEEN, 21st July, 1825.

" May it please your Lordship,—Although somewhat late, I presume to present my most grateful acknowledgments, and the delighted homage of a numerous list of poor, relieved by the humane and timeous beneficence of your lordship's feeling heart. Many whom you can never see or know are sighing out their gratitude in the retirement of poverty and distress, and blessing the hand that ministered to their unknown wants. The consideration of this, I am persuaded, will operate as a soothing and sweet compensation in a breast which requires no other return for acts of kindness to poor, suffering fellow-creatures.

" As acts of real charity and true religion are nearly connected, the heart that is susceptible of the one being more or less so of the other, I have proposed to augment your lordship's gratification by

O

associating religion, in the most pure and simple manner, with gratitude on this day of fasting, humiliation, and prayer.

"I venture to subjoin a copy of the Holy Scriptures with my letter of thanks, which I hope you will deign to accept. I do this, my lord, not because I suppose you are unacquainted with the Word of God, but as your lordship has treated me like a marquis, I attempt to return the compliment as a minister of God. I am pretty certain you never saw a copy of this edition of the Bible before; you see it is portable, and will occupy little room in your travelling-trunk, and you will find upon trial that it is the very best and dearest companion, both in life and death. . . . . . As those who surround your person and approach your presence are so far excelled by your superior accomplishments, blended with condescension, kindness, and generosity, they exert all their faculties to please and obey—therefore, life exhibits a picture by far too flattering for reality; but this book, my lord, will detect the counterfeit, remove the veil, and present men and things as they are. It speaks equally to the sovereign and the subject. It teaches that each man at his best is wholly vanity; that a man must be born again before he can enter into the Kingdom of God; that the Son of God is a Saviour, able to save to the uttermost all that come unto Him; that the Holy Spirit is a comforter, sanctifier, and guide to eternal life; that faith and repentance are required of every rational soul who hears the Gospel; and that Heaven, the place of the Divine residence more particularly, is the reward of all who are found in Christ at last. Such a book, my lord, I presume to offer for your acceptance. Would it not become every nobleman and prince in the four quarters of the globe?

"Such blessing as it holds out to the righteous I implore for you; deign to accept of my present and my best wishes.—I have the honour to be, my lord, your sincere and humble servant,

"JAMES KIDD."

To His Excellency JAMES MONROE, Esquire, President of the United States.

"May it please your Excellency,—The country over which you preside as Chief Magistrate is the country of the happiest days of my life. The remembrance of it ever has, and always will, draw forth the strongest and most patriotic emotions of my heart. As a testimony of my sincerity, I presume to send herewith, and present to your Excellency, my works on the most important of all subjects, and the most interesting of all sciences. May I entreat your candid perusal of them? I do this in the name of your ancestors, who professed their faith in the doctrines I have endeavoured to develop. I do this also on account of the very humbling consideration of the conduct of the first legislative body of the United States, who have made choice of a Unitarian to be their chaplain. While I entertain the highest respect for that august body, I deeply lament that the rulers of the country I love have done so. It shows an indifference to Christianity, and bids fair to issue in infidelity. I address your Excellency as the representative of God, among the many thousands over whom you bear rule, and to whom, in your administration, you are to imitate God, the moral governor of the universe. I presume your Excellency well knows that the origin of infidelity is ignorance of the foundation of the moral law. Most philosophers say this foundation is the human conscience alone, and this is a fatal error. Many Christians say it is an abstract of the ten commandments; this is also a mistake, but not so fatal as the former. The true foundation is the related character of the Moral Governor and the moral subject, together with the manifestations which the Moral Governor makes of Himself to the moral subject, and the benefits He confers on him, so that the moral obligations are constituted by His providence and grace.

" If you trace the history of the English infidels you will find that scepticism on this point was the rock on which Hobbes, Bolingbroke, Hume, and Gibbon split. How contrary were the sentiments of Milton, Locke, Addison, Clarke, and Newton. If you look back on the history of your own happy country you will find that the inhabitants who effected the Revolution were the well-informed descendants of pious ancestors and not infidels. Just so in France of late; your Excellency may well remember that in Britain the American Revolution was called a Presbyterian Revolution.

" And may I venture to say your great country is in danger of nothing so much as infidelity. I hope I may also add that a chief magistrate, who is indeed the representative of God, can never be such a blessing

to those over whom he rules as when he supports
justice in the State and religion in the Church of
Christ. This is representing the Great Almighty,
moral governor of the universe, who rules both in
justice and mercy. The churches of New England
resemble the churches of lesser Asia. They have
departed far from their original purity. Nor is there a
stain on the character of the famous statesman, John
Adams, except that of Unitarianism. Alas! that
they knew so much of human policy and so little of
the Book of God. Unitarianism and infidelity are
the same in nature, though distinct in name. Surely,
most excellent sir, you cannot suppose that natural
philosophy and chemistry, and all other sciences,
should have their difficulties, and the science of
theology, the deepest of them all, should be without
its mysteries. We are puzzled beyond measure and
uncertain how we came by the knowledge of duration
and space; and are we to know the deep things of
God without long and patient study and research?
If ever the United States fall, they will fall by infidelity, of which the first step is Unitarianism. The
greatest friend of the United States is the man that
promotes true religion most. I am no persecutor,
and am for full liberty of conscience. I am, however,
a great advocate for vital Christianity, which has for
eighteen hundred years been the basis of all real
liberty, and will be so till the end of time. A few of
our king-ridden, sceptical, deistical men would soon
overturn your free institutions. Unitarianism in New
England would do it much sooner. To prevent all
this, the only thing in my power is to present you,

excellent sir, with the accompanying volume, and at the same time to wish and to pray that your valuable life may be long spared as a blessing to your family and as the benefactor of your country, and that the United States may enjoy liberty until the last trumpet blow.—I have the honour to be, most excellent sir, your sincere, humble servant,

" JAMES KIDD."

To Rev. LEWIS ROSE, Nigg.

" ABERDEEN, 7th April, 1826.

"REVEREND AND DEAR SIR,—I offer you the impression of my best thanks for your kind letter of the 19th May. God send you to us full of the Gospel of our Lord Jesus Christ. Since reading yours it has occurred to me that you might call at my house in passing to the Assembly and spend what time you can. It also occurred to me to say that, if you could know of any of your brethren going to the Assembly or coming to Aberdeen about the first Sabbath of July, it would relieve us of some fatigue if you could prevail with such a brother to come and stay in my house and give us some assistance at our solemnity. Think of this and let me know as you pass. But be sure, take no lodgings but my manse in passing both to and from the Assembly. May the tender mercies of our covenant God for ever rest on your person, and family, and flock.—I am, dear sir, your sincere humble servant,

" JAMES KIDD.

" Rev. Lewis Rose."

(To the Same.)

"ABERDEEN, 15th March, 1828.

"VERY DEAR SIR,—Mrs. Rose has informed me of a young man who goes home from the Old Town College by your house. I take the opportunity to write by him, and the first piece of news I give you is that the Secretary of the United Associate Synod has introduced the Rev. Thomas Morrice very conspicuously in page 72-73. I have this moment written to him to that effect. Mrs. Kidd has been very dangerously ill, but is now a little recovering. If the Lord will, we all expect you on the first Sabbath of July next. I hope God is doing something among my flock; I think I see His hand among the young. I shall be glad to hear from you at leisure. You have no doubt heard that Mr. Elder is going to Bressa in Shetland. We expect Mr. M'Donald in the Gaelic Chapel in the first Sabbath of next month. I am, dear sir, your sincere humble servant,

"JAMES KIDD.

"The Rev. Lewis Rose, Nigg."

To Mrs. SMITH (Daughter of Dr. Adam Clarke).

"PALATINE HOUSE, 25th August, 1828.

"MADAM AND PUPIL,—I avail myself of a moment to contemplate yourself, your husband, and family. As far as I can perceive, tranquility reigns both in the heart and the home of all the family. This is what I ever wished; your happiness in life was ever dear to me, and it is so still.

"I look upon your rising little ones, and I look forward with great anxiety; you cannot give grace, and your dear infants need it. This will bring you often to the Throne of Grace, and while you have the pledge of the name of the Father, and of the Son, and of the Holy Ghost upon yourself and upon your dear infants, you have still a warrant to plead with God; and God is a prayer-hearing and a prayer-answering God. The Lord hear thee in the day of trouble; the name of the God of Jacob defend thee, send thee help from the Sanctuary, and strengthen thee out of Zion; remember all thy offerings and accept thy burnt sacrifice; grant this according to thine own heart and fulfil all thy counsel.—Ever yours,

"JAMES KIDD."

(To the Same.)

"ABERDEEN, 25th May, 1833.

"VERY DEAR MADAM AND PUPIL,—After very long and deep silence, I venture once more to speak and to say that it is with a trembling hand and a sorrowful heart I sympathise and lament with you the death of the Rev. Dr. Adam Clarke. At first I did not write, believing that you and all the family would be quite absorbed in mourning. May the Lord in mercy support you all. You can have no belief of the powerful effect the mournful tidings had upon my mind—our birth was at nearly the same time—then, say I, my days are at an end, and a voice cried ' Be ye also ready, for in such an hour as ye think not, the Son of Man cometh ; your friend, your fellow labourer is now gone, and the place which knows him now shall know him no more.'

" And since the removal of the worthy head of the Methodist communion, Dr. M'Leod of New York is gone, and the Rev. Rowland Hill and Samuel Drew are gone; and I look across the Atlantic, I review a period of forty years, I look to the graveyard, I look toward the Eternal World, I look to myself, and say this is not the place of my rest. O, how solemn to give an account for a family, and for a flock, and for time, and for the Bible, and for the Sabbath, and for the office of the ministry, and for preaching Christ.

" My trials have been many, and my sins more. My oldest daughter has been lately left with six of a family. For some time past I have given up all public meetings and public interviews of every kind, except official duty, so that I am become an obscure individual, yet I have great cause to be thankful that I have omitted no part of duty, either in the college or the church. I think, also, that God, in mercy, is countenancing my labours. I perceive several marks of his kindness among my flock. It will give me much satisfaction to learn that your dear mother and all concerned are enabled to submit patiently to the divine will.

" James Kidd.

" Mrs. Mary Ann Smith."

(To the Same.)

"ABERDEEN, 4th July, 1834.

"VERY DEAR MADAM AND PUPIL,—When your letter came with the news of your kindness and success in behalf of my little grand-daughter Agnes [Oswald], I intended to thank you immediately, but I found myself unable, for want of expressions suitable to your goodness and my obligation. I said, 'I shall defer until I recollect some sentiments of gratitude more ample than I now feel'; and the longer I waited the task became the more difficult. And I must just say now what I might have said at first—I most sincerely thank you, madam. I never was able to compete with you either in conversation, or in writing, or in beneficence. And it is just at present, what it has always been, I am unable to meet your benevolence either in word or deed. I entertain a deep sense of my obligation to Mr. Smith. I hope God is supporting your mother and yourself under the calamitous dispensation in the death of your worthy father—*you* feel much, the Church and Christianity feel much also, but *he* feels none of this. This should be your consolation. May it be so.

"I see myself on the borders of the Eternal world, and am looking to the hour appointed for all living. Best wishes to Mr. Smith and your dear mother.— Ever yours,

"JAMES KIDD.

"Mrs. Smith."

CHAPTER XXI.

THE REFORMER AT WORK.

DR. KIDD's first stroke in the field of reform showed him to be a doughty champion of the people, but a swordsman who was untried, and somewhat reckless in the use of his weapon. In 1816 the country was suffering from the depletion of resources caused by the long-continued and expensive European wars, and there was great distress, which was felt most acutely by the classes who were near the bottom of the social scale, and had the narrowest margin of earthly estate to fall back upon. Trade was dull, food was scarce, prices were high, and in many places the poor, in desperation, were making demonstrations which threatened disturbance. Aberdeen was also feeling the paralysis of trade and incipient famine. The Gilcomston shepherd evidently thought that the grain merchants and meal dealers of the town were, in some selfish way, combining to keep up the prices. Coming among the people every day, and seeing, as no other public man did, their straitened condition, his heart went out to them, and against the men whom he regarded as their oppressors. The probability is the dealers were not nearly so much to blame as he supposed, though such a thing has been known in our world as men profiting by the distresses of their fellows. At all events, the Doctor felt it his duty to rebuke those men from the pulpit, which he did in no measured terms.

From the archives of a legal firm in the town we have obtained a document containing evidence that was gathered regarding Dr. Kidd's utterances on this subject. Some of his co-presbyters were so scandalised at the violence of the language used in the sedate, law-abiding town of Aberdeen, that they evidently intended to proceed in some way against the Doctor, and were collecting material for that purpose. We print part of the contents of this document:—

"John Manson, Tacksman of the Mill of Ferryhill, informs that on a Sunday, about a month ago, he was present at divine service in the Chapel of Ease, Gilcomston, both in the forenoon and afternoon; that the Rev. James Kidd, minister of that Chapel, preached both in the forenoon and afternoon; that both in the forenoon and afternoon Mr. Kidd took occasion in his sermon to censure dealers in grain and meal as extortioners and persons who ground the faces of the poor; and in his prayers he prayed for their destruction at the hands of God and man. And in the afternoon, just before the blessing, he said there were men sitting before him who dealt in grain and meal who ought to be excluded from the Lord's

Table and be driven out among society, and added that, if he had the law in his own hands, he would slit their noses and their ears to let them be known, and to carry the mark of it to their graves.

"Aberdeen, 17th October, 1816."

The sting of it all, however, it would appear, lay not so much in what Dr. Kidd himself said as in the observations the aggrieved persons' acquaintances felt themselves at liberty to make:—"That the informant, on the Sunday, was not out of the Chapel door until the people were crying to him, 'The minister had given him it to-day'; and there has scarcely a day passed since, that the informant has not had it cast up to him, and been *advised to take care of his nose!*" That advice, "To take care of his nose"—given to him every day, too—must have hastened the crisis, and brought the Doctor's invective beyond the point of endurance. Other witnesses give similar testimony. One says, " He understood Mr. Kidd's observations applicable to grain and meal dealers were generally approved of by the congregation, except in so far as he spoke of slitting their noses, which the people thought was going too far." They knew, however, that Dr. Kidd did not really mean harm to anyone's nose. To speak in that fashion was just a way that he had, a touch of Oriental profusion that seems to be natural to the natives of that occidental island from which he had migrated.

Further on in life the Doctor became more self-restrained, but not less zealous in his efforts on behalf of the people. Veteran politicians in the north speak of Dr. Kidd as the man who gave the first impetus to the great modern popular movement in this part of the country, the force of which will not be spent for years to come. He was far removed from the professional or partizan politician. He did not care a pin point for politics, except as a means to the improvement of the condition of the people; but every measure that was likely to benefit them was sure to have his blessing and his push.

The three letters which follow are evidently answers to communications from himself, and are interesting from various points of view. The first is from Joseph Hume, a name that is held in honour wherever sterling integrity and constancy in the service of the people are valued:—

" BRYANSTON SQUARE, 21st February, 1827.

" MY DEAR SIR,—I had the pleasure to receive your note yesterday, and on presenting your petition last night, I stated the fact of 600 being fed from the public kitchen as an argument for promoting a change in the laws respecting corn. I concurred entirely in the prayer of the petition, and supported it in presenting it.—I am, yours sincerely,

" JOSEPH HUME.

" Dr. Kidd."

The second is from Mr. Bannerman, who represented the city, and did valiant service on its behalf : —

"LONDON, 15th June, 1834.

" DEAR SIR,—I yesterday forwarded you a copy of the Bill, which will be read a third time to-morrow evening (Monday) in the House of Lords. From the tenor of your former letter, I fear you are but ill informed by your friends of what passes here, of the share which the Government took in this measure, or of the sensation it created in Edinburgh and Glasgow, and from many other places which have sent deputations to London. In short, I think the whole of your church affairs are placed in the hands of well-meaning but injudicious men, who would puzzle and perplex a Government of angels. I wish you were all safely in the hands of the Tories again, although I see little prospect of it. There will yet be time to present your petition to the House of Commons if you wish it, and I will be guided by circumstances, after speaking to some of your friends here.—I remain, dear sir, yours truly,

" AL. BANNERMAN."

The third letter, from the Bishop of London of that day, does credit to him who gave and also to him who received it : —

"LONDON, 20th May, 1834.

" REVEREND SIR,—I have to acknowledge the receipt of your letter, and beg to assure you that I

take a lively interest in the success of Mr. Colquhoun's
Bill.   I have had some communication with that
gentleman on the subject, and have endeavoured to
interest the Earl of Rosebery in the measure.   I
shall do all in my power to promote its adoption.   I
thank you sincerely for the assurance of your prayers.
As the servants of one Master, contending for one faith,
we may assist one another in *this* way at least.—
Believe me, reverend sir, your faithful servant,

"C. J. LONDON."

The Doctor in his old age became a temperance reformer. The cause was then in its infancy,
and the steps that were taken by him, and most
of those associated with him, were cautious and
tentative.   In the year 1830, a Temperance, not
a Total Abstinence, Society was formed in Aberdeen, with which Dr. Kidd became associated, as
one who deeply deplored the vice and misery
which he daily saw in the train of the prevailing
drunkenness.   On the evening of 16th February,
1832, "a soiree or evening's entertainment," as it
was called, took place in the Trades Hall.   They
met at five o'clock in the afternoon, Dr. Kidd
being in the chair.   The "Aberdeen Magazine,"
for March, 1832, gives a rather satirical account
of the proceedings.   There were some present
who were certainly not the sons of temperance,
and had not come to further its interests.   Their
intention evidently was to introduce confusion,

and bring ridicule upon the budding cause. They shouted and whistled, and tried to drown the voice of every speaker. The Doctor, as chairman, was not the man to allow such wanton disturbance to pass with impunity. "Some of you," he exclaimed, "are half drunk. It was expected that all who came here would behave like gentlemen, instead of which many of you are conducting yourselves like ruffians." The Doctor brought forward a proposal that a deputation should be appointed to wait upon the Magistrates, urging them to deprive all publicans of their licences in whose houses any persons were found in a state of intoxication. Soon, thereafter, a brickbat was thrown through one of the windows; and, amidst the wildest confusion, the meeting was broken up. But such violence only brought the cause of temperance still more prominently before the public eye, and made Dr. Kidd and others more decided in their action.

Many stories are told of what the Doctor did on behalf of drunkards. We close this chapter with a specimen. A poor woman received a penny from the Doctor on the street, and he, curious to know what she would do with it, followed her till she came to a public-house. The Doctor, going right into the shop, before the woman had time to leave it, said to the publican, who was a strong young man—"What did you give that poor woman?" The reply was—"She

P

got a pennyworth of whisky." The Doctor at
once said—"Give her back her penny. I wanted
to give her food, and you have given her poison.
You ought to be ashamed of yourself, sir, to
spend your life standing in a place like this
selling whisky to poor wretches. You ought to
go and carry a hod, sir—go and carry a hod, and
be a useful, honest man."

CHAPTER XXII.

LECTURES ON POLITICAL ECONOMY.

DR. KIDD's political economy was the offspring of a warm heart, shaped by a strong intellect. He, as the minister of Gilcomston, was brought into close and daily contact with the poor, and he was impressed with the necessity for a better distribution of the good things of life, and a more general participation in the benefits of an advancing civilization. Moreover, his own independent and unconventional mind, the freshness of which remained unspoiled to the end, gave him a high appreciation of the worth of man as man, and the justice of his claim to all the prerogatives of manhood. His residence in America doubtless opened his eyes to a few things not so clearly seen in an old country, where unjust laws and effete institutions are often viewed through the transfiguring haze of patriotic sentiment. He was also impressed with the fact that the poor could do much by their own exertions to improve their condition.

He felt that the poor, as well as the rich, needed to have explained to them the great laws which regulate the creation and distribution of wealth. Having added the subject of political

economy to the studies he carried on, he determined to give the benefit of his knowledge to
the public. He arranged for a course of lectures
on that subject on week days. The *Aberdeen
Observer* gives a report of Dr. Kidd's introductory
lecture delivered in the Mechanics' Hall:—

"Political Economy was not a science of speculation but of fact; the beneficial results of its operation
were not the result of any legislative enactment, but
arose from the individual desire which each man had
to rise in the world, and which desire, aided by a true
knowledge, led to the most happy results. The
business of the political economist was with man in
the aggregate, not with what would interest only a
few, with States, not with families, with the passions
of the whole human race, not with that of any solitary
individual. Nothing was more common than to hear
great men broaching and acting on speculations at
variance with facts; this conduct certainly did enrich
a few, as monopolies generally would, but when it
could be proved that it was against the nation at
large, it was a bad course which was pursued; decidedly against monopoly he certainly was, and would
so continue, until it could be shown that what was put
into the pockets of a few was not taken out of those
of the whole nation. The passion for accumulation
was far more prevalent among the human race than
that for prodigality, witness the forests which had
been cultivated, the marshes which had been drained,
the roads which have been made out, the bridges
erected, and the cities which have been built, all

arising out of that passion for wealth, and of the force of the accumulating principle. The wealth of a nation did not so much depend on the salubrity of its climate, or the richness of its soil, but on the skill, judgment, and perseverance of its inhabitants, which could overcome every effect of a bad climate or soil, and could make an apparently uninhabitable and barren country rich and luxuriant; while, on the other hand, a nation without these principles would, in a country blessed with all the gifts of nature, wander about in hordes, spectacles of ignorance, want, and wretchedness. The Doctor next referred to the necessary connection between capitalists and labourers; without capitalists we could have no implements, no machinery by which to obey the divine command and till the ground, labour could not be carried on, and we would of necessity live on the scanty and unassisted bounties of nature. The Doctor then went into the principle of combinations, stating that if it could be proved that they eventually led to a depression instead of a permanent advance of wages, and curtailed the resources, and cramped the exertions of the capitalist, they ought to be abolished, quoting a passage from Mr. Hume's speech at Glasgow to the operatives, to prove that combinations did so, and Mr. Hume was the best friend the people ever had seen in Parliament—(cheers and hisses). Many a mechanic at the present day was a much greater adept in political economy than many legislators at the beginning of the present century—(cheers)—and in the heart of England, where M'Culloch had lectured, they would find a journeyman mechanic rise up in any large assembly, and discuss the most abstruse points in this science, with such depth of thought, force, and eloquence, that the orations of Pitt and Fox were fairly outshone—(cheers). No man without careful observation would believe the march of mind which had taken place since the suicide of Londonderry—(loud cheering). After explaining the system he meant to pursue in his ensuing lectures, the Doctor said that they would be worth the attention of the mercantile speculator, as they would give him a knowledge of foreign trade in all its bearings with this country; political economy was to him a polar star to guide him in his speculations. The tallow monopolists seemed lately not to have acted on this science, they had bought up all that they could find of that article, and now they would soon be bankrupts with making good bargains—(laughter). Referring to the benefits of the cultivation of intellect, the Doctor said he might quote the beautiful passage of Dr. O. Gregory, and ask what was Arkwright?—a barber. Ferguson? —a peasant. Herschell?—a pipe and tabor player. Watt?—a mathematical instrument maker. Brindley? —a millwright. Nelson?—a cabin boy. Ramage? —a currier—(loud cheers). These benefits exalted nations as well as individuals. What made William IV. the greatest monarch who now sat on a throne? Not the extent of his territories, not his army, not his navy, but because he reigned over a free, educated, thinking, and inquisitive people—(cheers). Ignorance of their rights had once been cried up as the best way to make an obedient people; but the days were gone by for having the book of knowledge sealed, and education now ennobled the very lowest in degree of the human race into men! 'Many a clown who stands in dumb and seemingly stupid gaze at the majesty of a full moon rising through a hazy horizon in an autumnal evening, or at the flash of the forked lightning, or at the fantastic shape of a transient cloud edged with gold by the gleams of a descending sun, who listens with ignorant but keen attention to the rolling thunder through the stupendous vault of the " overhanging firmament," or whistles as he returns from his daily task in sympathy with the minstrels of the grove, would, had he the benefit of education to brighten the rough diamond, and give scope to the " genial current of the soul," shine forth a Watt or an Arkwright in mechanics—a Washington or a Wellington in arms—a Nelson or a Cochrane on the wave—a Fox or a Canning in the cabinet—a Sheridan or a Mackintosh in the senate—a Chalmers or a Thomson in the pulpit—a Jeffrey at the bar, or a Brougham on the woolsack'—(cheers)."

There is a pile of carefully-written MSS. among his papers, in which, from the headings of the chapters, it is evident that he presented the various aspects of political economy as it was then taught. In those lectures there was the gathered result of an enormous amount of well-digested reading put into popular form.

There are some who might say that a man who has been in this world for nearly threescore years and ten should have been thinking of another economy than that which is needed for the present scene. But Dr. Kidd was too realistic and matter of fact for sentiment of that kind. He was not prosaic, but he was full of strong sense and healthy feeling; and he was of opinion that as heaven, a place, was not yet before him as the earth was, it was his business, as long as he was here, to do his utmost to make a heaven of the present world. Is it not wisdom, as well as piety, to stand by the post of duty till the time of release comes?

At the close of his course of lectures the Doctor was presented with ten volumes of Locke's works, beautifully bound in morocco. They are now in the possession of Dr. Robertson Nicoll, who has kindly furnished us with a copy of the inscription, which is tastefully done in copperplate, except the name, which is printed. It is as follows:—

" Presented to the

Rev. Dr. KIDD

By the gentlemen who attended his Lectures on Political Economy in 1824-5, as an expression of their gratitude for the instruction received, and of their high esteem for his superior talents."

CHAPTER XXIII.

CONTROVERSY WITH PRIEST FRASER.

HAVING an active mind that delighted in intellectual exercise for its own sake, along with a keen sense of responsibility that was alert to catch the call to arms, though it was not sounded with trumpet tones, he was ready for single combat with Papist, Infidel, or any other modern Goliath who entered the lists against Evangelical doctrine. Priest Fraser, of the Roman Catholic Church, Aberdeen, in the year 1830, delivered a course of lectures, on Sabbath evenings, which were largely attended by Protestants as well as by the persons who regularly went to the chapel. In those lectures Mr. Fraser took up some of the leading points of the controversy between the Roman and the Reformed Churches, and, of course, drove home the arguments as forcibly as he could in favour of his own creed. Dr. Kidd was not the man to allow such an industrious sowing of tares in the field for which he was so largely responsible to go unchallenged. His upbringing as a staunch Presbyterian in the north of Ireland, had begotten in him a horror of the doctrines of the Church of Rome, which subsequent study and observation had not diminished, and he felt he could not allow this poison to be distilled in the minds of the citizens of Aberdeen, without an attempt at supplying the needed antidote. Accordingly, he challenged the Rev. Charles Fraser to public debate on the questions raised in the lectures.

Mr. Fraser's reply, which, in some of its personal allusions, and its general tone and temper, was quite unworthy of him, indicated that he could not agree to a public discussion, but he was willing to debate the points at issue in the Latin tongue, and before professors of the University! In his second letter, Dr. Kidd replied that, as he had in view public instruction and edification in proposing a discussion, it should be before the people, and in a language they could understand. This drew forth another scornful effusion. Dr. Kidd did not lose his temper, but conducted his part of the correspondence like a Christian gentleman, who did not stoop to personalities, but was so intent upon the furtherance of public interests as to treat with dignified silence what was meant to wound, but had nothing to do with the business on hand. As this correspondence was one of the memorable incidents in Dr. Kidd's life, and excited an interest in the town, of which certain peppery pamphlets, still to be found in old libraries, are the witnesses, we give the letters which passed between priest and presbyter:—

Dr. Kidd's First Letter.

" To the Rev. Mr. Fraser, Roman Catholic Priest.

" SIR,—You have, in your Sabbath Evening Lectures on ' Purgatory, and Invocation of Saints,' advocated tenets which I maintain to be contrary to the Word of God in the Old and New Testaments.

" I therefore invite you to a discussion of these and the other doctrines of the Church of Rome, respecting which Protestants and Roman Catholics are at issue.

" I propose that we shall carry on our discussions before a general audience in one of the public halls of this city.

" Respectfully requesting to be favoured with your reply to this letter on or before Monday, the 15th instant,—I am, reverend sir, your obedient humble servant,

" JAMES KIDD, D.D.

" Chapel Street, Aberdeen,
    " 9th November, 1830."

Mr. Fraser's Reply.

" Doctori Kidd, Carolus Fraser salut. plur. dicit.

" Accepi, non sine voluptate, tuas, et non, tuas litteras ; a te nimirum subscriptas, sed alia prorsus exaratas manu.

" 'Siquis,' ait Divus Paulus, ' domui suæ præesse nescit, quomodo Ecclesiæ Dei diligentiam habebit ? '

Hoc Apostoli effatum iterum iterumque acri judicio perpendas velim; neque per inordinatum captandi vulgus amorem 'maculam atque execrationem tuæ senectuti conquiras' 'nam qui amat periculum peribit in illo.'

" Cæterum ad controversiam, te inter et me, quod attinet, libentissime signa conferam: non equidem in in [sic in MS.] concessu [consessu] inscitæ plebeculæ, neque sermone vernaculo, sed coram professoribus Universitatis, coram tuis superioribus, coram Sacrosanctæ Romanæ Ecclesiæ sacerdotibus, atque lingua ut Theologos decet latina. Tum enim vero in corona illa hominum eruditissimorum, quid tu, Doctor, ni fallor. Transatlanticus effeceris; quid ve egomet indignissimus Ecclesiæ sacerdos, apis more modoque operosus fingam, palam fiet.

" Præterea, quoniam tantus decertandi te tenet amor, adest in præsentiarum amicus mihi conjunctissimus, qui triginta omnino annos est in plagis Orientalibus versatus, qui tecum de Sacra Scriptura linguis orientalibus disputabit: quique plurimos jam jam libros hisce de rebus vulgavit.

" Hæ conditiones an tibi placeant nec ne, certum me facias velim, et quam primum.—Vale.

" IVto Ante Idus Novembres, A. 1830."

Translation of the above Letter.

(AS PUBLISHED BY DR. KIDD.)

"Charles Fraser to Dr. Kidd, with best wishes.

" I had the pleasure of receiving your letter, if indeed it can be called yours; for it is subscribed by you, but written in quite a different hand.

" 'If a man,' says St. Paul, 'know not how to rule his own house, how shall he take care of the Church of God?' This maxim of the Apostle I would have you to consider over and over again with the most serious attention, and not, through an inordinate desire of alluring the multitude, 'get a stain and a curse to your old age'; 'for he who loveth danger shall perish therein.'

"In regard, however, to a discussion between you and me, I have to say that I shall most cheerfully enter the lists; not, indeed, in a meeting of the ignorant rabble, nor in the vernacular tongue, but in presence of the Professors of the University, in presence of your superiors, in presence of the Priests of the holy Roman Church, and, as becomes Theologians, in the Latin language.

"Then, indeed, in that assembly of most learned men, will it be known what you, a Transatlantic doctor, if I mistake not, have accomplished; or what I, a most unworthy priest of the Church, like the bee, laboriously produce.

"In addition to this, as you have such a desire for controversy, there is here at present a very intimate friend of mine, who has resided just thirty years in eastern countries, who will dispute with you on the Sacred Scriptures, in the Oriental languages, and who has already published a great many books on these subjects.

" I will thank you to let me know, as soon as possible, whether or not these proposals meet with your approbation.—Farewell.

"10th November, 1830."

Dr. Kidd's Second Letter.

" To the Rev. Mr. Fraser, Roman Catholic Priest.

" Sir,—My object in proposing a discussion with you, on the points at issue between Protestants and

Romanists, is public instruction and edification in the establishment of the truth as it is in Jesus.

"The use of the Latin language in our discussions would effectually prevent general instruction and edification.

"You promulgate your religious tenets in the English language before a general audience; and I call upon you, in like manner, to maintain them.

"If you do not accede to my proposal, I shall conclude that you are either ashamed or afraid publicly to defend the Roman Catholic system in your mother tongue; and I shall feel myself at liberty to publish our correspondence.

"I decline offering any comment on the first paragraph of your letter.

"A discussion in the Oriental languages would neither instruct nor edify the public.

"May you and I be led to search into the truth with a single eye to God's glory and the good of immortal souls; and ever to contend for truth, in the spirit of meekness, and of love, and of a sound mind. —I am, reverend sir, your obedient humble servant,

"JAMES KIDD, D.D.

"Chapel Street, Aberdeen,
"12th November, 1830."

Mr. Fraser's Reply.

"Doctori Kidd, Carolus Fraser, salutem plurimam dicit.

"Pervenerunt iterum ad me litteræ cujusdam ignoti, tua tamen, de more, subscriptæ manu.

"Ex his satis superque patet, quod mihi quidem ab initio in suspicionem venerat, te ex tenebris prosiluisse non ad veritatem defendendam, stabiliendamque, sed ad captandum vulgus retia tua laxavisse. 'Heu nihil invitis fas quemque [quenquam] fidere divis.' Causa, quidmirum, cecidisti, non mea utique culpa, sed propria peremptus manu. Professor Universitatis ferox ad pugnam ultro progressus 'nubes et inania captare' somniasti; verum subito expergefactus, ac de improviso ad certamen majus et discrimen salutis provocatus, 'serpis modo humi tutus nimium timidusque procellæ.'

"Quæ de Instructione publica atque edificatione [ædificatione] laute, lepide, belle deblateras, illa quidem neque plebi fucum facere queunt; quis etenim sanæ mentis est, qui nesciat, singularia de Religione coram multitudine certamina non ad publicam instructionem, sed ad bilem movendam, non ad edificationem, [ædificationem] sed ad destructionem extitisse. Clamat hoc tibi nequidquam charitas non ficta, clamat virtus, clamat pax, clamat per orbem terrarum experientia rauca.

"Quae cum ita sint, Vale, tibique persuasum habe, homines suis opinionibus inflatos turpiter irrideri, et in maximis versari erroribus. In æternum Vale.

"Pridie Idus Novemb. A. 1830.

"Ad (Quere Æd.?) D. Petri."

Translation of the above Letter.

(AS PUBLISHED BY DR. KIDD.)

"Charles Fraser to Dr. Kidd, with best wishes.

"I have received another letter of a person unknown, but subscribed by you in your usual way.

"From this letter it is abundantly evident, as indeed I had suspected from the first, that it was not for the purpose of defending and establishing the truth that you left your obscurity, but that you were spreading your net to catch the vulgar.

> ' All human confidence, alas, is vain,
>   When heaven opposes.'

"As was naturally to be expected, you have lost your cause, certainly not through my fault, but being ruined by your own hand.   You, a fierce Professor in a University, advancing unprovoked to a conflict, dreamed of ' soaring to the clouds and aerial regions'; but being suddenly awakened, and unexpectedly challenged to a greater contest, and a struggle for your life,

> ' You, in cold safety, creep along the shore,
>   Too much afraid of storms.'

"What you finely, pleasantly, prettily babble about public instruction and edification, cannot indeed impose even on the common people, for who is there, of a sound mind, that does not know that single combats on the subject of religion, in the presence of the multitude, have not been productive of public instruction, but have served to stir up wrath, and have not tended to edification but destruction?   It is in vain that this is proclaimed to you by unfeigned charity, proclaimed by virtue, proclaimed by peace, proclaimed by universal experience.

"This being the case, Farewell; and be assured that men who are puffed up with their own opinions are objects of shameful derision, and are labouring under the greatest errors.—For ever, Farewell.

"12th November, 1830,
     "St. Peter's Chapel."

Dr. Kidd's Third Letter

" To the Rev. Mr. Fraser, Roman Catholic Priest.

" Sir,—Seeing you decline publicly to maintain the truth of those tenets which you promulgate, in presence of a promiscuous assembly, in your Sabbath Evening Lectures, I call upon you to publish these lectures, and I pledge myself to publish replies to them.—I am, reverend sir, your obedient humble servant,

" James Kidd, D.D.

" Chapel Street, Aberdeen,
" 13th November, 1830."

(Dr. Kidd received no reply to the above.)

While he was ready to spring into the arena on behalf of truth, he did not condescend to petty sectarian squabbles. As showing the magnanimity of the man's nature, and the soundness of his heart, which were ever conspicuous even in the championship of orthodoxy, an incident may be related that has a connection with the Wesleyan denomination. Being a strong Calvinist, Arminianism was one of the forms of heresy which he fiercely denounced. He gave notice of a course of lectures which he was to deliver against that system of doctrine. But before the first one was delivered a district meeting of the Methodists was held in Aberdeen, at which some eminent men of that body were present. One of the leading local Wesleyans, Mr. Gordon Gilchrist, invited Dr. Kidd to meet those ministers at a

Q

private gathering. The Doctor came, and was so
delighted with the intercourse he had with those
godly and able men on topics of common interest,
that he felt convinced that Arminianism could
not be such a very pernicious thing when
Arminians were such excellent men. The lectures were never delivered !

He had a very warm heart for the Seceders.
Sage, in his " Memorabilia," tells us that Dr.
Kidd rejoiced greatly in the union of the two
branches of the Secession under the name of the
Associate Synod. Donald Sage, who was minister of the Gaelic Church in Aberdeen, heard
Dr. Kidd say he believed the union was entered
into by both parties under divine guidance ;
for, he added—" Had such a proposal been made
many years ago, and the very angels of heaven
had come down among them to recommend it,
the Seceders would have driven them away
with pitchforks."

His relations with the Independents of the
town were generally of a most friendly character. Occasionally when a member left the large
and somewhat mixed multitude of Gilcomston
for a more select fellowship, he would, half in
earnest half in jest, accuse them of " poaching
upon his preserve." Their zeal for Sabbath
schools was emulated by his, and a little friction
might arise now and again when they came too
near to each other. But so little of a bigot was

he that when a Congregational Church was formed in a needy part of the county, he, out of his limited means, subscribed £1 to the building fund. His signature for that amount is still standing in the records of the Church.

But the Doctor had rather a smart theological skirmish with an Independent minister of the town, Mr. James Spence, the first minister of Blackfriars Street Church. The latter was accomplished and widely read, acute and logical in mind. He had dared to assail the position which Dr. Kidd took in his treatise on the Eternal Sonship of Christ. Mr. Spence had a good deal to say for the view he took of the Sonship as part of the subordination connected with the " humiliation " of Christ, the term Son being applied, he maintained, to the second person in the Trinity after the incarnation. The wordy war, like many other theological strifes, degenerated somewhat in tone as it went on.

CHAPTER XXIV.

THE ANTI-PATRONAGE BATTLE.

OF all the questions which have agitated the Scottish part of the ecclesiastical world since the period of the Reformation, Patronage has been the most disturbing and the most irrepressible. In some form or other it has never been far from the front during the greater number of those years, and has made itself felt as an appreciable force in almost all the conflicts which had to be waged for the completed emancipation and deepened spirituality of the church.

The Anti-Patronage battle was just another phase, in a higher sphere, of that sturdy independence which, at such a cost and with such success, was maintained by the Scottish people in their long-continued struggle for nationality. The right of lay patrons to present a minister, without any regard to the preferences of the members of the church who were to receive his ministrations, though sanctioned by the law of the land, was never admitted by the best of the people; and the more anxious they were for an uplifting ministry the more intolerable was that arrangement felt to be. In the dark days of spiritual indifference and formalism there might be considerable patience under the yoke; but as soon as the Church as a divine institution came to be of any consequence to the people, the more disinclined were they to submit to the imposition of men whom they had not chosen as pastors. Secession after secession from the Established Church took place, mainly on that ground, and for a considerable part of Dr. Kidd's public life he took a prominent part in the popular agitation which culminated in the historic event of 1843.

At a meeting of the local Anti-Patronage Society, held in the schoolhouse of Bankhead, Newhills, on 20th March, 1834, Dr. Kidd is reported, in the *Aberdeen Journal*, as having said "that Jesus Christ has all along acted as the sole Patron, Head, and Lawgiver of the Church. The Rev. Doctor pointed out the reasonableness of what was claimed by the Society. If liberty were enjoyed in the choice of a physician or a lawyer, why not in the choice of a minister? He also showed that it was the mind of Christ. The Doctor held it clear from the light of both reason and revelation that whatever is devoted to God cannot in whole or in part be retained at the same time by devoter, either by himself or offspring."

But long before that date his mind was exercised on the subject, as the subjoined letter shows :—

"ABERDEEN, 21st October, 1824.

"DEAR SIR,—A pamphlet has fallen into my hands entitled 'An Appeal to All Classes on the Subject of Church Patronage in Scotland,' &c.

"This pamphlet is very defective in information concerning the steps to be taken, either how to get the right out of the hands of patrons, or how to proceed to get a Chapel of Ease on the Establishment. Towards this latter object please permit me to turn your attention. Should security be gotten to the Court of Tiends for a stipend to the minister of a Chapel of Ease, which may be put on the Establishment? Can the patron of the parish claim the patronage of this new church in the parish? Can he do so by law, or will the law give it to him? I wish all the legal information which the publishers of the foresaid pamphlet can give, and as soon as possible. Your kind attention to this will be a great favour, as the place where I officiate is a Chapel of Ease, and as there is a motion in Aberdeen to put the Chapel of Ease on the Establishment, and mine being in the neighbourhood of the city, I wish to use all means lawful to put my Chapel on the Establishment. In answering this as soon as possible you will greatly oblige, dear sir, your sincere and humble servant,

"JAMES KIDD."

"Please address Dr. Kidd, Aberdeen."

The following, from his bosom friend, the minister of Nigg, bears upon the same subject, and gives a glimpse of Dr. Kidd's movements :—

" Manse of Nigg, by Parkhill,
" 9th January, 1827.

" My Very Dear Friend,— . . . . I intend, God willing, to be with you on the first
Sabbath of July, and if anything interferes to prevent me you shall, of course, have timeous notice.
Previously to my receiving your letter, I had seen, in
the Edinburgh *Observer* newspaper, a most humorous
account of your Anti-Patronage Society meeting in
Edinburgh, in which your speech was not represented
as more ridiculous than the speeches of the other
orators. Your potent auxiliary, Mr. Simpson, was
said to have failed in everything but one, viz., his
having convinced his audience that his tongue was too
large for his mouth. These squibs, however, will do
good. Their extravagance will prove their antidote,
and their weight will be only that of pebbles on the
shield of Hercules. The hissing of the old serpent
may be still looked for by the seed of the woman ;
and, in the present case, it is a sufficient proof that
the Society in question is viewed by the serpent as
inimical to his interests. Having said thus much in
favour of the Society's object, I must now give you
my opinion of its plan and probable success. As to
its plan, I think it, like all human devices, objectionable. It would require, however, more space and
time than I can afford to specify all my objections.
Suffice it to say, that the idea of giving to all the
male communicants, or heads of families in a parish,
the choice of their minister is, in the first place, too
strong a temptation to unworthy people's becoming

communicants; and, in the second place, a manifest
deviation from the original constitution of the Church
of Scotland. The choice of a minister ought to be
vested in the kirk-session and such resident heritors
as are communicants. And if this were the case, your
opponents could not deny you credit for endeavouring
to restore the law to what it was in the best and
purest state of the Church.

" As to the probable success of the Society, I am
sanguine in the measure contemplated and published
by its original founders. And it would be vain to
expect from it anything more. The Society, however,
will do more good indirectly, and by influencing public
opinion, than directly. By the by, if I were concerned
in the management of the Society, I would have
opposed the purchase of Colinton and Dairsie, and
recommended rather the purchase of some parishes in
Aberdeenshire, Berwickshire, Argyllshire, &c., where
the patronage would not be so expensive, and where
the benefit would be much greater. The strongholds
of moderation ought to be first attacked.

" As to my instituting an auxiliary Society in this
parish, the thing is impossible. The parish is small,
and poor, and divided, so that nothing can be expected." . . . .

Dr. Gustavus Aird, of Creich, tells of scenes
in connection with the anti-patronage battle in
the Highlands, in which Dr. Kidd took part :—

" So far as known to me, the first time Dr. Kidd
was in Ross-shire was about 1817, but I scarcely

remember it. In the parish of Kiltearn, in the Presbytery of Dingwall, a sad intrusion was perpetrated about 1816; few of the parishioners ever entered the parish church during the incumbency of the intruder, and refused to acknowledge him as a minister in any way. Dr. Kidd felt much sympathy for the people; came to Kiltearn and tried to effect a reconciliation. A large number of children were unbaptised. It was at length arranged, with the intruder's consent, that Mr. Macdonald, Ferintosh, should preach in Gaelic and Dr. Kidd in English on a week day, in the open air, at a part of the parish called Drummond, and baptise the children. Such of the parents as understood Gaelic stood on one side, and those who understood English stood on the other side; a passage intervened. There must have been upwards of a hundred children; some of them were four or five years of age and could speak, and gave utterance to their displeasure at the sprinkling of the water reaching their new clothes, exclaiming in Gaelic—' Fliuch, fliuch, chuir an duine uisge orm ''; English: ' Wet, wet, the man has put water on me.'

" The Doctor preached for one or two Sabbaths there, did all in his power to effect an adjustment, but all his efforts were in vain. In the month of July, 1830, he assisted at the Communion in the parish of Nigg, Presbytery of Tain, during the late Mr. L. Rose's time there, and also during the following week in Rosskeen, where Mr. Carment was minister. Large crowds were present, and many of the Lord's people were edified, comforted, and delighted. The first time I heard and saw him was in Nigg, Ross-shire, on

Saturday all day from Revelation xxi. 16-27; on Sabbath from Genesis iii. 15, the first promise; and on Monday all day from I. John i. 3—all of them very remarkable and precious sermons."

The following letter from the Rev. Donald Mackenzie to the Rev. Dr. George Morrison, Banchory-Devenick, which we lighted upon through the good offices of the late Dr. Edmond of Kingswells, describes the Kiltearn scenes from another standpoint:—

"MARYFIELD, 13th December, 1817.

" MY DEAR SIR,

     .   .   .   .   . " I have for several weeks proposed writing to you respecting the conduct of your Great Apostle among us. With great satisfaction I therefore embrace the opportunity you have given me of stating the facts of this case. The account you saw in the *Times*, was written by a member of our Church who preached for me on the preceding Sunday, accompanied me to Alness, and witnessed the scene he describes. Notwithstanding the humorous strain in which that paragraph is given, I can assure you that every fact related in it you may rely on as correct. Mr. Kidd's visit to Ross-shire was as unexpected and entirely unsolicited by the minister of Kiltearn—or any individual known to him, or to any of his friends —as the present destination of the Algerine squadron, said to be infested with the plague, and accompanied with evils of nearly equal magnitude, to him and to every lover of peace and order in our corner of the country—yet with an arrogant and self-assumed degree of importance which it requires all the effrontery of that gentleman to justify. . . . .

" To you, who can form some idea of the temper of many of our parishioners, and of the incalculable evils that must arise from fomenting and encouraging such measures as I have described, I trust it is unnecessary to enforce the necessity of fostering some strong and decisive constitutional measure for punishing past transgressors of laws so essentially connected with the peace, discipline, and best interests of our Church, and to prevent the repetition of these disorders that have disgraced those who sanctioned them, and been a source of so much vexation and distress to all peaceable and orderly Christians among us. To the Presbytery of Aberdeen we look with confidence as the steady and well-tried friends of our Church constitution, and the liberal supporters of a very few individuals who are willing to sacrifice many objects extremely desirable in themselves to the suppressing of these tumultuary measures so prevalent among us. —My dear sir, sincerely yours, &c.,

" (Signed)   DONALD MACKENZIE.

" The Rev. George Morrison, Minister of the Gospel at N. Banchory, by Aberdeen."

CHAPTER XXV.

DOMESTIC LIFE.

MRS. KIDD was a quiet, gentle woman, whose sphere was home. She did her unobtrusive part as a dutiful wife, and served the public by ministering to the comfort of her husband, and attending to the wants of her children. She never shrank from her share of the not inconsiderable household burden which her husband's exacting conscience and exuberant generosity imposed.

The children she bore who reached maturity were three daughters and two sons. The daughters were Agnes, who became Mrs. Oswald; Jane, who died in 1824; and Christiana Little (after his first American friend James Little), who was married to George Thompson of Pitmedden, at one time Lord Provost and M.P. for Aberdeen. William Campbell, the elder son, was educated for the ministry, and entered upon a charge in London. He was a singularly gifted and promising man, but died prematurely. Benjamin (after Dr. Benjamin Rush) studied medicine, and took his degree; he also was a youth of brilliant parts; he died in Aberdeen in 1840.

Dr. Kidd, like many other good and able men, had very heavy family trials. Here is the utterance of his heart about the death of his daughter Jane : —

"ABERDEEN, 11th August, 1824.

" This has been one of the most sorrowful days of my life. My daughter Jane was in the lowest state of existence, labouring under weakness, which has affected her for three years. All day her distress has been very great; she has submitted all along with much patience and resignation. As soon as I appeared, she began the 23rd verse of 73rd Psalm herself. Her voice seems as if from the grave, yet clear, collected, and distinct ; we sang this Psalm to the end. She then began the 63rd, then the 23rd, then the last paraphrase, next the 100th Psalm, in long metre; we sang these as she desired. I then began to converse with her about Heaven, its angels, its spirits of just men made perfect, about Christ and the happiness of Heaven, and all the views of the future world, in all which she joined with the utmost readiness, and with a cheerfulness that was quite surprising and most comforting to all present, and soon afterwards she passed away."

Dr. Kidd's household was increased in a way that was quite characteristic, though some might call it romantic, if not indeed quixotic. He often urged heads of families to show their love for Christ and humanity by taking in, housing, and schooling fatherless children. He maintained that charity which took that form was the highest and most useful example of Christian benevolence. What the Doctor preached he tried to practise. Among the many criminals that Dr. Kidd took a friendly and helpful interest in was one Peter Young, a gipsy, who, before his execution, was humbled before God, and professed to be a changed man. He left two legacies, one a piece of ingeniously carved work of his own to the Doctor; and "the only legacy," he said, "he had to give to his son was the 102nd Psalm in long metre, and he prayed earnestly he might believe in the Lord and lead a good life, instead of the wicked one his father had done."

Dr. Kidd took the boy into his own house, clothed him, and sent him to school. Once or twice he disappeared, and on his return told his guardians that his father's tribe was determined to get him back to their wild, lawless life. They lay in wait for him, and frequently, when he went out, there was some one at hand to entice him or seize him by force, so that it had to be arranged that a member of the household should always accompany him as he went to and from school.

But in spite of all the precautions of the Kidd household he disappeared and could not be found, though diligent search was made for him. Years passed, and towards the close of the Doctor's life a handsome soldier called at the manse, who was closeted with him for a long time. He was the long lost gipsy boy turned into a rising man in His Majesty's service. He had been captured at last by the tribe, taken to England, closely watched; but he never could forget his father's legacy and the Doctor's home, and he intensely disliked the life he had to live. At last he enlisted under an assumed name, conducted himself with propriety, and had risen to the rank of sergeant. He was passing through Aberdeen with his regiment, and it was a great joy to him to have the opportunity of expressing his indebtedness for what was done for him when he was a castaway.

In Dr. Kidd's old age his son-in-law, Captain James Oswald, died, and the widow, with her two boys and two girls, were in the minister's house for some time. Nothing could exceed the warmth of the enthusiasm of the grandson, from whose journal we have already quoted, when describing the domestic life of the Doctor. He writes:—" On Saturdays my brother James and I went with him, one on each side, up Chapel Street and on to the toll of Rubislaw and home. During our walk he would direct our attention to some object of interest and instruction, sometimes to what was lying on our path, sometimes to the books we were reading, or the passing events of the times, always making it a pleasure for us to listen. We felt our minds opened out to view the subjects, whatever they were, in a new and fresh light. We went regularly to him at a certain hour on the same day, when he drilled us in the Shorter Catechism, asking us the questions from the beginning to the First Commandment one week, and the next from the First Commandment to the end. He never had a Catechism before him, but knew every question and answer accurately in its order, word for word, as if he were reading them. Here is a gleam from the past in that journal:—"On returning from church, the household assembled, and each read a portion of Scripture in order."

The Doctor, who did so much for others, was not without his little material tokens of popular appreciation. His people presented him with the house in Chapel Street, where he resided for years. A sideboard came from an unknown donor to put into it, which was supposed to be from an opponent whose heart was softened. The young men of the congregation gave him a large Bible, which was used at family worship. People delighted to honour him in their own way, and according to their taste and means. An old gillie of Lochiel gave him a stick presented by "Prince Charlie," which was, unfortunately, lost or stolen. The Doctor must have inwardly grinned when a painter drew in oil colours the coat of arms appropriate to the name of Kidd. Another member of his congregation very sensibly handed him a pair of silver spectacles when the eye was becoming dim with years.

One thing was set over against another in the Doctor's life, the bitter never being far removed from the sweet. A prisoner on the Bass Rock said quaintly, "I dwell at ease and live securely. The upper springs flowed liberally and sweetly when the nether springs were embittered." In like manner Dr. Kidd knew where to go for consolation when earthly sources of gladness were dried up. This is how he relieved his heart in writing when his wife was evidently nearing the gates of the other world :—

"10th May, 1829.

" The foregoing sermon on Hebrews ii. 12-15, and the following, I. Corinthians xv. 26, were delivered while Mrs. Kidd was lying on her deathbed. I cannot describe my feelings on both Sabbaths during delivery. May God bless them to my family and my flock. I bless God I was supported all day ; may I be humble and thankful. My dear wife has been ailing and very low, and I have been greatly troubled about her."

And he adds :—

"7th June.

" I have had great distress this week. Mrs. Kidd died on 14th May, and the variety of emotions and experiences of my mind I cannot describe. May God in mercy bless this sad event to myself and my children, and may all things work together for good to me."

R

On the Sabbath after Mrs. Kidd's death, and
while her body was lying in the manse waiting
interment, Dr. Kidd preached in the Chapel as
usual, only with an added pathos and solemnity.
Some of the elders remonstrated with him in
vain.   "What good could I do," he replied,
characteristically, "sitting beside a dead body,
when my people are waiting to hear God's
message from my lips?"

That home which was now breaking up,
had not been without its helpful testimony.   It
had been the abode, not of angels, but of human
beings, with many of their frailties and some of
their sorrows; and yet the people of Aberdeen
felt that God was in it.

Dr. Paul, in his "Past and Present of Aberdeenshire," says:—"In my early days family
worship was, in this quarter, much neglected,
even among the clergy: among the laity it was
seldom heard of." In agreement with that statement, Dr. Kidd found that his house, for years
after he came to Aberdeen, was a centre of
wondering interest to the neighbourhood, when,
in the course of family worship, the psalm was
sung.   People gathered round the door to hear
the unfamiliar sounds on a week day, and in a
private house.   With characteristic hospitality
and readiness to seize any opportunity that came
in his way of doing good, Mr. Kidd opened the
door and invited them to come in.

CHAPTER XXVI.

THE GILCOMSTON PASTOR FROM HOME.

IT is surely superfluous to observe that the above heading is not meant to convey the impression that the Gilcomston pastor was ever from home in Gilcomston Chapel. No king who believed in the divine rights of his order was ever more firmly seated upon his throne, and no father in his armchair among his children was more at home than Dr. Kidd in the "chapel of ease." It was his place, if ever a man had one in this world. He was not at all times equally at ease, nor was he uniformly felicitous in his address, for, like other mortals, he had his moods; but, for better or for worse, the place and the man were one as long as there was breath in his body. A brother minister once asked his advice as to whether he should accept the opportunity of translation to another sphere. The answer was promptly given—"I consider that no field is so worthy of being cultivated as the one where my master saw fit to place me. I have often been urged to higher worldly posts, but here I stay while I can do His work, and you should do the same."

Moreover, as a worker, Dr. Kidd believed in

concentration, and therefore was not addicted to
gadding about, dissipating energy over a wide
surface. But, while a faithful " keeper at home,"
he was too generous-hearted a man to close his
ear and heart against all the numerous invitations which were urgently given to come and
help elsewhere.

In the early days of his ministry he found it
exceedingly hard to resist the demand for his
services, as in this place the need at that time
was so great. In a city one of the leading
ministers of which regarded " prayer meetings
as nurseries for spiritual pride," it can easily be
supposed that Dr. Kidd sometimes wished he
could overcome the laws which condition physical bodies and be in twenty places at the same
time.

He, with a few of the members of his church,
established a Sabbath School in Old Aberdeen,
and some of them were stoned for their pains.
He had numerous meeting-places throughout
the town, one of them being in that part which
is now called Holburn Street, where, according
to the testimony of one who occasionally attended,
the Doctor had sometimes to be precentor as
well as preacher. But he had not the same
affluence of resource in the one department of
duty as in the other. Indeed, he was rather
poverty-stricken when he came out as a leader
in song, for, whatever the psalm, the fitness of

things, as determined by Dr. Kidd's abilities, made it imperative that the sacred words should be wedded to the ancient tune of "Blackburn," the merits of which have not, I believe, been recognised by modern compilers of tune-books. Alas! too, for the limitations of humanity even in its noblest developments, no single specimen combining in himself all the talents and attainments, living witnesses bear evidence to the fact that the execution did more credit to the heartiness of his feeling and the strength of his lungs than to the tunefulness of his voice and ear. Dr. Kidd had no desire to displace the precentor: he believed in division of labour. When a psalmody leader was present at a comparatively small meeting, the Doctor joined in lustily, and was so loyal in his support as to be a positive embarrassment. It would be difficult to say what part in music he took. The sound was a kind of accompaniment not unlike what the intermittent and distant mutterings of thunder may be supposed to be to the songsters of the grove. In the big assembly of Gilcomston Chapel, it was not possible even for him to "drown" the other voices; but in smaller gatherings for him to come in as an ally was to bring all the other singers into captivity, not certainly by the skill of his tactics, but solely by the overpowering vehemence of his onset.

From the Brig o' Balgownie to the old Bridge

of Dee, he was to be heard from time to time in
different places speaking on behalf of righteousness and Christ. Dr. Anderson, of the Gym-
nasium, some years before he died, gave this
witness:—"When I came to Old Aberdeen I
had a strong prejudice against Dr. Kidd, but in
going about the people, I found that most of the
true Christians of a certain age, whom I met,
traced their conversion to the instrumentality of
Dr. Kidd, so that I have changed my opinion of
him, and now venerate his memory."

The Doctor was often asked to bring his
warm heart and eloquent tongue to the service
of any good cause or benevolent institution need-
ing pecuniary support. He begged with an
importunity and success which no other man in
Aberdeen could rival. He, on more than one
occasion, anticipated the biting sarcasm of the
modern preacher who remarked that when he
surveyed his audience he wondered where the
poor were, and when he looked upon the collection he was equally at a loss to know where the
rich were; for Dr. Kidd protested against the
costly dresses and jewellery worn by professing
Christians, when God's cause was languishing
for lack of support, until some of the ladies
present were seen to blush and furtively cover
the too patent proofs of selfish extravagance and
pride which they carried about with them.
Some were known, under the spell of Dr. Kidd's

thrilling eloquence, to have put rings and other expensive articles of ornament and attire into the plate. He once preached in the West Church on behalf of the Shipwrecked Mariners' Society, and no less a sum than £100 was the result, which was an extraordinary one for the time.

Dr. G. Aird of Creich writes:—" A railing was erected around the Gaelic Chapel. The Doctor was asked to preach on a Sabbath afternoon for raising a collection to defray the expense. He took for his subject the contributions given for erecting the Tabernacle. Towards the conclusion of the sermon he exhorted them to contribute liberally. 'Perhaps,' said he, 'you may say, "What did you yourself give?" Well, you all know James Kidd is not a rich man, but he gave a little, and in order that you may give more—Beadle, get the plate'! when he threw into it a crown piece, and then exhorted them to do likewise. He exhorted a lady who had a fine muff to put it into the plate, another to put her silk mantle into the plate, and another lady to put her boa into the plate; and, addressing a gentleman, 'G—— C——, you have a fine gold watch and chain and a number of gold seals; put the whole into the plate. And you, E—— M—— (one of the elders), you have I know not how many houses, and none to leave them to but a wife as old as yourself; put one of them into the plate." Had the exhortation been complied with, ere all was over, the plate would have contained what might well help to repair the church.

It was not often that the Doctor was in circumstances to avail himself of the privileges of hearer, and when he did so he usually mingled a little speaking with the hearing, as we now proceed to show. Dr. Macdonald, of Ferintosh, was a life-long friend of Dr. Kidd, and one of his great favourites as a preacher. When the "Apostle of the North" came to Aberdeen, which he did once a year or so, to preach in the Gaelic Church, Dr. Kidd went occasionally, with as many of his congregation as could be accommodated, to the evening service. One Fast-day evening when Dr. Macdonald was preaching in the Gaelic Church, Mr. Mackenzie, son of the minister at that time, tells us that Dr. Kidd was a hearer. Five minutes before the hour of service Dr. Kidd was seen to enter the church, and go into the minister's seat (then immediately below the pulpit). Several times during the five minutes that had to elapse before the hour, Dr. Kidd was seen to look round to the clock. The beadle (a character in his way, as all beadles were in those days), came in with the Bible and psalm-book, and while passing the minister's seat on his way to the pulpit, was accosted by Dr. Kidd—"Donald, is the minister not coming yet?" to which Donald replied, with becoming dignity of manner, "He'll come at his ain time, sir." Dr. Kidd again looks round to the clock: two minutes from the hour. At last the clock strikes the hour; Dr. Kidd's patience is exhausted: up he rises and goes to the pulpit and gives out the psalm. During the singing of the psalm, Dr. Macdonald and Mr. Mackenzie are seen coming in from the vestry, by the side door. Dr. Macdonald, seeing that the pulpit is occupied, is for following Mr. Mackenzie into his seat, but Dr. Kidd is all the time observing everything from the pulpit, and, leaning over it, signs upon Dr. Macdonald to come up higher. Dr. Kidd, after the singing was over, engaged in prayer, and then Dr. Macdonald rose up and gave out his text, Dr. Kidd remaining seated in the pulpit until the end of the service.

The discourse was a powerful one (as all Dr. Macdonald's usually were), and on this particular evening he was dealing out the terrors of the law to his hearers, and while doing so, Dr. Kidd, who was sitting at his back, took hold of his coat tails and, giving them tug after tug, called out audibly to the congregation, "Give it to them, John, every villain of them; many a time have I told them, but they would not believe me."

Sage, in his *Memorabilia Domestica*, gives us this additional incident in connection with the Gaelic Church:—One Sabbath evening Dr. Kidd and his people, with many others, had come to the Gaelic Chapel doors a little before six o'clock and found them shut. The crowd was immense, and the crush to get in was likely to be serious, as the numbers outside were increasing. Dr. Kidd demanded why the doors were not opened, and receiving no answer, called out—"If they are not opened instantly, break them open." The elders were, as might be supposed, greatly scandalised at this unseemly violence on a Sabbath day, and sent a deputation of their number to Dr. Kidd to remonstrate. He apologised to the Gaelic elders by saying that, being a native of Ireland, he was suddenly seized with an Irish fit, but that he had no sooner uttered the words than he repented of his rashness and felt that he had spoken unadvisedly.

In one of the rare visits which he paid to the Metropolis, he went to hear the great Edward Irving, who has, perhaps, as good a claim to the epithet "a misguided archangel" as any one of past or present times. That wonderful and lovable man was then in the zenith of his glory as a popular preacher, who, by the splendour of his genius, could attract statesmen and members of the aristocracy in London to a Presbyterian Church. But Dr. Kidd was not satisfied with what he heard. He thought dishonour was done to Christ by something that was said about His nature and work, and he refused, at the close of the service, to shake hands with a man who

could so speak of Jesus Christ. There was not,
to the public eye, the most distant premonition
then of the coming storm in Regent Square, but
Dr. Kidd discerned tendencies which soon obtained fuller and flagrant development.

The Rev. D. K. Auchterlonie, of Craigdam,
tells us of a visit Dr. Kidd paid to Arbroath :—
" An uncle of mine, John Wannan, worked for
some time at his trade at Arbroath, and he often
spoke of a memorable scene of which he was a
witness, and in which Dr. Kidd was chief actor.
Dr. Kidd was in the habit of preaching once a
year or so in one of the parish churches in the
town of Arbroath, and on one of the occasions in
which he visited that town my uncle was a
hearer in the church in which he preached. The
service got on prosperously till it came to the
time for the Doctor to give out his text. At
this stage he seemed to be in a state of considerable annoyance and confusion. He turned over
the leaves of the old pulpit Bible from Genesis
to the Revelation. Then he took the Bible up
and shook out all the numerous stray leaves on
to the floor of the pulpit. He took up the stray
leaves one by one and examined them carefully ;
he crammed them back into the Bible again, he
shut it, and gave it a violent knock with his fist,
saying, ' Do you call *that* a Bible ? My text is
not to be found in it ! ' Then to a man in the
nearest pew—' Here, sir ; give me the loan of
your Bible.'

"And thus, under difficulties, he started his sermon, and was well on, and in the full flood of his eloquence, when suddenly he hitched up, saying, ' I don't know how long I have preached ; you have no clock in the front of the gallery, as you should have, to admonish me, and I have nothing (pulling it out) but this old rattle-trap of a watch, which goes an hour fast one day and an hour slow the next.'   Then (raising his voice) ' I'll tell you what, my friends ; I'm coming back next year, and if by that time you don't have a new Bible on this desk, and a new clock in the front of that gallery, I'll let you hear about it on the deafest side of your heads.'   My uncle testified that the new Bible and clock were both in their appropriate places long before Dr. Kidd's next visit ! "

On one occasion the Doctor was in Dundee to preach in a certain church on Sabbath evening.   He was present at the morning service, when it was intimated that Dr. Kidd from Aberdeen was to preach there in the evening at a quarter past six o'clock.   He could not bear to begin a service so many minutes after an hour. "No, no," said the Doctor from the pew in which he was sitting ; " I'll have no trifling with time : I'll preach here at six o'clock precisely."

Regarding one of his visits, the Doctor has left it on record—" On leaving Dundee, where I had been called to assist at the dispensation of the Lord's Supper, Mr. Kirkcaldy gave me 'Pearse on the Best Match,' and I have received more knowledge and experience of the heart work of faith from that than ever I did from any book except the Scriptures, and I have had great comfort ever since. 'Owen on the Person and Glory of Christ' for the general knowledge of Christ, and 'Pearse' for the experimental knowledge of Christ, are the best uninspired books I have read on the subject."

One Saturday evening he arrived in Rhynie, being engaged to preach in the Parish Church on the following day. Before going to bed he took a walk in the outskirts of the village, and he met a man, to whom he put the question, " Do you pray to God?" The man replied that he could not truthfully say that he did. "Well," rejoined the Doctor, putting his hand into his pocket and taking out half a crown, "take you that if you'll promise to me never in your life to pray." The man immediately took the money, and went away dumfoundered. He had not taken many steps, however, till he felt he had sold his soul for half a crown, and, coming back, he said—"Here's your money : I winna hae't." But what happened made him think and think till he became a changed man.

CHAPTER XXVII.

KIDDIANA.

Most public men, notably ministers of religion, who have reached a high place in popular favour, and gained a reputation for racy humour and free, quaint speech, have many witticisms and funny stories laid to their credit, some of which are evidently, from their character, worthy of all rejection as spurious. Rowland Hill and Spurgeon, like Dr. Kidd, besides the numerous and veritable offspring of their own facetious genius, have to bear the imputed paternity of vagrant and questionable jokes, which have been doing service from time immemorial. It is rather a delicate task to attempt to draw a dividing line between what is genuine and what popular rumour has made them adopt. It is all the more difficult when it is remembered that even saintly men occasionally, in moments of exuberant spirit and fancy, not to say touchy temper, affirm more than is befitting the "old man" who is struggling to keep his hold. When such occur, we have to remember the Chinese proverb—"Better a diamond with a flaw, than a pebble without it." Too many know Dr. Kidd only by the laughter-provoking stories which are fathered upon him with more or less truthfulness; but to know Dr. Kidd in that way is to know a stream only by the froth it casts up. We have been at pains to verify the "Kiddiana" in these pages by a reference to the judgment of those who, from their family connection, or from special information, were able to discriminate.

On the occasion of the accession of George IV. to the throne, Dr. Kidd prayed openly for him in this wise—"Grant, O Lord, that he may be a better King than he has been a Prince Regent," and when called to account by the local authorities for this utterance, the Doctor nonplussed them by asking—"*And where's the man that can't improve?*"

He went into the shop of one of his members, who, with bent head, was absorbed in some piece of work. As he was not expecting to see the Doctor at the time, his face could not but express surprise when he looked up. Ever ready to improve the occasion, the Doctor, gazing earnestly upon him and grasping his hand, said, "Did you expect to see me?" "No." "*What if it had been death?*" Whereupon he stepped out.

One Sabbath morning, Dr. Kidd hurriedly entered the pulpit, and, without sitting down, he looked all round the church, and in stentorian

tones exclaimed, "Go to hell! Go to hell! Go
to hell!" The people were, of course, greatly
surprised at the use of such language by their
revered pastor, but were soon relieved when he
addressed them as follows:—"These awful
words, my brethren, I heard used by one young
man to another a few minutes ago on the street,
as I was walking along towards this church. Is
this the fruit of all my labours among you for
the last twenty years? Is this my reward for
going in and out among you all that time, willing to spend and to be spent for you, that I
should, within my own parish, and almost within
a stone-throw of this sacred place, have my ears
profaned by such dreadful language, and that,
too, on the morning of the Lord's Day? I pray
that I may never again have such a startling
and painful experience while I am spared to
stand in this pulpit."

One Sabbath he was annoyed by a man
coughing repeatedly during the sermon, without
any attempt being made to suppress it, and, unable to endure it any longer, he exclaimed:—
"Give over that coughing, sir; you're disturbing me. Do you cough that way all the week?
It's my opinion that a number of people come
here once a week *just to clear their throats!*"

A man who had on a very noticeable red

waistcoat was sitting, one warm Sabbath day in summer, directly under the minister's eye. He began to nod his head, giving thereby clear indication that, if not asleep, he was on the verge of that condition, which roused the wrath of the Gilcomston pastor. "Waken that man," thundered out the voice from the pulpit. He was pinched and roused by his neighbour. But he awoke only to fall asleep again. "I say, waken that red-breasted sinner there," pointing with his finger to the unfortunate culprit. But all efforts were of no avail, again he was over. At last, patience exhausted, the Doctor seized a small pocket Bible lying at his hand on the pulpit cushion, and sending it with unerring aim, struck the sleeper on the side of the head, adding, "Now, sir, if you will not hear the word of God, you *shall feel it !*"

While preaching on a Sabbath evening, his eye caught a showily-dressed youth, who was looking in every direction but that of the pulpit. But, after wandering all over the place, his eyes always settled with an evident complacency upon his articles of attire, more especially upon a very attractive white vest, and a fashionable hat and cane. "Young man sitting in the breast gallery," cried Dr. Kidd, pointing in his direction, "your hat and stick will do very well, and your waistcoat is exceedingly nice; and you and I being

s

now quite satisfied on these points, perhaps you will be able to give me a little of your attention."

Dr. Kidd had a strong dislike to people who spoke of "hopes" only, in regard to religious prospects. On one occasion, while visiting an aged woman in illness, he asked her of her salvation; and, being roused by the frequent repetition of her "hopes" that she was safe, the Doctor lectured her soundly on her want of true grounds of assurance. When the Doctor had finished, the old woman raised herself from her sick-bed, and in piteous and earnest tones exclaimed, laying her hand on the Doctor's arm— "*Eh! puir man, have ye nae hope?*"

Dr. Kidd could be very kind and neighbourly to individual Roman Catholics, but Popery, as a system, was to him what the red rag is to the bull. In the year 1832 or thereabout, one of the many failures of the harvest in Ireland took place. Amongst other efforts to relieve the distressed, there was a musical performance given in the Roman Catholic Chapel in Aberdeen. Dr. Kidd took his own way of rendering help. He got a box made with a slit in it, placed at his garden gate, labelled, "Dr. Kidd's charity box for the poor Irish!" After a week's exposure, he announced from the pulpit the amount collected, about £21, which he gratefully acknowledged. He could not refrain from expressing his "satisfaction that his little box had produced more money than all the fiddling and whistling in the chapel in Justice Port!"

In Dr. Kidd's "Book of Skeletons of Lectures on Prophecy," the following striking marginal note is inserted:—"A.D. 1848: This year Europe may republicize." Again:—"France in revolution--most likely one of the family of Buonaparte will, after a time, ascend the throne of his great ancestor." Let it not be forgotten that this forecast was made by a man who died in 1834.

A lady reports that, after the solemnities of a communion season, she and a friend were walking along Union Terrace behind the Doctor and several of his brethren who had been assisting, when they heard him say—"Can you tell me how it is that though I can bear great troubles as well as most men, the petty annoyances of life irritate me so that I say things which cause me much grief and shame afterwards, bring discredit on my Saviour's cause, and give the enemy cause to blaspheme." The answer came from Mr. Rose, of Nigg—"Yes, brother; you carry your great trials to God, but the little ones you try to manage for yourself, and so fail." "Aye, aye; that is the true cause, I believe."

Seek Him, Then.—In pressing home the necessity for instant religious decision, the Doctor's patience was often tried by answers which were meant to be regarded as humble and pious, but which were, in fact, only evasive. In the course of his personal visitation he met a man whom he could not move in one way or another. He could not elicit any confession from him more satisfactory than the general observation—"Oh, yes, God is good if we seek Him." "Well, seek Him, then," urged Dr. Kidd; and taking out his watch, said, "I am a busy man, but I am willing to wait a whole hour here till you seek and find Him."

One Sabbath morning when entering upon the last part of his discourse, which dealt with the tender mercy of God, he observed an old woman rise from her seat and go towards the door. As his eye caught the retreating figure, he, full of the surpassing interest of his theme, and throbbing with desire that his hearers might feel it, called out, "Come back! come back! and hear of the mercy of God." When she persisted in going out, he turned to his audience, with a wondering and pitying expression, and remarked, "Is she not a strange old woman to run away from the mercy of God?" From that circumstance he proceeded to make a most thrilling and solemn appeal to those before him not to despise the mercy of God.

He was very fond of interpreting the prophecies, particularly as relating to coming events, as the downfall of Antichrist, the inbringing of the Jews, the Millennium, &c. He had an idea that something very particular happened every seventh year, and when the seventh year came round, he would find some striking event in it, and say, I do not profess to be a prophet, but I have always observed that something of special importance happens every seventh year. He used frequently to attack the errors of the Roman Church, and would say that Napoleon was the best missionary that was ever sent out against her.

In proof of the deep and wide interest which Dr. Kidd awakened, not only in the city of Aberdeen, but in surrounding districts, it may be mentioned that persons came great distances— from Skene, Inverurie, and other parts—to hear him on Sabbath. The Rev. James Johnstone, of Belhelvie, says that a late office-bearer of the Free Church in that parish, Mr. Robert Harvie, was accustomed to walk from his farm at Whitecairns every Sabbath, a distance of about eight miles from Gilcomston Chapel.

CHAPTER XXVIII.

MORE KIDDIANA.

In his usual reading of Scripture one Sabbath day, the passage selected being from the eighth chapter of the Gospel according to Matthew, Dr. Kidd came upon the sentence, "And when Jesus was come into Peter's house, he saw his wife's mother laid and sick of a fever." After he had read the verse, he lifted his eyes suddenly from the Bible before him as if he had made a discovery, and, looking at the people, exclaimed, "What! Peter, the great head of the Church with a mother-in-law! The thing is impossible. I am sure our Romish friends will join me in saying so. There must surely be a mistake. Let us read the passage again. Yes; there it is, in my Bible at least. Is it so in yours?"

———

The Rev. D. K. Auchterlonie, of Craigdam, writes:—"An aged friend, a great admirer of Dr. Kidd's, happened to be present at an ordination within the bounds of the Presbytery of Aberdeen, at which Dr. Kidd gave the charge to the young minister. The majority of the ministers present

were Moderates, and Dr. Kidd's charge was a
prolonged satire directed at the typical Moderate
clergymen of the day. My informant indicated
that it was perfectly evident from the restive
conduct of the ministers present that they were
conscious of the fact that they were the persons
alluded to. Dr. Kidd's remarks were somewhat in
the following strain :—' My young brother, you
have now been set apart to the office of the holy
ministry. Whatever you do, be sure that you don't
overwork yourself. Why should you die before
your time ? There are some foolish people, as you
may be aware, who go in for Sabbath schools,
prayer meetings, and Bible classes ; but, my
beloved young brother, I counsel you carefully to
avoid all that sort of nonsense. And then there
are other simple-minded ministers who are so far
left to themselves that they will preach three
long sermons on one Sabbath day. Could there
be more preposterous folly than that ? My
brother, you may consider that you do well if
you preach one sermon a week. And on no
account let it be longer than twenty-five minutes.
Indeed, the visitors and the gentry will be better
pleased if it is only twenty minutes long. And,
now, here's an important word of advice—whenever you pronounce the benediction, hurry away
down among the people, shake hands with all
the heritors, and salute the principal farmers
cordially, and ask them " *how's nowte.*" In this

way you will become a very popular and a very successful minister of the gospel.'"

Owen's works had a high place in the appreciation of the Doctor. He once said publicly— "I read Owen on 'Communion with God' once a month; Owen on the 'Person and Glory of Christ' once a quarter; and Owen on the 'Spirit' once a year. Were I left on a desolate island with the Bible and these three books, I would seek no more and could get no better."

Dr. Gustavus Aird, of Creich, tells us of the curious and characteristic account which Dr. Kidd himself gave of the beginning of his acquaintance with Owen's works. In dealing at his evening service with the question—"What is the misery of that estate into which man fell?" he found that he must speak on the subject of communion with God, and he was not satisfied with what he himself knew of the subject. He told the congregation that on the following Sabbath they would revise the ground they had gone over, so as to make sure work of it. Next day he went to all the booksellers in Aberdeen, making enquiry for a book on communion with God. At last, in the Gallowgate, he entered the shop of a man who sold old books, an old-light Seceder, father of Dr. Knight, Professor of Natural Philosophy in Marischal College, who presented him with a second-hand copy of Owen on "Communion with God." And, the Doctor added, "to prove that I have perused it well, this is the third binding it has got since it came into my possession."

The Rev. Duncan Grant, of the Gaelic Chapel, and Dr. Kidd, spending a social evening with some friends, happened to refer to Edwards' work on "Divine Sovereignty." They could not agree on a sentence that was quoted, and both men being remarkable for tenacious memories, the one would not yield to the other. By-and-bye the company separated, Mr. Grant going home to his bed and Dr. Kidd to his library, searching for the disputed passage. At last, finding it to be as he had said it was, he, in a very jubilant frame of mind, at once went to Mr. Grant's house. It being late, the door was locked and everybody in bed. The Doctor knocked loudly, and to the question put by Mr. Grant's brother—"Who is there?" there came the answer—"Is the Pope in?" Mr. Grant was told there was a man at the door who must be a madman, as he is asking if the Pope was in. "It must be Dr. Kidd," was the reply, "go down and bring him up." Up Dr. Kidd marched and into the bedroom with Edwards under his arm. The volume was placed in Mr. Grant's hands as he lay in bed, and he was asked, to his own

discomfiture, to read the sentence and acknowledge he was wrong. The Doctor then left him
to his slumbers with this parting shot—" Never
again to contradict a man so strenuously who is
older than yourself."

When the late much-respected Dr. A. Dyce
Davidson was presented to the South Parish
Church, Dr. Kidd came up to him on the street
and gave him his hearty congratulations. It was
quite fashionable in those days for young men to
take snuff, students and ministers not being
behind others in that respect, and Mr. Davidson
was just in the act of transferring a pinch from
between his fingers to its destination, when the
Doctor seized the defaulting hand and said,
" Let an old man give you three good advices—
Don't be in a hurry to marry, else you will fall
into debt; don't be much out of your own pulpit
if you expect your congregation to stick to you ;
and, lastly, let snuff be kept in some other place
than where you are about to put it."

The Gilcomston pastor was present at a
private baptism in the house of one of his members at Woodside, where there were friends
present belonging to other churches. Being the
friend of all evangelical denominations, he, in
his usual open and hearty way, asked the
various persons present what was their church

connection. In passing the question from one to another, he took no notice of a rather showy, consequential young man in the company. Piqued at this want of attention, the youth asserted himself by remarking—"You have not asked me, Doctor, what I am; I am a free-thinker!" cocking his head at the same time as if proud of the distinction. The minister, eyeing the conceited youth, and measuring him at the same time, replied—"Free-thinker! is that all the length you have got? I know a young fellow in Aberdeen who says he is an atheist."

The Doctor had no love for the "pipe," and when he saw young people indulging in that way he never failed to remonstrate as only the paternal despot of Aberdeen could do. He dashed the pipe from their mouths, at the same time uttering the maxim, "Young smokers make old beggars." Not unfrequently the young rascals took their revenge, when they were a safe enough distance away from the Gilcomston pastor, by shouting, "Mealy pouches! mealy pouches!" referring to the appearance of his coat pockets, into which were often stuffed bread and oat cakes, with which to meet the wants of any hungry ones he might meet.

The Doctor had a great horror of debt. When parting with a friend whom he did not

expect to see for some time, he would exhort him
to "Fear God, and keep out of debt." He had
the savings of the greater part of a life-time
locked up on deposit receipt in Maberly's bank.
On the Sabbath after the failure of that bank he
referred to the suffering and ruin which had
followed in the train of the catastrophe. The
amount of defalcation in Aberdeen was £62,000.
He said—" Sixty-two thousand cries from Aberdeen ! When a robber attacks your house with
intent to steal, you may have the opportunity of
meeting force with force ; but when a genteel
thief, with smooth words and fair promises, gets
hold of your property, you are disarmed and
wholly at his mercy."

Out of consideration for the weaker brethren,
who, from exposure to the open air or other
causes, felt drowsiness creeping upon them when
seated in church, it was understood that any
were at liberty to stand up for a few minutes
during the service, that by a change of posture
they might succeed in mastering the inclination
to fall asleep. As many as thirty or forty on a
summer day might have been seen at once in
different parts of Gilcomston Chapel standing up
in acknowledgment of the sincerity of their
desire to do all that could be done to insure
wakefulness. Some of them, however, abused
the privilege, by remaining longer upon their

legs than was necessary, and gazing about in a way which indicated wandering thoughts. The Doctor noticed this one day, just as he was reading that part of Scripture in which the Pharisees were rebuked by our Lord for seeking the chief seats in the synagogue. He paused and then said—" My friends, there are modern Pharisees, both in back seats and in front seats, who stand up and stare like statues."

The late Dr. R. Simpson, of Kintore, once took the opportunity of gently remonstrating with the Doctor for speaking with such severity against Roman Catholicism. " Ah ! " replied the redoubtable Ulsterman, "you have not seen Popery as I have; you have never lived in Ireland; you have never felt the *whisk* of the cow's tail."

The Rev. James Sutherland, of Turriff, remembers being at a meeting in Old Trinity Church where the controversial feeling was very strong. An enthusiastic Roman Catholic in the gallery was doing his best for his party, by occasional interjections, which had a most disturbing effect upon the speakers. The Doctor, who was on the platform, submitted to the interruptions till they became intolerable, and, at last, standing up with umbrella in hand, he, pointing to the delinquent, shouted in stentorian tones—"Put out the dog; put out the Papist dog!"

A menagerie came to the town, and it was advertised on the bills that working men would be admitted at half-price. The Doctor presented himself at the door for those who paid only half-price. The proprietor, looking at him, objected, and said he must pay the full fare. The Doctor, pointing to the bill, said, "There is not any one in Aberdeen more of a working man than I am, from three in the morning till eight at night."

Like every genuine lover of humour Dr. Kidd could enjoy a joke, though it went against himself. In calling upon one of the members of his church who kept a grocery shop, he met a woman who was also one of his congregation. In addition to buying bread and other necessaries, this woman, standing before the counter like himself, ordered in his hearing an ounce of tobacco. "Tobacco!" exclaimed the minister, "why spend your money on that?" "It's the only luxury we have," was the defence. "Luxury! what need have you or I for luxuries? If we get the plain necessaries of life let us be thankful." "Weel, Doctor," the good woman drily remarked, at the same time glancing significantly at the Doctor's portly frame, "the 'plain necessaries' of life have done mair for you than for me." The Doctor looked upon the thin, scraggy figure with a beaming countenance, and, as he left the shop, laughingly said, " Good, very good."

Dr. Kidd had a cat which had been in the house for years, and for which he had a strong affection. On going out one morning it met a neighbour's dog in the back yard and was worried. When the body of his favourite cat was brought into the house, and he was told how it had been killed, he was speechless with rage. He rushed out of the house to the owner of the offending animal and demanded, in no measured terms, why he kept such a ferocious brute. He threatened legal proceedings, and almost made his neighbour feel as if he had been a murderer, and not merely the owner of a dog which had behaved as dogs usually do. When the two separated it almost looked as if a wall of implacable and eternal enmity lay between them. But before the day was done the Doctor came back with a different expression on his face. He said, " I have come to express regret for having used such strong language in the morning. The dog was only following its instincts; and it is written that we are not to allow the sun to go down upon our wrath."

The late Mr. Hogg, a native of Woodside, and formerly well known as a missionary in Glasgow, bore witness to the following incident:—Passing down Hutcheon Street one day the Doctor came upon a little group of women gathered round an old body who had just been evicted by a cruel landlord. As she lay upon the pavement, the Doctor asked the wives if none of them had a place they could take her into. A cellar in the back yard was the only available offer, so the Doctor lifted the feeble old woman in his arms and carried her in there. As he bent down trying to soothe and comfort her, a strong hand was laid upon his shoulder, and a nautical voice disturbed his kind ministrations—"Avast, there! Avast, sir! that's my mither." The woman's sailor son had just returned from a long voyage. Taking in the situation at once, and reading the filial affection in the youth's manner, the Doctor was deeply moved, and turning his face upwards as he knelt beside the woman, he exclaimed, "Take off the tiles! take off the tiles! there must be angels looking down."

The Doctor was a lusty singer himself, and liked to hear a "loud noise" made in the worship of the sanctuary. He was accustomed to say that "the praises of God should be like the roaring of the ocean's wave." He could not bear to see people with their lips closed when a psalm was being sung. It looked to him like an affront to Jehovah to remain silent when the call came to join in praise. One Sabbath he was preaching in the parish church of Leslie, where the psalmody was exceedingly spiritless. The Doctor was fretted with the dull, lifeless way in which the praises of God were being sung. An old woman, rather dull in hearing, was, according to the custom of the times, seated on her stool at the head of the pulpit stairs. She, like too many in the congregation, had the psalm book in her hand without emitting any sound. She was sitting quite close to the minister, and yet did not seem to catch any of his demonstrative enthusiasm at the psalm-singing. One who was in church that day reports that the Doctor, out of patience with what he regarded as an unseemly silence, caught the old dame's arm, and shouted into her ear, " Sing, sing; you old sinner ! "

Intent upon his business as a spiritual shepherd, and ever alert to catch wandering, or thrust forward slothful, sheep, he could not bear to see people standing at the church door when they ought to be inside. An old man tells us that when he was a youth he had occasion one Sabbath to wait at the church steps for a friend. The minister, who was later than usual that day, came upon him, and without waiting to get a word of explanation, collared him, and said, " Are you waiting till the plate is taken away. Go in at once and put in your bawbee."

T

The late Rev. Wm. Mitchell, of Free Holburn Church, was accustomed to tell of a friend who, on passing the minister's house very early one Saturday morning, heard a night watchman being severely scolded by Dr. Kidd for making a noise opposite his study, and interrupting him in his preparation for the Sabbath. The watchman had been doing nothing but what was usual in those days, telling the hour of the morning and the kind of morning—as, for example, "Half-past five o'clock, and a fine morning!" Perhaps, as Mr. Mitchell suggested, the Doctor had not been going forward very successfully in the preparation of his sermon; and that may have accounted for his extreme irritation in running out upon the watchman, and, with considerable demonstration of manner, pressing the question—"What right have you, sir, to come opposite my study and disturb me in my preparation for Sabbath?" The poor watchman was able at last timidly to stammer out an excuse or vindication of his conduct. "Please, sir, I've nae allooance to dae aitherwise, because the Magistrates wish it daen." "Well, then, sir," rejoined the Doctor, conscious that he had rushed into a strait place, and was desirous of getting out of it as nimbly as possible, "if it must be done, let it be done properly;" and the poor man stood speechless before the Doctor, as he put him through his "facings," criticising severely his defective articulation, and making him attend to correct pronunciation, and then finishing his gratuitous and much-needed elocutionary lesson by the order, " Now, say it after me, sir. ' Half-past five o'clock——,' " the stentorian voice awakening not a few of the sleepers of Gilcomston.

———

A woman came out of her house, chasing her boy, and when the little fellow was out-running his mother, she in her rage called after him, " Come back, you devil." The Doctor, who was passing at the time, said to her, " Woman, if that be the devil, run the other way; don't go near him ! "

———

On sacramental fast-days he often began the service himself with prayer; and on one occasion, when confessing the sins and short-comings of the congregation, he referred specially to the elders thus:—" God have mercy on the elders; for they are a set of inefficient men, as they seem to think when they manage to gather the pence at the church door on the Sabbath, they have discharged their whole duty: God have mercy on the elders."

———

The Rev. James Johnstone, of Belhelvie, tells of an elder of his church, long deceased, who was present in Gilcomston Chapel when the

following occurred :—On a fast-day, while sitting in the elders' seat in front of the pulpit, the
Doctor, as the minister assisting for the occasion
was preaching, observed a man in his neighbourhood sleeping with head on book-board.
Seizing his large umbrella and quietly reaching
across the seats, he gave a poke to the sleeper,
saying aloud, "Sit up, sit up, sir." This startled
the preacher in the pulpit and he stopped.
"Go on, sir," said the Doctor, and added, having
an eye to a proper division of labour in the
circumstances, "Go you on; I'll keep the fellow
awake."

The Doctor believed thoroughly in the activity of the prince of the power of the air, and
was not ignorant of his devices. In one of the
passages of his church there were pegs for persons hanging their hats upon. A sudden gust
of wind on one occasion burst open the door and
sent the hats rattling along the floor, making
a great noise, and diverting the attention of
the congregation just as the Doctor was making
a very earnest appeal. "Oh, never mind!" he
interjected, "take no notice of it. I know who
has done that; never mind, he wants to
withdraw your attention from this solemn
truth."

A man was taking home in a barrow from

the brewery two sacks full of "draff" for his cow, but having drunk too freely before he started, he could not get along in a very straightforward manner. The Doctor, passing along the street, saw the man's predicament, and volunteered to take his place for a little. But the man becoming utterly helpless as they went along, he pitched him on the barrow above the sacks, and went on with the heavy load. At last arriving at the door of the house, out of breath and a little out of temper, the Doctor said to the man's wife, "Come out and take in your brute!"

The Doctor often said that all he had baptised and admitted to the Lord's table he would follow with his prayers as long as he lived. To a person asking baptism for his child, regarding whom Dr. Kidd was doubtful, he said, "Now, tell me, man, that you are not to pray for this child, and I'll not bind you in; for if I bind you in, and you do not do it, you perjure yourself. I have great doubts of you, man, and that makes me speak as I do."

A man lying drunk was accosted by Dr. Kidd, who asked him what he was and why he was lying there. "Do you not know me, Doctor? I am ane o' your converts," was the reply. "Very like my handiwork," rejoined the Doctor;

"for if God had converted you, you wouldn't be where you are."

Occasionally he stationed himself at the door of the passage to observe the ways and manners of the people as they entered in. One day he saw a man stalking along the passage with his hat on. The Doctor was soon at his heels with the command, "Take off your hat, man; coming into God's house with your hat on; your Maker and you are surely on very familiar terms!" Another day he saw a number of people standing at the church door. "Walk in, walk in to the house of God," he said, "and not serve the devil at my church door." "I was looking for my wife," mildly interposed one. "Sir, walk you in, and I'll be caution for your wife."

It was his practice to go poking about in all sorts of places. One morning he went to the harbour, and was able to act as the unexpected champion of a servant girl who had been sent to buy fish from the boat as it came in. A scoundrel who was loitering about took some of the fish from her, and when she cried out, slapped her on the face, saying as he did the unmanly deed, "Take you that." "And take you that," was the rejoinder of the Doctor, scarcely seen in the grey morning, as he delivered a blow which sent the fellow staggering in dangerous proximity to the water.

When the man was executed for sheep-stealing, referred to in another page, it is said that Dr. Kidd, who attended him during his imprisonment, stood by while the hangman was adjusting the rope, and, observing the rough way in which he was doing it, he severely rebuked him, and actually did it himself, and in a very gentle manner.

Professor Masson speaks of the Doctor having been seen with a poor woman just out of a fever leaning on his arm in a mean neighbourhood of the city, making a round of the shops!

Fraser of Kirkhill, grandfather of Donald Fraser, of Inverness and London, was once preaching in the Gaelic Church, Aberdeen, in the hearing of Dr. Kidd. The Highland minister was of gentlemanly appearance, and bestowed more pains upon his toilet than Dr. Kidd did. But beneath the neatly-combed hair was a good head and a warm heart, as was abundantly shown in his preaching. The Doctor was overjoyed, and his groundless prejudice melting away, he could not help ejaculating, " Well done. I'll never judge a man by his hair again!"

CHAPTER XXIX.

OLD AGE.

OLD age is usually associated with decay. Often, too, the decline which is perceptible in the body is only too well reflected in a man's outward activities and interests. Along with the lengthening shadows there is a chill in the surrounding atmosphere. A man begins to feel that he is of less account than he once was, that he is not reckoned as in the days of yore among the forces of society; the men who stood alongside of him in the prime of his manhood have dropped away one by one, and a generation has sprung up that does not look in his direction when choosing its leaders. The tide of practical efficiency and usefulness is ebbing. The humbling feeling comes home to a man that he is spent. The instrument that is blunted with long use is laid aside. The bitterness of death is experienced before the end comes, and even the Christian man needs all his faith and patience to gain the victory over pride which is not content with its "day." But it was not so with Dr. Kidd. It could not be said of him as it was of old King Lear—"He but usurped his life." To the end of his days he maintained his position of usefulness in Aberdeen. His popularity was undiminished, and activity can scarcely be said to have slackened till he had passed the allotted threescore years and ten. He did not become an "extinct volcano" in the city, for the moral and religious interest of which he had laboured so assiduously.

This perennial freshness of interest was due partly to his splendid physical constitution. Sound, and even robust, in every part, regular in his habits, of a contented and cheerful disposition, he was able to carry a measure of youthful buoyancy into his old age. Another most important contributing factor to his sustained popularity and usefulness was the alertness of his mind. He was alive every day to all that was going on in public life and the world of literature. Too many men, when they reach a certain age, become "fossils," in the sense that their shrunken sympathies are wholly with the thoughts and things of the past. The most intimate companions of their brooding minds are shades and memories. They do not keep their souls sensitive to the touch of the times. Passing events are to them the shadows, and the recollections of times gone by are the realities. Can it be wondered at that such persons lose their hold of the rising generation, and are, therefore, practically dead before their time? When a new book was being cut up by Dr. Kidd, he did say, a year or two before his death,

"It is not for me, at my age, to spend my time this way;" still, we are told that he wished to have any publication that was recommended.

In one respect his old age was a decided improvement upon previous stages of his life. He became wonderfully mellowed. The flame of his piety was more clear and pure, and had less smoke and fewer sparks. He mourned over the indiscretions into which he had fallen, and laboured hard to bring his mercurial spirit under subjection. Some of the entries in his journal indicate the severity of the struggle he often had with his own nature, and the depth of his sorrow when temper was to him what a runaway horse is to the driver:—"I bless God for the help of the Sabbath, and though I felt a little of my own spirit, yet I trust God overruled it, and will bless my labours:" "I felt greatly uneasy for speaking to a man sleeping. I afterwards thought this unbecoming in one who had been so lately at the Lord's Table. May God forgive me:" "I was somewhat unwatchful in my procedure, and I pray that I may be forgiven."

As at the beginning, so towards the close of his ministry, Dr. Kidd put upon paper his self-communings. We give part of the later journal, which has been preserved:—

"11th March, 1827.—I have great cause to bless God for His gracious assistance all day, but in particular in the afternoon. God's name for ever be blessed for the effect which the sermon had upon ———; it appears to have savingly awakened her to God for the first time, notwithstanding that she has heard me all her life."

"July, 1831.—God appears to have been very gracious to me and my flock. Outward things were comfortably conducted, and I have just cause to bless Him for health and strength, for inward composure and rejoicing, and for calm serenity of mind, and, I trust, real communion with the Father and with Jesus Christ His Son. May my covenant engagements be ratified for ever—that God may be my God, and I may be His son. Amen."

"27th July, 1832.—This is Monday, and until Saturday last I never understood fully the real meaning or nature of the Gospel as glad tidings of great joy to all people. In reading ' Colquhoun on the Law and the Gospel,' his view of the doctrines, the promises, the offers, the invitations of the Gospel— all so free, so gracious, so merciful, so suitable, without command, without threatening—astonished me much, and, notwithstanding that I had read the book before, I did not see the Gospel so clearly, and notwithstanding I had endeavoured to preach the Gospel from the day I was licensed, yet I never saw or perceived what the Gospel is so clearly. Blessed be God! I hope I do now understand it in some degree. Oh, what a mercy the Gospel is! How precious! How sweet! All free grace! All free gifts!"

"July, 1832.—I thank God from my heart for the gracious countenance shown to my people and myself on this solemn occasion. The weather was fine —cool and dry—the assistance of the ministers seasonable and suitable, the arrangements of the tables more regular and composed, the appearance of the communicants was grave, solemn, and devout. As far as man could see, the time was a time of love, and life and soul satisfaction. As for myself, many things call for thanks and praise. I found ease and readiness, and, I hope, Divine assistance; my labour did not over-fatigue me, and my spirits were supported; yet, on several occasions, I had presentiments of approaching separation from the services of the house below, and I look forward to this with a degree of desire and patience. Years and failing strength, with ' a desire to depart and be with Christ, which is far better,' all unite in declaring 'that here I have no continuing city.' May I be prepared for the ' City which hath foundations, whose builder and maker is God.' "

" January, 1834.—I have been mercifully assisted in many ways since the last record I made at the end of my sermons. My views of Christ have been more clear, ardent, and satisfactory. The object of Faith has been more direct and steadfast, and I have more joy in believing."

" April, 1834.—I avail myself of a moment's leisure, and of the vacant place in this book, to record, for my own sake and for all near and dear to me, the great advantage of studying Christ constantly. I have tried the study many years, and find it progressively experimental. My views of Christ at first were ardent and elevated, but rather uncertain and confused; but from time to time I have had gracious and enlarged views and experiences, and still receive more light, more life, more strength and satisfaction. I would not part with my knowledge and impressions of Christ to-day for all the world. Oh, what a blessing to have fellowship with Christ Jesus! J. K."

"May, 1834.—This day, and at this time, I revolve in my mind 33 years of my ministry. And I know not where to begin, where to pause, or where to stop, nor hardly what to say. Have I been faithful? Not so much as I ought to have been. Have I been successful? God only knows. During all the time sin has had a very strong hold, and yet I am not without some gleams of grace. I must at present, as when I began, leave the matter in Christ's hand. Oh, my Lord, in mercy help and pity me and my flock. I am conscious of much sin in conduct, but not error in doctrine. I have to lament many grievous falls, and yet I must say I have never been altogether deserted. My poor sinful heart has betrayed me many a time, and my God has still spared me and carried me through. Were I called into judgment I must condemn myself, but I trust I would not let Christ go. Every view I get of Him, by faith, supports me more and more—so precious is Christ to the downcast soul. Let me be ever near Him, ever be with Him, in union and communion. Amen."

The letters we now give to the public have much autobiographical value:—

To Mrs. SMITH (Daughter of Dr. Adam Clarke).

"ABERDEEN, 26th September, 1833.

"VERY DEAR MADAM AND PUPIL,—I have had a busy time since I received the Life of your worthy and venerable father. It is one of the most useful memoirs that has been published for several centuries past. Gratitude, diligence, piety, and love to God and man appear displayed as far as human imperfection could go. At the same time modesty, humility, benevolence, and Christian zeal operate in wonderful uniformity. Few men have raised themselves in the scale of society by mere personal efforts. All the family and all the connections of the late Dr. Adam Clarke must read the Life with sound satisfaction and pure approbation; the name of Adam Clarke will adorn the works of the Wesleyan Methodist body as long as men read; and the same name will dignify the annals of his posterity. May the Lord give grace to all concerned to improve the warning and the call. You will not feel the loss so severely as your dear mother, and the reason is your home, Mr. Smith, and your family. I shall be under the necessity of writing to Mr. Smith to prevent your exertions, if you do not promise to spare yourself. I am sure no woman can stand the fatigues of a family, and make the other exertions you do. I pray you, my dear pupil, consider what I say. I fancy I see Mr. Smith in tears, and your dear infants looking for their mother. O, you little know what would be the state of your dear family without you.

"When I imagine I see your bustle in your family,

your midnight hours in writing the life of your father, your engagements in society at different meetings—I say my dear pupil cannot stand all this; her vigorous imagination, her ardent· zeal to do good, her natural womanly genius will weary her beyond what nature can bear, her strength will fail, and, unless she retire, she must sink. Say, my dear pupil, does Mr. Smith ever speak to you in longings like the above? if not, he must be blind, and if he do, for my sake, for his sake, for your children's sake, and for your own sake, give in to your affectionate tutor! Please cause Mr. Smith to read this—but I doubt you will be afraid—and ask him what he thinks of it. He will answer, it is just what I have been saying to you. I write only by my own impressions without ever having heard what Mr. Smith says, but strongly believe I am right. That God may spare you long is my earnest wish.

" With best wishes for Mr. Smith, and most sincere prayers for the eternal welfare of yourself and dear children, I ever am, very dear madam and pupil, your sincere and affectionate humble servant,

" James Kidd.

" Mrs. Smith.

" P.S.—May I ask a line when you can."

———

(To the Same.)

" Aberdeen, 15th November, 1834.

" Very Dear Madam and Pupil,—I embrace the opportunity of my son-in-law going to your city to ask how you do, and how is your husband, and how are your children, and how is your mother? I have no news worth mentioning, everything here is stationary; the political aspect of Europe is clouded, and a storm is gathering. I shall be glad to hear that my dear little Agnes is pleasing you. I am much concerned about her, spiritually and corporeally. Little Robert is his mother's pet, and the union between them is indissoluble. He was in his arms when his father died and became his substitute; therefore the endearment is inexpressible. You know a parent's heart. Long may you be exempted from a parent's trials.

"I perceive from your letter that you are constantly engaged. Pray do not forget God! The devil has lost his moral purity, but none of his natural capacity and power, which, according to the Scriptures, appear to be very great. May God keep you! You know my affection for you and your family. Forgive my freedom. I have laid aside all study and all books but my *Bible.* I am preparing to leave the world. May the God of all grace, very dear madam and pupil, bless you and yours.—Ever yours,

"JAMES KIDD.

"Mrs. Mary Ann Smith."

CHAPTER XXX.

THE END.

DR. KIDD's attitude of mind, towards the close of his earthly career, was a remarkable illustration of the power of that Christian faith which can so grasp the unseen and spiritual as to make them more real than the passing things of time. "The righteous shall hold on his way, and he that hath clean hands shall be stronger and stronger." Death was not to him one of those facts for which no place is found in the general scheme of life. "What if I had been death?" was the question he put to one of his members as he stepped into his shop, and evidently took him by surprise. That readiness to go when the call came, which he urged his people to seek, he himself possessed. For some time before the end came, and while attending most assiduously upon daily duty, for which he had a wonderful measure of strength, he felt like a sentinel at the post of duty who might very soon be relieved by his superior officer.

Dr. Kidd died as he had lived, thinking not of himself, nor of anything else but the duty of the hour. He felt that strength was given to him to be used, and as long as he could crawl

U

to the desk or the pulpit he would. Ease to him was inglorious. Life was nothing if it did not mean service. What was he but an instrument, and what was it for but use? The resolute, onward spirit which did so much for him at the beginning, did not desert him at the close of his earthly career.

His daughter, Mrs. Oswald, tells us he did not rise at his usual early hour on the morning of 19th December, 1834, as he had been seized with a faintness or stupor on attempting to leave his bed ; but, on next day, Saturday, his medical attendant found him writing, in preparation for his Sabbath duties. The doctor told him he ought to be in bed, and on no account was he to think of preaching next day. Dr. Kidd pleaded hard for permission to appear among his people. "To-morrow," he said, "is our collection day for our Sick Man's Friendly Society, and surely a sick man pleading for sick people would have good effect." But the physician was inflexible. "Well, doctor," he said, "I have a high opinion of your skill, and much esteem for yourself : I obey, but there is not another man in Aberdeen would keep me from my pulpit."

The courageous, soldierly spirit which could brook no surrender, carried him on, and the poor declining body was obliged to do its part, until it actually fell down from sheer exhaustion. "To please the doctor," he lay in bed on Monday after his "silent Sabbath." On Tuesday, the day preceding his death, much against the earnest wishes of his family, he insisted upon going to Marischal College to meet his students. He was obliged to stop by the way and call a conveyance to reach the classroom.

The students were awed by the death-like pallor on his face, and the subdued pathos of his opening prayer. It came to them with the solemn effect almost of a voice from the other world, as their professor was evidently at the very border-land. He translated with them the first chapter of the book of Job, and made some remarks upon the general contents and character of the book. He went on to offer some observations of a practical nature to the young men before him as aspirants to the ministry. He maintained that every one could make a great deal of life by constant application, and he cited Poole, the author of the "Synopsis," as an example of diligence worthy of imitation. He also said some things, which the circumstances made specially striking and memorable, about the necessity of an inward and spiritual change, in order to the real possession of religion. He then gave out the lesson for next day, pronounced the benediction, and went home—with great difficulty.

He came back saying he thought he was better by going out; but he had not been in the

house ten minutes before he was seized with
apoplexy, and in other ten minutes he lost all
consciousness. Next day he passed away quietly
at half-past one o'clock, surrounded by his sor-
rowing family and several of his most intimate
friends. He did not have to linger long at the
threshold. He was spared what might have
been irksome to one like him, who was stronger
on the active than on the passive side of his
nature, and was better able to go forward than
to sit still; so the end of his usefulness here was
the beginning of the higher activities of the
other world. He died on 24th December, 1834,
and was buried in St. Nicholas Churchyard.

The absence of his strong and vivid personality was keenly felt by all—old and young.
An old man, still amongst us, remembers well
what a feeling of loneliness came over his spirit
when he, as a boy, heard that Dr. Kidd, who
had often " blessed " him, was gone. It was as
if a dominating height, familiar, yet grand, had
suddenly, as by a stroke, been effaced from the
landscape.

On his funeral day, work was suspended in
the city ; the inhabitants of Aberdeen constituted
the mourners. The professors and students of
the University; the members of the Town
Council, and representatives of all the churches
and institutions of the city were present. A little
incident connected with the funeral, reveals

more than could pages of the most elaborate description, and one that does credit to all concerned. As the minister of St. Paul's Episcopal Church was going to take his place in the funeral procession, he saw two old women trudging along King Street Road; he stopped his carriage, saying—"I am sure you are going to the funeral," and, finding his surmise correct, he took them in beside him, and placed them down at a convenient spot in the town, where they could see the long procession as it passed.

At one of the services in Gilcomston Chapel on the Sabbath after the funeral, the following "Farewell," found among Dr. Kidd's papers, was read. Never was such a scene witnessed in a church in Aberdeen, as sentence after sentence of it fell upon their ears. The place was a Bochim. For once the people broke through their natural reserve, and, as they heard this voice from the dead, a wail of lamentation came from the vast multitude. We bring this book to an end by giving the "Farewell" as it was penned by Dr. Kidd:—

" ABERDEEN, 3rd October, 1833.

"I feel myself advancing fast to the grave, and upon a back look of past life I can say, in truth, that God has been very merciful to me, and now I leave my testimony to His providential care of me, from my infancy hitherto. He has given my heart's desire to me in my standing in society, and I bless and praise Him for all, and am willing to lay down my Professorship and my Ministry when He may please to call me to do so.

"I now bid adieu to the Universe, and to all things beneath the Sun. Farewell, ye Sun, Moon, and Stars, which have guided my wanderings in this valley of tears, to you I acknowledge much assistance in all my attainments.

"Farewell, thou Atmosphere, with thy clouds, and thy rains, and thy dews, thy hail, and snow, and different breezes, which contributed so much to my life and comfort.

"Farewell, ye Earth and Sea, which have borne me from place to place, where Providence has ordered my lot, and with your productions have supported my bodily wants so often and so long.

"Ye Summers and Winters, adieu!

"Farewell, my native Country, and every place where I have had my abode. Adieu, Aberdeen! May peace and prosperity for ever be in you; to all your Inhabitants I bid farewell.

"Farewell, Marischal College and University, in which I have had the honour of a Chair so long, may Learning and true Religion flourish in you till the latest posterity. Adieu, ye Members of the Senatus Academicus, may ye enjoy many years of health, peace, and prosperity.

"Farewell, all ye who studied under my care, may you be useful, faithful, and successful Ministers of the Gospel.

"Farewell, Chapel of Ease. May peace be within

thy walls; for my friends' and brethren's sake, Peace be in thee, I say.

" Adieu, ye Eldership, ye Heads of Families, ye Young. May the Lord in tender mercy bless all I have baptised, and all I have admitted to the Lord's Table for the first time. I follow all with my most earnest prayers as long as I live.

" Farewell, ye little children in general all around, whom I have so often met in kindness, and saluted with my best wishes for your good. May all good be your portion in this world and the next.

" My own Children, I commit you to God in life and in death. May He fulfil to you the promise, Psal. xxvii., ver. 10. With mixed distress I leave you under the care of Him that is able to keep you from falling, and to present you faultless before the presence of His Glory with exceeding joy. Farewell!

" I bid adieu to my Library, and to my *Bible*, which has been my companion from my earliest days. I leave the Volume, but I carry with me, as the ground of my sure hope, the contents found in Psal. lxxiii., ver. 23-28; John xiv., ver. 3; Psal. cxxxviii., ver. 7 and 8; and Psal. xxiii. These I take before God as my dying support and comfort.

" Farewell Time!—Welcome Eternity! Farewell Earth!—Welcome Heaven!—Amen, and Amen.

" (Signed)   JAMES KIDD."

APPENDIX.

DR. BAIN'S* RECOLLECTIONS OF DR. KIDD.

My recollections of Dr. Kidd date from the earliest moment that I could be supposed to take any notice of what was going on around me. I was baptised by him, and attended his church with my father till I was about ten years of age. During the last two or three of those years I can distinctly remember his appearance and behaviour in the pulpit, but not any passages of his discourses. At the same time I perfectly remember the talk about him and his ways that went on among his congregation. My father ceased to attend him, although still preferring him to everybody else, because he could not find accommodation for his growing family. For a year or two after that time I was doomed to listen to the driest of the dry among his contemporaries. But about 1830 or 1831 I went back to him on my own account, and was in close attendance on his church till his death. From those years I am able to recall a good deal of his discourses and ways. Of course, I have a very vivid remembrance of his strong, burly figure, although then in a very advanced age. He was slow in his gait, and not much given to out-of-door exercise. But his power of endurance showed itself in the

*Alexander Bain, LL.D., Emeritus Professor of Logic, and Ex-Lord Rector of the University of Aberdeen.

astonishing capability of keeping up three discourses every Sunday till within ten days of his death. Not satisfied with his pulpit work, he used to give twenty minutes before the morning service to wind up a class in the schoolhouse, and then took possession of the pulpit a quarter before the regular time. At five minutes to eleven punctually he rose to open the service, with a view, he said, of being very punctual in the dismissal of the congregation at 12.30. He did the same in the afternoon. In the evening he mounted the pulpit at a quarter to six, and began the service immediately, so as to observe the same punctuality of dismissal. Having only two psalm-singings—the beginning and end of the service—he stood on his feet continuously during the opening prayer, the sermon, and the closing prayer. He declined wearing the pulpit gown, having only the bands, which he assumed before leaving home. His costume was characteristic and unchangeable. His broad-tailed dress coat and knee breeches were coupled with a broad-brimmed hat, and, only in bad weather, a very slight overcoat. In fact, weather seemed to have affected him very little. Having in my early days attended the Gilcomston day school for three years, I was very familiar with his transit on the way to Marischal College by the corner of Skene Terrace, and, of course, remember the usage of the boys in going up to him with bare heads to have his benediction. I think it is incorrect to say, of his later years at least, that he was in the practice of visiting his enormous congregation at their houses. I have no doubt this may have been the case in his early years, but certainly

not in the period when I remember him. I know he
occasionally gave out from the pulpit that he was to
have a certain day of visiting the members of the
congregation in a particular street, but I am quite
sure that he never was in my father's house, although
he had been at least ten or twelve years a member of
his congregation. Nor did he often attend funerals
if he could get some licentiate to take his place.
Baptisms, of course, were all in the church, and the
size of his congregation made these of weekly occur-
rence, both in the morning and in the afternoon
service.

I cannot pretend to enter into a minute analysis
of his preaching style and manner. These told upon
a whole generation so effectually, that tradition sufficiently represents them. His choice of strictly religious topics was sufficiently wide, but I should say
that he was singular in the degree that he dwelt upon
the function of the Holy Ghost in the work of redemption. His preaching of Christ was necessarily the
leading theme, and was sustained with every possible
variety of illustration and circumstance. But the
matter of his discourses was not so much the characteristic part of him as the manner—in other words,
the language and the delivery. He had a wonderful
command of the choicest English vocabulary, so far
as serving for simplicity and pathos, and the effect
was aided by a remarkably fine voice and well-
modulated delivery. The first occasion when I
resumed attending his church, after the experience
that I have mentioned, I was taken all of a heap with
listening to his first prayer. The easy flow of

language, the choiceness of the topics, and the brevity
of the whole, came upon me like a new revelation,
and from that hour I stuck to his church.   I can only
choose a few illustrative points which have clung to
my memory.   His baptismal prayer was fixed into a
set form, but yet the touches it contained seemed
never to tire by repetition.   Two passages in particular I am able to quote.   The first was returning
thanks to God " for His goodness to the mother in the
time of nature's sorrow," with a petition to perfect
her recovery.   More striking still was the passage
where he prayed for " all who have ever been baptised in this place," adding, " Wherever they are, by
sea or by land, we follow them with our prayers, that
none of them may be lost on the morning of the great
day."   The preservation of some copies of his prayers
would be even more interesting than his published
sermons.   It was understood that he made a point of
meditating and choosing the topics, so as to vary
them from one Sunday to another.

In the time that I speak of, many minds were
engaged upon the great problem of the plan of salvation, with a view to reconcile grace and free will.
Dr. Kidd, of course, knew the difficulty, but, by his
strong language, rather aggravated than eased the
solution.   He was never afraid of pushing a thing to
its utmost extreme in the view of rhetorical effect,
and, if he had been taken literally, he would have
landed thoughtful persons in serious difficulties.   But
to satisfy the understanding never was any part of
his aim, and, indeed, it did not lie within the compass of his mind.   His amazing power consisted in

keeping up the interest of a congregation for so long a period under such frequency of services. He was not unaware of the necessity of varying his topics, and one well-known resource was to enter largely into the exposition of prophecy. This led him into a quantity of historical matter, which, coming upon the fresh curiosity of youth, was interesting enough. He gave, after a time, a series of discourses upon the two great prophetic books—Daniel and Revelation. He had settled the date of the commencement of the millennium as 1864, to be followed by 1000 years of the reign of Christ, and a subsequent interval of about 300 years, when Satan would be in the ascendant, which was to bring us to the day of judgment.

Although mainly devoted to the New Testament for his topics of discourse, and for the exhibition of the work of Christ and the Holy Spirit, he had strong sympathies with what was peculiar to the Old Testament, and lectured through the historical and prophetic books, a chapter at a time, in his forenoon discourses. He could dwell upon the Old Testament characters with especial unction. It was one of his peculiarities to go through the Psalms consecutively in the forenoon service at the first singing. In so doing he expended a few minutes in an exposition of each, which he was able to sustain with a wonderful degree of interest. His choice of Psalms (he abhorred paraphrases and hymns) at the other diets was extremely limited—in fact, it was the recurrence of a very small number of passages from a small number of Psalms.

Much is said about the extent of his studies at

home. I have no doubt that his reading was very various, but I cannot undertake to specify it more particularly. He did not confine himself to theological literature, although he probably knew the best thoughts of the best theologians of the old school. Among the heavy prolixities of John Owen, I remember his lighting upon one book as a kind of oasis, and recommending it from the pulpit, the work entitled " The Person and Glory of Christ." Another of his book recommendations was somewhat more peculiar. I can recall the time when Galt's novel " Ringan Gilhaize " made its appearance, and from the interesting picture that it gave of the Covenanters, he enjoined his congregation to read it, which a great many of them did as soon as they could get a copy into their hands. Novel-reading in general, of course, he did not encourage, and it was probably unknown to the generality of his hearers.

One of his distinctive usages consisted in assiduous attendance upon condemned criminals during the six weeks between sentence and execution. Almost every day of that period he went to jail and communed with them, in the view of bringing about a frame of mind suited for their fate. The Sunday evening after an execution he gave a discourse to improve the occasion. This, however, he managed very delicately, and refrained from entertaining the audience with the secret confession of the unhappy beings.

As a very great deal is made of Kidd's eccentricities, I may give some authentic references to a few of these. One of his most noted peculiarities was his habit of wakening sleepers at church. This was a matter of fact, but I think the frequency of the practice was very much exaggerated. In a period of between three and four years, I can recall only three occasions of his wakening anyone at church. One was a woman who had caught his eye at a distant part of the building, his exclamation to her being, "Madam! wake up!" with nothing farther of an energetic accompaniment. The second occasion was an old man, the retired schoolmaster of the Gilcomston School, who usually sat on the seat at the bottom of the pulpit. This old man he caught dozing one afternoon, and ordered him to waken up with the somewhat odd remark, "If it were not for my respect for you I would expose you," as if he had not done so sufficiently already. The third took place on a hot summer day just before the communion, whether man or woman I cannot say, but the Doctor's remark was, "If I knew your name I would refuse you a token"—an illustration of his very small respect for either law or justice in dealing out church censures. The only other instance that I can produce was not in church, but in an address to a Sunday School, I myself being the subject. It was during the summer play, when he went the round of the Sunday Schools and gave an evening address to each, the pupils being duly assembled for the purpose. It so happened that on the day that I had to attend him at Gilcomston School, I had been out for a long excursion in the country, and, of course, fell asleep during the service. The Doctor soon caught me, and in his deep, energetic tones broke out, "Rouse him up like an old cat, the little monkey; why do you let him sleep before me!"

Whoever had charge of me must have been sufficiently uncomfortable, but, for my part, I was rather proud of his attention than otherwise.

In distributing the tokens to the communion he made a point of presenting them in his own person, an elder standing by with the communion roll. If anyone came up that he knew to have become disreputable, he put his hand to his shoulder and shoved him on. The communion being only once a year, at midsummer, it assumed a character of more than ordinary interest and solemnity. The number of communicants exceeded the number of sitters in the church. There were ten table services, with not less than two hundred at each set of tables. The services began at nine in the morning, and lasted till between five and six, with merely a half-hour's interval to the evening sermon. Kidd's own discourse on the occasion was usually of a very solemn character.

At one time—I do not know for how long—he was accustomed to put to fathers who came to him for the baptism of a child this question—" What good do you think baptism has done yourself?" This, of course, was a poser, and it was not likely that any of them could answer it off-hand. He then added a second query—" Why do you come to me for baptism to your child when you do not know that it has been of any use to yourself?" His usage having become known, an attempt was made to concoct a reply that would extricate the applicants from the fix. One form that this reply took I can remember to be that " it was the means of introducing them to membership of the Church, and, when completed by admission to the Lord's Table, they were put upon the line of the Christian life, and humbly trusted that they were properly desirous of fulfilling its duties." Some such formula, I was given to understand, was received as satisfactory, none of the applicants having either the ability or the courage to give the proper answer that it was not left to them to judge of what was a Christian duty.

My next remarks relate to Dr. Kidd's career as Professor of Hebrew at Marischal College, an office that he held for forty years. His Chair gave him a personal interest in the students of Divinity, and one mode of displaying this interest was to devote an evening service annually to addressing them in a special discourse. He obtained for them on the occasion the front pews of the end and side galleries, which they generally filled. His usual plan was to select a special topic, which he handled for their edification. As far as I can remember, his last discourse took the form of a compendious view of the plan of salvation as a whole, and the handling struck me as in his very best manner, combining expository skill with rhetorical point.

The last year of his life saw his admission into the church courts, by the action of the General Assembly in taking in ministers *quoad sacra.* He sat in one Synod, and attended the usual Synod dinner at the close of the sittings. The young minister of Dyce ventured to single him out for a chaffing toast. He ought to have known better. The Doctor retorted in a parallel toast, which made the future Principal come off second best. There was no malice on either side.

Extract from the records of Marischal College relative to Dr. Kidd's family :—

"*Agnes*, born 18th January, 1785; *Janet*, born 20th January, 1791—(said Janet's death, 18th September, 1794); *William Campbell*, born 2nd October, 1795; *Benjamin Rush*, born 31st December, 1799; *Jane Allan*, born 17th June, 1802; *James Little*, born 15th November, 1804—(said James died 16th September, 1805); *Christiana Little*, born 12th September, 1806; said Agnes was *married* 14th February, 1814, to Mr. James Oswald, shipmaster, Aberdeen; said Jane Allan died 11th August, 1824; said William Campbell died 1st August, 1825; said Jane Boyd, spouse, died 4th June, 1829; said Christiana Little *married* 12th July, 1830; said Dr. James Kidd died 24th December, 1834."

Mr. Thomas Kyd tells of the impression Dr. Kidd left by his occasional visits to Dundee :—"Forty years after Dr. Kidd's death, my father, Mr. David Kyd, was stopped by an elderly woman as he was walking in the neighbourhood of Rose Street, Dundee. She wore an apron, under which she seemed to carry a parcel. This she took from its hiding place just as my father and she met each other. It was a little portrait in a paltry frame, the same likeness of Dr. Kidd that does duty as a frontispiece of some of his books. 'You'll mind wha that is, Mr. Kyd,' said she. My father looked at the engraving, and replied that he well remembered the Doctor. 'I'm but a

v

puir body,' continued the woman, 'I get aff the Buird' (the Parochial Board), 'but I saw the pictur' a while syne in a broker's shop—it was ninepence, and I saved up till I was able to buy it.' And then she told how the Doctor used to preach in the Chapelshade Kirk on fast days or communion Sabbaths when she was a lassie, and how much spiritual good she had got from his ministrations there, few and far between as his appearances must have been. 'I sometimes think,' added she, 'that I can hear his voice reading in the Revelations yet.'"

Dr. William Alexander has favoured us with the following extracts from MS. of Dr. James Foote, East Free Church :—

"I attended Professor Kidd, of Marischal College, two sessions for Hebrew. As a Professor he was lively and zealous; and as a minister (for he became minister of Gilcomston Chapel of Ease) he was indefatigable in his preaching, and characterised by a natural Irish eloquence, amounting often to eccentricity. [About A.D. 1801-3.]

"After being present, towards the end of October, in Marischal College at the prescribing of the exercises for the competition for the bursaries in the forenoon, I returned along with the Professors to the examination of the exercises at five o'clock p.m., and sat in the old Divinity Hall—a small room with a very large fire—hardly ever rising from my seat for upwards of twelve hours. When we left the Hall, between five and six o'clock in the morning, it was a sharp frost. I returned home, walking very slowly, in consequence of having Dr. Kidd, then becoming infirm from age, leaning on my arm. The result was that next day I was seized with rheumatism."

The attack became severe, developing into fever, and he was not able to enter his pulpit for the next sixteen Sabbaths. The year was 1828.

In 1831 the Popish controversy was being somewhat vehemently carried on, and on 9th December of that year, Dr. Foote received what he termed "a characteristic letter" from Dr. Kidd, addressed to him as secretary of the Aberdeen Auxiliary of the Reformation Society, and bearing on that Society's alleged slackness in dealing with certain "heresies," &c. He had been about to draw up a remonstrance to the Society when the receipt of certain official communications had altered the complexion of affairs; and, says he, "you will perceive that there is yet hope of our friends in Exeter Hall adhering to the truth. Thanks to the uncompromising promptitude of the Institution's best friends, its Directors have been awakened to a sense of the impending danger. Still it strikes me that an auxiliary, seeing auxiliary it is, ought to communicate with the parent Society, expressing satisfaction with the decision come to, and earnestly beseeching that the embryo ulterior measures relative to these agents may be broadly stamped with a *veto* and a *ban* anent the promulgation of Irvingism, and every other *ism* opposed to the principles of the Reformation. I feel delighted that the special meeting has done its duty. Yet it is evident that part at least of the committee are tainted with heresy. The first vote seems to me decisive on this point. *Latet anguis in herba ;* therefore, let us watch and warn," &c. . . . " Let the world know that the Aberdeen Auxiliary Society's committee will give no countenance to the heretical *whim-whams* of deluded visionaries."

INDEX.

PRINTED AT THE "FREE PRESS" OFFICE, ABERDEEN.